TRICK OF FATE

Connell O'Keeffe

&

The Pen Caer Legacy

Patricia Watkins

A novel

Published by Down Design Publications
Fishguard, Pembrokeshire SA65 9AE, UK
All rights reserved
© Patricia Watkins, 2012
ISBN 978-0-9572104-5-5

www.downdesignpublications.com

Cover illustration by Elizabeth Lake

It is February 23, 1797, and actor, Connell O'Keeffe, is on his way home to Ireland from Fishguard, Pembrokeshire, after performing in Haverfordwest. Unaware the French have invaded Pen Caer, he passes through Manorowen just in time to witness an event that is to change his life forever.

CHAPTER 1

"Whoa there! That was close." I was lying on the rain-soaked ground, in amongst the heather, gorse and grey limestone rocks, taking a rest and gazing with little interest at some bees braving the early spring sunshine. There was little cover here though, so if anyone had thought to kill me with that shot, he should not have had much trouble.

There was silence, and after a minute or so I dared to poke my head up. "Don't shoot. I'm not armed." Nothing happened, so I put up my hand and waved. "See. I'm not armed."

Why was I so calm? Here was someone who had just tried to shoot me, and my shoulders had sagged, rather than tensed up as one would normally expect when being shot at. Maybe it was because so much had happened to me in the last weeks, I was resigned now when trouble came, rather than alarmed. I was weary, and this was yet another trial for me to overcome or endure, and the will for the former was no longer there.

"You! I need to see both your hands. Now!" It was a woman's voice, and she emerged from behind a massive boulder, musket in hand. Had she not already fired it at me, I would have been tempted to smile, as she resembled some overly-dramatic actress making an entrance on stage in some melodrama.

But she *had* fired it, and when I hesitated, she started walking towards where I lay. "Now! I said."

"Sorry. Can't do that." She had come up close now and was standing within six feet of me, and having reloaded the musket with an efficiency unusual for a woman, was pointing it at me. At that distance, at least I wouldn't know much about it if she decided to shoot at me again, and I continued to lie there, looking up at her. She was about my age, and if there was any beauty in her face, I did not see it; all I saw was the hate. That, paired with the loaded musket, should have made a frightening combination, but, as I said, I was no longer roused by anything. Resigned to whatever was going to befall me this time, and not caring, all it did was make me flippant. I started to get to my feet, and the musket went off, so I ducked down again.

"You put both hands up where I can see them, I said, or next time I won't be firing into the air. I'm a good shot too."

This was no country peasant-woman dressed in traditional Welsh clothing with bonnet, beaver hat and shawl. Bare-headed, and wearing a well-tailored woollen pelisse, she looked like a gentlewoman. She spoke like one too. What was a gentlewoman, or any woman, doing out on the moors in the early morning, on her own, carrying a loaded musket and trying to kill people?

I could have pointed out to her that at six feet, being a good shot was of no high priority, but I didn't. "I've no doubt you are, Madam," I said, "and have no wish to argue the point with you, but let me stand, and you'll see why I can't do what you ask."

She nodded. "Any tricks though, and I *will* shoot, believe me."

I thought to make a frivolous reply, but decided against it. She did scare me now, the first woman ever to do that, and I stood up. I and my warm woollen coat and fine waistcoat had parted company a couple of days before, and I stood there in my once-white linen shirt open at the neck, my breeches only partly done up, and my muddy boots. I must have looked worthy of anyone's contempt, especially a woman's. The chill easterly wind caught the empty right sleeve of my shirt, and it flapped in the breeze. "Satisfied?" I stretched across, grabbed it, and tucked it into the top of my breeches, offering a wry grin, but she ignored it.

"Empty your pockets. I need to see if you have any hidden weapons -- a knife perhaps."

All that emerged as a result of that was a very soiled handkerchief, an apple, a piece of stale bread, and a lump of greasy cheese, covered in grit.

"Now your boots."

"Now my boots what?"

"Off."

The location of our confrontation was not the best in which to be without boots, covered as it was with prickly gorse bushes, the springy, woody heather, and scattered with sharp stones. I hesitated. "Why take my boots off? You can see I don't have any weapons."

"I don't want you running away."

Her voice was harsh and unforgiving, and her face told me she would as soon shoot me as not, and I had no heart to argue with her. I sat down again, and started to pull them off. "That would be stupid of me, considering you have a musket pointing at me."

"It would, but I don't intend to give you the opportunity to try anyway. Besides, I don't want to have to kill you myself if I don't have to. I'll leave that to someone else."

"Generous of you..." I had removed my boots, a lengthy business, especially as they had not left my feet for several days, and stood up again. "I hope we don't have to go far. Walking on this will be hard on bare feet."

She made no answer, but, impatient with my slowness and showing no sympathy, waved the musket in the direction she wanted me to go.

I really did hope we did not have far to go. Apart from the effect on my feet of this wild north Pembrokeshire terrain, I had not slept for several nights, and such food as I had on me, and was saving until I was desperate, was what I had left after starting out three days previously, and had been meant to last me only the one day. The weather was cold too, and without the warmth of my coat and waistcoat, I was shivering.

That I looked like nothing more than a dirty vagabond there was no doubt, and I suppose she could be forgiven for thinking I might be a threat of some sort, although in what way, I had no idea. If only she knew it, I was ready to drop at her feet with exhaustion and pain too, for I had already discovered that the cold east wind somehow made my arm that was no longer there suffer from a variety of aches from the tips of its vanished fingers to the tiny part of what still remained attached to me. Most of the time I felt I wanted to nurse it in my other arm to keep it warm and comfortable. I would even find myself trying to do that, so real was the sensation of it still being there.

"How about lowering that musket? You know I'm not going anywhere, and if you were to trip, and it went off, you'd most likely succeed in killing me anyway... And since you say you'd prefer someone else to do it..." I plodded ahead, too weary to think of anything witty with which to finish the sentence. Besides, flippant I might be, but real humour was not something in which I had felt like indulging for a while now.

Apart from everything else that had happened to me, my confidence where young women were concerned had already been battered but a few days before, when the reaction of one had convinced me I was no longer attractive, she having made it obvious she found the sight of me repellent. This woman's contempt for me now only confirmed my conviction, removing all trace of whatever confidence I might have had left.

She did lower the gun, however, and we had gone about a quarter mile when my bare toe ploughed into a solid chunk of rock. I wanted to let out a yell, but saw no reason to give her that satisfaction, and I stood there, holding my breath, waiting for that initial jolt of pain to ebb.

"Come on. I can't wait here all day."

"You're a hard lady, I have to say. Where are we going anyway, and why? Why not simply let me go on my way? I've not done anything to harm you."

"There are still some Frenchie invaders who haven't been captured, and there's a reward for any that are found... Oh, do hurry." She waved the musket at me.

Now she did have me scared. It was a long story, but I couldn't afford to be handed over to the authorities, and if it had been possible, I would have tried to escape right then, but there was no hope of that. I was not foolhardy enough to take any risk with an irate woman, armed with a loaded musket, by trying to escape barefoot, or even with my boots on. I started moving forward again.

"But you can tell I'm not a Frenchie."

"Yes, but you're Irish, and there were some of them amongst the invaders too. They're wanted for treason against His Majesty King George III, so you're even more valuable."

I didn't answer. It was clear she would not be of a mind to listen to what I might have to say, which would have taken too long to explain anyway, given her level of impatience, so I kept trudging ahead until we came to a house.

I don't know what I was expecting, but it was quite a grand house, a squire's mansion. She marched me into the cobbled stable yard, where a groom was currycombing a fine mare. By now I was unsteady on my feet, and even light-headed. He turned and came over. "Ah! Miss Saunders! What have we here then? A poacher?"

"No, David, not a poacher. Put him in one of the unused stables for the time being, will you? Give him some straw to lie on. Oh, and find him some food, please."

"Yes Miss Saunders." He had not noticed, and went to grab me by my arm, but grasped instead the short stump of what was left of it. I yelped, and he stood back, shocked. "Miss Saunders? Did you know about this?"

"Well, I know he's got only one arm, if that's what you mean."

"Yes, Miss, but this is a recent injury, not yet healed. Are you sure you want me to lock him in the stable? Perhaps the servants' kitchen might be more appropriate. By the look of him, I don't think he's going to harm anyone."

"No. He's much too dirty. We can't have him in the house like that. Besides, he's one of the invaders, and we don't want anyone like him in our home at all."

"Whatever you say, Miss Saunders," he said, and took me over to one of the stables. "In you go then. I'll get someone to bring you out some food. You look as though you could do with it. I'll see if I can find you a blanket too." He shouted to one of the stable-boys to bring some straw, then locked me in, closing the upper door as well, although, given the state I was in, I don't think I could have climbed out over the lower one if I had tried. Besides, I was too exhausted to consider escaping now, even if both doors had been left wide open.

"Thank you." I lay down, and fell asleep almost at once. It was not a peaceful sleep though, being full of nightmares and horrors, and in the end I woke myself up shrieking, "No!" I was sweating, my shirt soaking, and I shivered, chilled throughout my body, even though someone had thrown a horse-blanket over me while I slept.

It was dark in the stable with both upper and lower doors being closed, but I could see it was still daylight outside. I got up, and found someone had left me food. There was a slice of cold beef, some bread, cheese and a mug of ale. It must have been there for some hours though, because the meat had been dragged off the plate, and there were nibbles around the edge of it, where a rat had been helping himself.

Too hungry to be fussy, I ate everything, following it with my apple and my lump of cheese. The stale bread from my pocket, though, had gone mouldy, so I threw it into the corner. Almost immediately the rat appeared, and carried it off. He was fat and sleek, with bright black, intelligent eyes, obviously well fed. I would have to watch he did not try nibbling at me too. I don't like rats, even healthy-looking ones; they can carry deadly diseases.

I felt better now I had some food inside me, but was still cold. My arm was bothering me too, for when it was not hurting, I felt other strange sensations in it, always as though it was all still there, and reminding me it had no doubt long since been fought over and eaten by the foxes of Pen Caer, and with it had gone my career as well.

I am, or was, an actor, a good one too, one of the best in Dublin's Royal Theatre, and known for my outstanding fencing displays. Audiences always looked forward to the duelling scenes in which I played Romeo or Hotspur, and I thought with regret of the excellent reviews I had received in the *Freeman's Journal*. I had loved my chosen career, and was well suited to it. I had found my niche in life, and could think of nothing else I would rather do.

When this Miss Saunders had found me, I had been trying to get back home to Ireland, although to what, I had no idea, my career being over now. All I had needed to do was to get to Fishguard. From there it would have been simple. A couple more miles, and I would have made it. Now I was a prisoner -- again.

I looked around me. The stable was part of a row of stone-built buildings. The only source of light was between the boards of the double doors, there being no window. It was too dark to see the roof clearly, but it smelt of rotting straw, and probably needed re-roofing. The floor was cobbled like the yard, and I was glad that at least I had been given enough straw to lie on, so did not feel the lumpy stones beneath me. Until a few weeks previously I had never slept in a stable in my life, and would never have imagined myself ever having to do so. I sighed. I, Connell O'Keeffe, had gone from highly esteemed gentleman-player in the Theatre Royal in Dublin, to a one-armed starving vagabond locked in the dark in someone's stable.

I heard the bolt being drawn back. The upper door was opened, and two silhouettes appeared against the bright light. I blinked.

"All right, Katherine, what have we here then, eh? You'll have to stop scouring the countryside like this. I've told you, all the stray invaders have long since been rounded up. There *are* no more out there."

"But this one's an Irish Republican, Father, a traitor, and I can't give up until I'm sure every one of them is in custody."

Her father, presumably Mr. Saunders, opened up the lower door and came in. He was carrying a riding crop, and pointed it at me. "You. On your feet. Have you no respect, man?"

I stood up. I was much taller than he, and he looked up at me. "So, my daughter has caught herself a stupid Paddy, has she?"

"If I could, Sir, I'd challenge you for calling me that."

"How dare you speak to me like that!" He went to swipe me across the face with his crop, but I ducked, and he missed. Tempted to snatch it out of his hand and beat him with it I may have been, but knew he had a stable yard full of hefty young men to back him up, and I had no wish to get into any more trouble than I already was.

He tapped the crop against the iron manger. "Now, the question is, what are we going to do with you? You were trespassing on my land, for which I could have you sent to jail."

"No, Father. He must be tried for treason. *All* the Irish invaders must be tried for treason. I want them all hanged." She pointed at me. "He could even be the one who killed Richard."

"I think that's unlikely, my dear."

"You're wrong, Father. The loss of his arm is a recent injury. Who knows how many innocent people he killed before that happened?"

With the bright sunlight behind her, and me having been in the dark, she was nothing but a sinister black shape,

9

which made her words that much more chilling and vindictive, and I stood there, too dispirited to think of anything, let alone something to say in my own defence.

"Possibly, possibly." Mr. Saunders shrugged. "Well, I'll have him taken down to the sheriff's office in Haverfordwest as soon as it's convenient." He looked around. "Until then he can stay here, I suppose." He pulled out a handkerchief and waved it in front of his nose. "My, but he stinks! Get David to see to it that he receives a wash, and get one of the servants to find some other clothes for him; he smells worse than a fox." He turned to leave. "Right my dear. This time I think you may indeed have found one of them."

Referring to me in the third person as they had done, it was as though they had been appraising a horse they had just acquired, and I felt even further degraded and sorry for myself; I had deserved none of this.

They left, leaving me once more in the dark, and a short while later David, the groom, appeared with a bathtub, followed by some housemaids carrying jugs of hot water. The tub filled, the maids left, leaving me with the groom. He watched me undress. "What happened to you then?" He peered at the cauterized stump of my arm, still red and ugly looking, and recoiled.

I said nothing.

"So you *were* one of the invaders then?"

"No... I wasn't." I stepped into the tub, and lowered myself into the warm water, sinking into it until my head was covered. It felt good, and I stayed there so long, David must have thought I was trying to drown myself, for he took me under my armpits and dragged me up.

"Are things so bad for you that you want to kill yourself?"

"Why is Miss Saunders searching the countryside for what she calls Irish traitors?"

David leaned back against the wall, resting one foot on the stones behind him. "Ah, a sad story, I'm afraid." He shook his head. "She was engaged to be married. The wedding was to take place this coming May, but her betrothed, Captain Richard McCaffrey, was killed by one of the invaders, and her grief is such that she's taken it upon herself to try to find the man who killed him -- an impossible task, of course. Mr. and Mrs. Saunders are most concerned about her, although she's always been a strong-minded and wilful young lady. I'd even say, spoilt too." He handed me a towel. "We found you some clothes. They're not your size exactly, but they'll do till we can get your own back to you."

I dressed in my borrowed clothes. At least being clean again raised my spirits somewhat, and for the first time in days, I was warm.

"That's better. Mr. Saunders was right. You stank," David told me, as if I had not been aware of it.

Not that I am a fastidious man, but personal cleanliness is important to me, as was my dress, always having been aware of the latest in fashion for a gentleman such as myself, and taking my sense of style as that being set by Mr. Beau Brummel. Following his style too, I wear my hair short, a la Brutus, as it's known, and my hair being wavy, it's a style that suits me well. Being a well-known actor back home in Dublin, and always recognized by the theatre-going public, how I presented myself had been important too, and before I lost my arm was always proud of my physique, which showed off my clothes to the best advantage.

I had not been able to have my hair attended to for weeks, and as it was now hanging around my shoulders again, adding to my vagabond look, David handed me a piece of string to tie it back, then realizing I couldn't do it myself, did it for me. I thought to escape while he was occupied, but a few of his stable boys had gathered at the door, blocking the way. No doubt they had come to see the oddity brought in by Miss Saunders. Tall-standing, well over six feet, and once full of self-esteem, I now wanted to shrink away and disappear into the background. I did not even have the confidence to tell them to stop staring at me, and to go away.

Now I was clean and tidy once more, David hung around, wanting, I knew, to find out more about me. "So, if you're not one of the invaders, what were you doing wandering around the countryside like that?"

I shrugged. "It's a long story."

"I'm listening."

"It's not a story I feel like repeating."

"Sounds like you're trying to hide something. Maybe Miss Saunders is right about you."

I said nothing, and he persisted. "It seems to me that a man, dressed in good quality clothes, who has recently lost his arm, and is found, bedraggled and filthy, wandering over the moors, has a lot of explaining to do one way or another."

I ignored him, and lay down on the straw again, turning my head away. I no longer knew whom to trust anyway, and decided the less I said to anyone, the better.

He gave up, and pushed himself away from the wall. "Right. I'd better get back to work, or I'll have Mr. Saunders after me as well."

He left, and once more I was alone in the dark with my own, increasingly sombre thoughts. I lay there on my back, my hand behind my head, and watched a shaft of dust-laden sunlight fall on the slime-covered stones of the stable wall, then move slowly around until it grew dimmer, finally fading away. Night was falling, and soon it was completely dark.

With nothing to do but stare into the darkness and contemplate, I thought back just over four months, when my life was one of laudable achievement, love, and excitement about my future.

CHAPTER 2

I had just arrived back in Dublin after a successful summer theatre season in Limerick and Cork, where I always enjoyed playing, and was looking forward to a break, before starting the winter season again at Mr. Daly's Crow Street Theatre. I had every right to be proud of myself. I had been acting under the management of Mr. Daly since I was twenty-one, and had already made a name for myself. I always received excellent reviews in the *Freeman's Journal*, which, apart from praising my acting skills, also noted -- well, why shouldn't I quote it? After all, it's all in the past now -- that such a *"tall, handsome young gentleman cannot help but draw the attention of the ladies, who come to see Mr. Connell O'keeffe himself, almost more than to attend the plays in which he so ably performs"*.

I think I could be forgiven for enjoying such flattery, although I did risk becoming spoilt by the attention, something to which any young man could not be averse, of course. I have to admit too that being waited for by the ladies at the stage-door at the end of the evening made me very confident about myself, although Mr. Daly would rightly bring me back down to size when he saw fit, preventing me from becoming arrogant and too self-important.

Even the gentlemen could be persuaded to come to see me perform Romeo in *Romeo and Juliet*. Though not normally a favourite play with the men, who prefer more action and displays of fencing, they *would* come to see my duel between Romeo and Tybalt, Juliet's wicked cousin though. It was one of the few instances in which Mr. Daly gave me free rein to continue the fight as long as I wished and, as the actor who played Tybalt was also a good swordsman, we gave the gentlemen a fight worth watching. The Freeman's Journal had even referred to my swordsmanship as *"spectacular"*, and me a man to be reckoned with if forced into a real duel -- not that I was ever excited about the prospect of fighting a real duel. I would stand up for myself if necessary, of course, but am not a naturally aggressive man, and would never be inclined to pick a fight.

The theatre, though, was a life to which, as I said, I was ideally suited. I could use my duelling talents without ever hurting anyone, or getting hurt myself, and I found the acting itself exciting and rewarding. Each new play presented a challenge, always providing me with something new. It was an excellent outlet for my higher-than-average level of energy as well, giving me that all-important feeling of self-worth and achievement at the same time. I was a happy, confident and contented young man with a most promising future. Life was good to me.

It was then, right after we got back from Cork, that Mr. Daly received a request for some Crow Street players to visit the town of Haverfordwest, in Pembrokeshire. The gentleman making the request was himself a Dublin actor from the old Smock Alley Theatre, who had made a similar trip to Haverfordwest nineteen years before, but had fallen in love there, married, and had remained there. Mr. Daly remembered him well, noting that Dublin had lost a first-class actor when he failed to return, and agreed that a small troupe should make a short trip to the west Wales town right before the winter season began. I was one of those selected to go. That was in early October of last year, 1796.

Haverfordwest still did not have its own theatre, and we were to stage two performances, one at the Blue Boar Inn, up near St. Mary's Church, and the other at the home of a member of the gentry. Most of the cast were housed in the busy Castle Inn, down on the square, not far from the quay, but I was fortunate to be invited to stay with the gentleman who had invited us, Mr. Potter, who lives on Tower Hill, and is now a well-known printer and bookseller in town. He was also sheriff a few years back.

My stay with him was memorable in that he was able to tell me so much about the Dublin theatre back in the 1770s, when he had acted alongside such greats as Thomas Sheridan and the famous playwright, John O'Keeffe, a distant cousin of mine, who is still one of the most-produced playwrights in London, mostly at the Haymarket. In return Mr. Potter asked me about my own career and what changes had been made to the theatres in Cork, Dublin and Limerick, where in his day, you had to go through a coach-maker's establishment and a kitchen to enter the theatre, something he had considered very unprofessional. He spent hours reminiscing, only too happy, I think, to find

16

someone who would know all the people and places he was talking about, and understand all his references to, and experiences in, his theatre life.

I was happy to listen to him, but he had invited me specifically, he said, because he had heard of my prowess with the sword. This was something for which he himself had been well known, and had even kept up his skill until his servant and mentor, who had taught him everything he knew, was killed by a smuggler seven years previously. That was a sad story, and it was clear he still grieved for this man, but did not go into detail, it seeming to be something he preferred not to talk about, and I respected that.

He was anxious to see how well he could still fight, so we went out into his back garden and set to. He was out of practice, no doubt about that, but even so, I could tell he had once been highly competent, having been trained as I had been to fight with two swords at once. He even regaled me with stories of some narrow escapes he had had while still living in Dublin. He is a man after my own heart, and I respect him greatly.

While I was there, he prevailed upon me to help him regain some of his prowess, and although now in his mid forties, by the time I left, we were able to amuse people with displays sufficiently spectacular to elicit many "oohs" and "aahs" from our audiences. As both Mr. Potter and I are born showmen, we had as much fun, of course, as those who watched us.

Mr. and Mrs. Potter are very sociable and love to entertain, holding elegant dinner parties and soirées at their Tower Hill home, or at the mansion belonging to Mrs. Potter's family on the outskirts of town. Mr. Potter sometimes entertains his guests with monologues he has written, and while I was there, he wrote a few small sketches for the two of us to perform together. As I was included in their friends' invitations to their homes as well, we succeeded in providing a great deal of amusement all round.

Apart from fencing and acting, I do have another talent for which I am appreciated, and that is singing. I am what is known as 'a fine Irish tenor', and once that was discovered, I was called upon all the time to sing, something to which I was quite amenable.

I was never bored when with Mr. Potter, and like him, I am a man to get bored easily if not physically active. Like him too, I feel the need to be always achieving, not liking to go bed at night without feeling I have accomplished at least something worthwhile that day.

"You're my dear husband reborn," Mrs. Potter would laugh, wagging her finger at me. "When you get married, you're going to drive your poor wife to distraction with your energy and schemes... And if you're like him in other ways as well, you'll be a tease too!" She put her arm round her husband's waist and looked up at him, smiling. It was obvious they were still very much in love.

It seemed I was destined to be like him as far as love was concerned as well, as I too, within days of my arrival, fell in love with a young lady there, and like Mr. Potter, did not return to Dublin when the rest of my troupe went back, my heart ruling my head. Mr. Daly was none too pleased with me, as I was important to his income. As a gentleman player, though, I received no remuneration for my performances, so he could not complain too much, and promised me I could return to the company, providing I did not stay away too long, something I assured him in my reply, would not be long at all.

Mr. and Mrs. Potter graciously allowed me to extend my visit with them during my courtship of my new love, whom I was convinced would be happy to marry me and return with me to Ireland. Mr. Potter, however, took me in hand and warned me to think carefully, and to be sure my young lady would indeed be willing to return to Dublin with me, for if she did not, it would, he said, be the end of my career as an actor, should we stay in Haverfordwest.

"Connell, young man, don't do as I did," he said. "That's not to say I regret marrying my dear Elizabeth, not at all, but if you're an actor at heart, as I am, you'll always find it hard to fulfil your own life here in Haverfordwest. Look at me. I'm a printer and bookseller. I own a library and a reading room, and am a respected member of the community, but I still yearn to be treading the boards. It was what I was born to do, and it's something I regret having had to give up. So what I'm saying is, be prepared to have to make a choice: your young lady, or your career. These Pembrokeshire girls, I warn you, do not like to leave their homeland."

Being young and hot-headed, and sure of myself too, my advances never having been rejected by any young lady before, I was convinced the object of my passion would be only too happy to return to Ireland with me, should I ask her to marry me, so I courted her in the full expectation that I could not fail.

I won over my new love's mother in no time, but her father was not too happy about me courting his daughter. Outside the cultured cities, such as London and Dublin, actors are still looked upon as being rather disreputable people. Although fun to have around you, especially at soirées and parties where actors, known for their wit and repartee, are good to have as guests, they are generally not considered good enough for your daughters to marry.

Gentlemen players, such as I, are just that, gentlemen who liked to act, but who can also survive off their own incomes. Some even have estates of their own.

Even so, in places like Haverfordwest, it has taken a while for the locals to accept that an actor can be a gentleman and a reputable person at the same time. Mr. Potter himself had been a gentleman player, so had battled some prejudice when he first arrived in the town. However, he married the daughter of a gentleman despite the prejudice, so I saw no possible reason why I should not do the same, and the object of my love was the heavenly Miss Julia Faraday.

As I said, Mr. and Mrs. Potter's social life is a busy one, and they themselves do much of the entertaining, holding sumptuous and lively dinners where wit and wine flow in equal measure. It was at one of these dinners I met my Julia. I thought her the most beautiful, most gentle creature I had ever met, and by the end of the evening had fallen in love with her.

I had courted young ladies before, of course, although I have to admit I had never had to exert myself much as they were always only too happy to accept my advances. This, however, was the first time I had fallen in love with one of them.

Miss Faraday occupied my thoughts and whetted my desires every minute I was awake, and I stayed awake as long as possible at night continuing with my adoration. I was supposed to be returning to Ireland just two days later, but was so much in love, the thought of forsaking her was impossible to even contemplate. For the two nights preceding my scheduled departure, I don't think I slept at all and, devastated at the thought of leaving, when the day finally arrived, decided to stay behind. Thus began my courtship.

She lived some way out of town in a fine mansion, so I hired a horse for the duration. It had, of course, to be a fine, spirited animal to suit what I felt was my personality and to impress the object of my courtship, and I appeared on their doorstep every day, smiling, dressed as well as I knew how, ready to step out with my Julia. Looking back now, I suppose it was presumptuous of me to assume I was always welcome, but I think that, even so, I *was* welcome, as there were always smiles to greet me. Mr. Faraday was never there, though, so I don't know how his welcome would have been. I fear that perhaps I was a bit full of myself after all, and Mr. Daly was not there to set me to rights, so I had no qualms about showing up every day, eager to see my lovely lady.

We were lucky in that it was an unusually fine autumn, and Miss Faraday and I went out almost daily, wandering around their estate, accompanied by our chaperone. She was one of Miss Faraday's younger sisters, who did not endear herself to me, in that she liked to avail herself of my other arm as we walked along.

My Miss Faraday was fond of birds and flowers, despite seeming to know very little about them, knowing fewer names than I knew myself, and I was no expert. Desiring to impress and to be everything to her though, I did my best to show an interest when she stopped to admire every plant along the way, and to point out every bird that warbled.

"It's too bad you're not here at night time," she told me on one of our walks. "There's a bird that sings then, and it has a beautiful song. Have you ever heard a bird that sings at night, Mr. O'Keeffe?"

"Yes. I assume you're talking about the nightingale, which does indeed have a beautiful song. I used to hear them when I was growing up on my father's estate near Dublin."

"Oh! How exciting! What did you say it was called? That bird?"

"A nightingale."

"What a pretty name! I'll remember that," but she didn't.

By the time I finally fell out of love with Julia, I think I had been shown every plant and bird on their estate. I myself appreciate Nature too, and I do take note of the birds singing and the flowers blooming. I know many of their names too, but it was not until after we parted company, that I realized how bored I had become with having to remind Miss Faraday of the name of every plant I *did* know, and of every bird that opened its beak to proclaim its presence. Perhaps I had even become bored at the time, because I do remember trying to introduce new subjects, without success.

"What books do you enjoy reading, Miss Faraday?"

"Oh lots."

"Any specific authors? What have you read lately?"

"Oh lots."

"How about Henry Fielding? You must have read some of Fielding, or Swift. Have you read any of their works?"

"I'm not sure. Maybe."

"I think you'd remember if you *had* read them. You should. You'd enjoy them."

"Oh I will, Mr. O'Keeffe. I will, to be sure. You're so clever, Mr. O'Keeffe. Listen. I can hear a bird singing. Now you did tell me what that one was. I remember it particularly. What was it again?"

"A blackbird."

"Oh! You're so clever, Mr. O'Keeffe."

"Why? Because I can recognize a blackbird's song?"

"Oh I don't know." She spun around. "Do you like my dress today? I put it on especially for you."

"You're beautiful no matter what you wear, my dear Miss Faraday." I could say that truthfully, although I would have found her even more beautiful with no clothes on at all, but that pleasure would have to wait until our wedding night, an event I was only too sure would take place in the very near future. That Connell O'Keeffe might be unsuccessful in his endeavour to gain the wife of his choice, was not even contemplated. It could not happen. Why should it?

"What else do you like to do then, apart from look at plants and listen to birds singing?"

"Oh lots."

"Like what?"

"Oh, I don't know. Oh look at that sweet, tiny flower. Don't you think it adorable, Mr. O'Keeffe?"

"Yes, indeed. Did you come to see my company perform *Romeo and Juliet*?"

"Oh yes, Mr. O'Keeffe."

"And?"

"And what? Mr. O'Keeffe."

"Well, what did you think of it?"

"It was lovely, just lovely."

"Any special scenes you liked in particular? The balcony scene, perhaps?"

"Which one was that? Oh I thought it was all simply lovely. There's a ball being held at Crowcroft mansion this Saturday. Will you take me?"

"I'd be delighted to accompany you."

The prospect of accompanying my young lady to the upcoming ball was so exciting, the days leading up to it went far too slowly. Still having some money available, I went out and attired myself in the latest fashion, and was most satisfied with the image I presented to myself in the long mirror in my room. Mr. Daly, where were you?

Full of myself I may have been, but there was no denying we made a handsome couple at the ball, and many a lady whispered from behind her fan when we passed. Of course, I assumed they were all compliments, but then, my Miss Faraday was perfection itself, and I had not done anything to disgrace myself. I knew I looked a fine figure of a man, so there was no reason why they should not have been compliments.

Unfortunately, and most unusually for a young lady of her class, my lovely Julia was not the best of dancers, which rather spoiled the impression, and after the first three dances, in which she trod on my foot several times, I tried to find excuses not to take to the floor, my own vanity making me ashamed to be seen dancing with a woman who kept tripping me up. I even resorted to a pretence that I had somehow hurt myself, and assumed a rather dashing limp to back up my assertion.

"Poor Mr. O'Keeffe," I heard her lamenting to one of her friends. "He has hurt something or other, and can no longer dance. He's such a magnificent dancer too," I heard her add. I don't know whether I could rightly be called a magnificent dancer, but I was at least proficient in the art, which was more than could be said of my gorgeous Miss Faraday.

I came and stood next to her and her friends. "Good evening ladies. May I join you?" A space was made for me, and I sat down. Female wit can be caustic and exciting, sharper than that of the men at times, certainly more biting. This should be interesting.

"Did you hear, Miss Faraday? Poor old Mrs. Jones is not well at all. She was walking down High Street a week ago last Wednesday, and tripped. She fell quite heavily, I understand, and had to be carried home."

"Oh really? Mrs. Jenkins too has fallen at exactly the same spot. They should do something about it. I'm sure I'm quite nervous when walking in that area, but then Haverfordwest has a reputation for being the most horrendous place in which to walk. Why, only a few days ago, I myself nearly fell... Oh! Have you seen the latest muslins at Mrs. Morgan's boutique, *Bon Marché*? I swear I must go there and buy several dress lengths. I think the lavender shade..."

My mind wandered, and after a respectable stay in their presence, I excused myself, and went off in search of Mr. Potter.

Looking back now, I wonder that I ever thought I could spend the rest of my life with Miss Faraday. There was no denying her beauty and her gentle manner, but at the time I failed to see beyond those two desirable qualities, which I finally realized were indeed her *only* desirable qualities. We had nothing to talk about, and almost nothing in common. For a lady in her position in society, she knew very little, and was not accomplished in any way that I discovered. Her conversational skills were so poor too, that I ran out of subjects to discuss; there are only so many times one can rescue a conversation, when each attempt is brought to an abrupt end by the simple response of "yes", or "no", or "lots".

Despite our obvious differences and lack of compatibility, my judgment was nevertheless clouded by those two desirable qualities, and I continued to court her, ignoring her -- yes -- lack of intelligence, and I continued to ask her to marry me and return to Ireland with me. I found her so attractive: her lithe, elegant body, her exquisite features, her long blonde hair, and I loved nothing more than to lift her onto or off her horse, help her over a style, or do anything that would give me an excuse to put my arms around her, or even to just touch her. She smelled so sweet too, like some of the flowers she loved so much, and I wanted her more than I had ever wanted any woman. It was good that we did have a chaperone, I suppose, although I would not have done anything too outrageous. I was too much of a gentleman to take that sort of advantage of a lady.

As it turned out, however, Mr. Potter was right, but it took several months of entreaties for me to come to the conclusion that I did need to make that decision between my love of acting and my love of Miss Faraday, and when it came to making that decision, I realized physical attraction was not enough, and decided my acting was more important to me. It was ironical, though, that within a week of my decision my acting career was over anyway. After all, how many parts are there for a one-armed actor? However, at the time, I was not to know what disaster was about to befall me.

I suppose the same could be said for my Miss Faraday when it came to making a choice: she loved her home more than she loved me, so neither of us was sufficiently in love to make sacrifices for the other, and our parting was, in the end, anticlimactic. There were no sobs and tears of desolation, no proper farewell even, and I am sure I was no sooner out of sight than another beau was there to replace me, and by that time he was welcome. The more I thought about her afterwards, the more gratified I was that she had *not* wanted to leave Pembrokeshire; our marriage would not have been a happy one.

When I told Mr. Potter about my decision, he was blunt. "I was wondering how long it would take you to realize she was not the right woman for you, O'Keeffe. You need a woman with spirit, a woman to stand up to you, keep you in line, bring you back down to earth," he laughed.

"Oh I do, do I?" I feigned offense. "I'm not sure how I'd react to a woman who tried to dominate me, or stand up to me. It would make for a lively union though, no doubt," I added.

He laughed. "I like you O'Keeffe, and shall be very sorry to see you go, but having seen you perform, I know you have a great career ahead of you, something you would not have if you stayed here. I can even see you ending up in Drury Lane, or at the Haymarket, acting for that cousin of yours, John O'Keeffe. He and I were good friends too, although it was sad to have to watch him gradually go blind after falling into that canal in his late twenties. Let's hope tragedy like that is not something common to the O'Keeffe family, eh?"

"I have to agree with you, Sir. I can't imagine not being able to act, and I know poor John O'Keeffe took to writing using the help of an amanuensis because he could no longer act on account of his blindness... I'm not sure how good I'd be as a playwright."

"Well, let's hope you're not put to the test, young man."

The weather being warm for the time of year, I decided to take a circuitous route to Fishguard. I was in no hurry, and had heard of the fine, ancient cathedral in the little city of St. David's, so being interested in church architecture, thought to go there first. This I did, after first hiring a good-looking gelding at the local hostelry, with the understanding that I would leave it in Fishguard on my departure from that town.

Mr. Potter, riding his wonderful old Irish horse, Hercules, accompanied me as far as Roch, where we shook hands. "Have a safe trip home, Connell," and he turned off towards the coast, where he planned to go to Druidston after leaving me.

Thus, on a fine February day, just a month ago, I set out on my journey back home to Dublin and my now one and only love, acting.

After saying goodbye to Mr. Potter, I passed through Roch, which had a small castle off to the right of the road, sitting on its small, elevated rock, and consisting of scarcely more than a single keep. There were exceedingly few fine carriages on the road. Those people I did meet, were riding mostly donkeys, and there were few of them too. Occasionally I would pass a wagon loaded with a bright, shiny coal, and drawn by two enormous oxen with immensely wide and fearsome horns, although they looked anything but aggressive otherwise, being quite docile as they plodded along, yoked together. Most of the people I saw appeared to be quite poor.

My ride was leisurely, and the weather remaining pleasant, I was able to take in the splendid countryside, although it was a bit on the wild side, with wide, heather- and gorse-covered moors stretching away to the Preseli hills in the distance.

By mid-day it was so warm I took off my wool coat and even my waistcoat, and rode along in the sunshine, wearing just my white-linen shirt, breeches and boots. I had plenty of time to think, and was now glad I was going home unencumbered by a wife, especially Miss Faraday, and could not imagine what I had seen in her. It was just the physical attraction that had lured me, and I was relieved I had come to my senses finally, although, had she accepted my offer of marriage, there was no knowing what would have happened, for, as a gentleman, I would not have been able to back out of the arrangement had I changed my mind afterwards. I breathed a huge sigh of relief; I had had a near miss.

Everyone seemed to be suffering from the unseasonal heat, and I passed through some areas where farmers were out planting their corn, but come noon, were leaving the fields, some of them commenting to me as I passed, that it was just too hot to keep on working.

I continued on my way, and thought about how I had written to Mr. Daly, telling him I was on my way back. He would not be too pleased with my having missed the first few months of the season, but he would get over it, I was sure. After all, as I said, my services as an actor came free, and although he enjoyed putting me in my place, he still recognized that I did bring him in a good income. I had not written to my parents though. I had told them earlier I would be staying over with Mr. Potter for a while, as I had met a young lady whom I was courting. Right now they were away on a grand tour in Europe anyway, having left home just before Christmas

I took my time, passing by a lovely long beach, shelved with great piles of stones, and through the pretty little village of Solva, where many small boats were moored, finally arriving at my destination by sundown, which was quite early, it being only February after all. It had been a most enjoyable day's trip, especially as the weather was so pleasant, considering the time of year, and I was happy and contented.

The bed was comfortable, and the inn relatively quiet, the innkeeper not permitting much in the way of drunken behaviour, and the following day I arose quite late for me, being normally an early riser. I dawdled over a fine breakfast, prepared for me by my most hospitable husband-and-wife hosts, with whom I spent some time chatting, although they had some problem speaking in English, often conferring with each other as to the correct translation of certain words. Even so, they managed to give me excellent information on what was worth seeing in and around the area, and it being another mild and pleasant day, I wandered around on foot, even walking out to the ancient St. Non's well, which, legend has it, will cure your ills if you drink of its deep, clear water.

Having no ills to cure, my pilgrimage there was not for that purpose, but I drank the water all the same, and found it most palatable and icy cold. I had also read the travels of Geraldus Cambrensis, and even had a copy of his writings with me, so was able to visit the locations he too had visited and commented on in St. David's, making my time there that much more interesting.

St. David's itself was little more than a village, despite being a city on account of its cathedral, and after spending another comfortable night there, I was ready to set off in the morning on the last part of my journey to Fishguard.

At breakfast that day I noticed what seemed to be quite animated conversation amongst the locals, but being now in Welsh-speaking Wales, and unable to understand the language, I had no idea what they were talking about. My hosts being too busy serving their guests to be able to give me the time to ask what might be going on, I was unable to ask them to explain either. There did seem to be quite a bit of grim animation in the conversations I overhead, however, accompanied by much gesticulating and pointing, and I wondered if the Welsh were always like this, or whether something special was afoot, and causing what seemed almost like consternation.

There certainly was not much jollity in them, and those not in the midst of their animated conversations seemed almost glum, something I put down to the Welsh having been taken up with the preachings of Mr. John Wesley, who had made frequent visits to Wales up until his death six years ago. I had been to a couple of services in one of the many non-conformist chapels that had sprouted up in Haverfordwest over recent years since his visits, and found it a rather depressing interpretation of our Lord and his will for us. Maybe everyone in St. David's was going around with the fear of Hellfire hanging over them like the sword of Damocles. Whatever it was, although I enjoyed my visit to St. David's itself, and its formidable cathedral, I can't say I was taken with the people, unless, of course, they did have some reason for looking out of countenance that I was unaware of.

The weather was fair again on this morning, and still exceptionally warm for the time of year -- people later claimed it was the warmest ever experienced. The distance to Fishguard was slightly longer than that from Haverfordwest to St. David's, but I was in no hurry, and ambled along, even singing to myself, and thinking that, all being well, I could catch a boat that night, and by the following week would be once again treading the boards in Dublin. I could not wait now, as it seemed so very long since I had last performed, and I realized how much I had missed it.

A magpie flew across the road in front of me, scolding loudly. I am not superstitious, or wasn't so at the time, but know many who are sure to take note of how many magpies cross their paths at one time, and I could not help reciting the old rhyme out loud, keeping in time to the lazy clip clop of my horse's hooves:

> One for sorrow, two for joy,
> Three for a wedding, four for a boy.
> Five for silver, six for gold,
> Seven for a secret never to be told.

By mid afternoon, as I approached Fishguard just a mile or so from the village of Manorowen, I began meeting people who appeared to be fleeing inland for some reason, but on enquiring what was going on, was unable to understand what it was they were telling me. They just kept pointing towards the coast. The weather was still calm and quite balmy, so it could not be a storm, and I had no idea what the problem could be. Even so, I was now in a quandary. I was fewer than two miles from Fishguard, but it definitely seemed as though there was something worth fleeing from, so the question was: should I too head back inland, or continue on my way?

I decided to get off the road just long enough to climb a nearby hill to see what it could be that was so terrifying to the local people, they felt it necessary to flee their homes. Off to my left I could see a rocky crag rising up. It was not far away at all, and if I climbed it, it should give me a good view of the surrounding countryside. There was even a style leading into the field out of which the crag rose.

I stopped and dismounted, and tied my horse to a nearby tree. Once over the style, I could no longer see my mount, the hedge being so high and thick, but had to assume nothing would happen to it, it being unlikely anyone would steal it as it was branded with a nick in its ear, which made it easily recognizable. It was also an unusually handsome horse, a pure black, with four white stockings and a white star that had attracted me to it in the first place -- a horse I would not mind owning, I had thought.

I had gone half way across the field, when I noticed two soldiers of His Majesty, dressed in handsome uniforms, standing alone a couple of hundred yards or so ahead of me. I had been so busy keeping my eye on the crag, I had not noticed them at first. Anyway, now I would not have to climb it at all, as they would no doubt speak English, and be able to tell me what, if anything, was going on, so I continued to walk towards them.

They did not see me, but then it dawned on me that they were in the middle of a heated altercation, with much shouting and angry gesticulations, although they were too far away for me to hear what was being said. I stopped, not wanting to find myself in the middle of an argument between two very irate men. I was even about to turn around and head back to my horse, when I was horrified to see the one draw his sword, and before the other had time to draw his, he had run him through, killing him outright. The soldier fell, and lay motionless, apparently run through the heart.

I stood, too shocked to move for a few seconds, then the killer, an officer I could tell now, saw me. I am no coward, but had no wish at all to come face to face with a murderer, especially one who knew I had witnessed his crime. I headed back down the field at a run.

Unfortunately, there was no visible path across the field, and in my haste to retreat, I forgot exactly where the style was, so was up against an impenetrable thorn hedge when he caught up with me, sword raised. It was a large cavalry sabre with a vicious point that had enabled him to do what he had just done. It was covered with blood, and the look on his face was one I shall never forget; he seemed almost demented.

I drew my own sword, and immediately found myself in a battle for my life. I had just seen him murder a fellow officer, and he had no intention of letting me leave the scene to tell the tale if he could help it. He no doubt also saw in me a scapegoat for his crime. We fought for several minutes, during which I nicked him several times. Unlike him, I was not out to kill; I simply wanted to make sure he could not kill me.

It was soon obvious to me that I was by far the superior swordsman, and it was not long before I was able to knock his sword from his hand.

In the past, my swordsmanship had been purely for show, sufficiently realistic to impress the male members of the theatre-going public, and I had never engaged in a serious duel, let alone killed anyone, and had no intention of doing so now. I was satisfied to know only that he was no longer in a position to kill me.

It must have been because of the extraordinary position in which I had suddenly found myself that I did not think clearly, even to the extent of assuming that, even though this man had just killed someone, he would still be a gentleman when it came to duelling etiquette. It was a ridiculous assumption, of course, but, as I said, one does not always think clearly in the heat of the moment, and when one considers that just a few minutes before, I had been ambling along the road, looking forward to arriving in Fishguard, and dreaming of being back in the theatre, I think I may be forgiven for not thinking clearly. Anyway, for whatever reason, I followed the etiquette by standing on the edge of his sword, then bending it until it snapped in two. I then tapped him on the shoulder with my own, and said the words, "I spare you your life." The convention in duelling then is, of course, that such a fight can never be re-activated by the loser, but if he does, then the winner has the right to retaliate.

I walked away, found the style, and greatly shaken, continued my ride to Fishguard, becoming more and more distressed about the whole episode as the experience sank in, and if I had not been so preoccupied with going over the horror of what had just occurred, I would no doubt have been quick-witted and alert enough to avoid what happened next: a disastrous mental aberration that was to change the course of my life in an instant.

I had gone barely a quarter mile when two men jumped me, and before I could escape, had taken hold of my horse's bridle. The one was the man whose life I had just spared, the other, an officer I had not seen before.

"That's him." The killer pointed at me. "He's the one who cut him down. I saw him do it. Make him show you his sword. It'll still have blood on it."

It was true my sword had blood on it, but it wasn't the victim's blood; it was his. "I've killed no-one," I protested, and pointed to the murderer. "He was the one. It was he who murdered a fellow officer, then came after me and tried to kill me too."

Both men laughed. "I see we have a typical Paddy liar here," said the second officer, laughing at what he no doubt believed to be my outrageous claim. They pulled me off my horse, and I landed with a jarring thud on the ground, and while I was still down, the one held me, while the killer seized my sword. I saw my mount canter off down the road towards Fishguard. Now I was in great danger, and my distress about what had happened back in the field turned to panic.

"I suggest we carry out justice right now," the killer was urging. "Save hauling him in as a prisoner. He deserves to die this instant for what he's done." He was waving my sword in front of me, making slashing motions with it.

The other shook his head. "No, we shouldn't do that. Besides, his body will be found, and there'll be questions asked. I don't want it on my conscience. We need to leave him to the authorities to deal with."

"But he's obviously one of the invaders. Why would he kill one of us otherwise? No doubt he was too much of a coward to stay and fight, and stole that horse from a passing gentleman."

"Yes, but if he's one of the invaders, why isn't he wearing a Frenchie uniform?"

"Probably stole those clothes too. He could have even murdered to get them." The killer seized hold of my shirt, which was all I had on above my breeches -- my coat and waistcoat still being tied to the saddle of my now vanished horse. "Good quality too. Probably killed the unfortunate gentleman. That horse he was riding was an excellent animal too." He glared at me. "Not only a killer of one His Majesty's soldiers, but of a gentleman too. If I had my way, you'd die right here, and now. You're nothing but a criminal. Nothing!"

My only hope lay in the second officer. "I don't know what you're talking about. Who invaded? And where? What uniform?"

This they found greatly amusing. "Kissed the Blarney Stone then, have we? Don't come over all innocent on us, Paddy," said the second officer. "We know exactly what you are, and you're coming with us, alive, and you can thank me for that. If it were up to my fellow officer here, you'd be dead already, so count yourself lucky." He shook his head in disbelief. "Doesn't know what we're talking about indeed," he laughed, then looked at me. "I'll say this for you, you're a good liar."

"But I've been in the country for nearly four months. I have witnesses who can prove it, and I've never killed anyone in my life. I'm an actor."

"An actor, eh? Well, if you *are* one, you're good at it for sure. Play the innocent like a professional."

"I left Haverfordwest only the day before yesterday, and have been staying in St. David's at the Cambrian Inn. Ask. I can prove it."

"Got your alibi from the poor gentleman you stole from and killed, did you? You're resourceful, I'll give you that," said the killer.

"You!" I pointed at him. "You know what you did. I saw you kill your fellow officer. What's more, you can't show us your own sword, because I broke it when you tried to kill me too."

"Broke my sword, did you? Then how is it I still have it right here, intact?" He drew out a sabre.

At first I wondered where he could have found another one, but then realized he must have gone back and stolen it from his victim. I pointed to it. "That's not your sword. That's the sword of the man you killed."

The murderer glared at me. "Nonsense! I myself saw you break my comrade's sword in half right after you killed him. It's still lying in the field, where you left it."

"But check that sword." I pointed to the one he now had in his other hand. "It'll identify the true owner."

They both laughed at that. "These are regulation swords issued by the militia. They don't identify the wearer."

I had no answer to that, and my case, as far as they were both concerned, was lost. This being so, the killer was even more anxious to carry out some form of justice on the spot. "Well, if we don't kill him, then I mean to make him pay personally for what he did to my friend. That much you'll have to allow me," he told the second officer.

The other man shrugged. "What are you going to do? Give him a good horse whipping? That I'll go along with. As long as we deliver the prisoner back to camp alive, that's all that matters."

I had never been more scared than at this moment. We had been standing in the middle of the road, but now, while the one held his sword at the ready, the killer went over to the gate to a field, and opened it. "Bring him in here, just in case someone comes by. Don't want any witnesses," he added.

They both then took hold of me, and although I fought back, my struggles were useless, as they were as big and as strong as I was, and with the murderer holding on to my left arm, and the other officer onto my right, they dragged me into the field, where they tore off my shirt.

For a few moments we all stood there, a grim tableau, while my panic rose. Then the killer drew out a hunting whip, the sort that can deliver a wicked, flesh-cutting lash when used efficiently, and by the way he was cracking it, it was clear he knew how to use it.

"Hold out his arm." The murderer's voice was casual. "Let me take a good look at this wastrel, before I have the pleasure of punishing him." He was standing right in front of me, legs apart, surveying me. The sabre was in his right hand, the whip now in the other, and the thought passed through my mind that he must be left-handed. The other man still held me firmly by my right arm, his own sword ready in case I tried to get away.

"Just raise it," he repeated. "That's it. Out straight."

I wondered what he had in mind. I had no shirt on, but was he going to confine his whipping to my right arm?

He could do serious damage if he were to concentrate on just that one area, but that's perhaps what he intended doing as punishment for my having beaten him in our duel. The last thing I could afford though, was for him to damage it irreparably; after all, my whole career depended on my right arm, and I started to struggle again.

"Stand still."

There were two of them against my one, and I stopped struggling, and then came the worst moment of my life. The other officer, not knowing what to expect, any more than I did right then, held out my arm as instructed. In that instant I knew what the killer intended. He was *not* left-handed. And I let out a shriek.

"*No!*"

My voice went echoing through the hills, but it did not save me, for in that instant he had raised his sabre, and brought the lethally sharp blade down, full force, striking a mere few inches below my shoulder, to cut straight through the bone, and slicing off my arm just an inch or so below the armpit. The second officer recoiled, and dropped my severed arm, the hand of which he had been holding, and I watched it fall to the ground, seemingly in slow motion, and fainted.

When I came to my senses, the field was moving beneath me, a trail of my blood dripping, spattering the blades of grass beneath me as I went. I was slung over someone's shoulder and tried to say something, but nothing came out. Then I tried to free myself.

"Keep still, or I'll drop you." It was the killer's voice. Then I was sick, and he did.

I was lying on the ground in an army camp, and all around me were men dressed in the same uniform as the killer. I turned my head to my side, where I was suffering the most agonizing pain. What was left of my right arm had a piece of wire wound tightly round it to stop the blood from gushing out. It looked like a shin of beef after the butcher has severed it with a cleaver, and I was sick again at the sight of it.

Someone came up and pointed his crop down at me. "Deal with this now before he loses any more blood, and dies," he ordered. "He may be the enemy and a killer, but do what's necessary to alleviate the pain. I'm not inclined to torture."

Panicking, I tried to get up, but couldn't. Then someone hit me on the side of my head.

This time, when I woke, it was dark, and almost everyone was lying around asleep. Even though I had a blanket over me, I shivered with cold, shock and pain. The pain was like nothing I had ever experienced before. It was impossible to keep still, and I writhed around, trying to escape from it, but it made no difference, and every way I turned I could smell my seared flesh.

"Will someone keep that stupid Paddy quiet?" I must have woken everyone, because someone came over and caused me to cough and splutter by pouring brandy down my throat, all the time complaining about the waste of good brandy. Every time I did swallow it, more would be poured down me, until I was silenced.

I do not know how long I had been unconscious, but it was morning when I was lifted onto a farm wagon. From the smell, I guessed it was usually used for carrying manure, and I began being sick again from a combination of the smell, the pain and all the brandy I had consumed. Being on my back I was in danger of choking, and someone rolled me over onto my side.

I was still in the wagon, still on my side, with stooks of straw packed tightly at my back and front to stop me rolling around, or even moving. It was claustrophobic, hot, with nothing but straw to see, but the midday sun was burning into the side of my head and the stump of my arm, searing it like the cauterizing iron itself had done. There was the sound of waves, and a tumult of voices beyond the straw, but it was the pain that overshadowed everything, an excruciating, unrelenting torture. The brandy, the heat and loss of blood produced a tremendous thirst too, my mouth so dry, my tongue stuck to the roof of it, and I tried to call out, but no sound came, and my body, finally overcome, gave me some respite, as I became unconscious again, and with it went the pain.

I am not sure what happened after that, but eventually I woke up in the church to which Mr. Potter and his family had taken me while I was living with them, St. Mary's Church, in Haverfordwest. Apparently it was midnight before we arrived there, so I had been unconscious for a number of hours, all during the slow procession from what I found out later had been Goodwick beach, right next to Fishguard harbour, which I had been so close to reaching before disaster struck.

I was stretched out in a private pew, where no-one would bump into me, and a woman was trying to give me some water. The whole church was reverberating with the sound of people moaning, shouting and banging. The stench was overpowering, and I was sick yet again.

"Please... please would you go just the few yards down the road to Tower Hill for me, and tell Mr. Potter, the printer, that I'm here. I'm not supposed to be here. I'm not one of the invaders. I'm an actor."

She patted me on the hand. "Not you mind, 'un'. You just lie there quiet now. Your 'ead's all mixed up." She forced some more water down my throat.

"No, no! Please. I'm not mixed up at all, I... I..." I must have fainted again, because when I woke up, she was gone. It was night again, and there was no sign of my Mr. Potter.

The moon was shining in through one of the windows, and I watched its light glide slowly along the back of the pew next to me, revealing the notches and cracks one by one, then hiding them again as its beam slid past. Apart from some moans coming from the very sick, the church was silent, but there was no sleeping for me because of the pain again, and I turned my head towards it. The small, useless stump, all that was left of the arm with which I had performed almost everything that had been of importance and pride to me in my life, lay there, inert, now nothing more than a source of agony.

Until now I had been in no state to consider all that was happening to me. Now though, shocked and in despair, I called out for help, my voice this time echoing around the stone-wall confines of the church, but no-one came, and the long night gradually faded into the indigo of the early dawn.

At first I was too weak from blood loss to even sit up, but a couple of local women who came in twice a day, bringing food to everyone, seemed to find something special about me, and saw to it that I received my share of nourishment, and I gradually improved. I think this was because, unlike my fellow prisoners, the real invaders, I had at least been well-fed and healthy before my encounter with the murderer near the village of Manorowen. The cut had been clean as well, and the cauterization had done its job, crude though it was, so I had no infection, and as my body began to rebuild its lost blood supply, so I gained strength.

I continued to ask if they could find Mr. Potter for me, but no-one took any notice, thinking my mind had succumbed to the strain, and I wondered what my former hosts would think if they discovered what had happened to their guest. If only I had been able to get a message to them, I know I would have been out of there and back in the security of their home within the hour, but I could not contact them, and here I was, helpless and unable to save myself.

The poor church, meanwhile, was becoming more and more of a cesspit as the days went by, and more and more desecrated and damaged by those who were still well enough to wreak vengeance on the building. The smell worsened daily as well, as we were all locked in there, and there was nowhere to take care of necessary bodily functions, other than right there in the church, one corner of which was designated for that purpose. Many had come down with the flux as well, and were dying of it.

I wondered too how my parents would react if they knew of my situation. Fortunately, I am not the most faithful of writers to them, and the last they had heard from me was that I intended staying in Haverfordwest to court the lovely Julia Faraday. As far as they knew, that was where I still was, and what I was still doing. My poor mother would be severely ill with worry if she knew, and my father would be on his way here to help his wronged son. If I had had the chance, I would certainly have contacted him, for, as a baronet, he would be able to bring pressure to bear to get me out of this. Even if I could though, I would not know where to find him as, as I said, just before Christmas he and my mother had left on a grand tour, and they were not expected back until the end of May at the earliest. I did not even know which country they might be in. It was most likely that they were in Italy, but where, I had no idea.

During my time there in St. Mary's, I also learned what all this was about, and that some fourteen hundred, mostly French, but a few Irish Republicans too, had landed not far from where I had had my encounter with the officers. The intention had been for the local peasants to join the invaders, and rise up against their English overlords. For various reasons, however, their invasion was a failure, and now they were all prisoners, the Irish ones, being all officers except for me, of course, being held for trial as traitors to our king.

I wondered what had happened afterwards in that field of mutilation on Pen Caer, and how the other officer had reacted to what was done to me, but one thing was certain, one or both of them had gone to the trouble of ensuring I looked like one of the invaders, by dressing me in a French uniform. This meant that I, being Irish, was being accused -- officer or not -- not only of having killed one of His Majesty's officers, but of being a traitor to His Majesty, King George as well. This being the case, I was in much greater danger than the French prisoners, because I faced being hanged for my crime should I come to trial. There was even a witness, the real killer, to what I had supposedly done, willing to swear to it, and how I had done it.

I lay on my back in my private pew, and thought about my chances of surviving this ordeal. As I said, with everything they had against me, I would be hanged if I did not escape. How I lost my arm was of no concern to anyone; it was assumed it was done in battle. That I had

44

supposedly turned traitor against His Majesty would outweigh all other considerations, and mark me for special retribution.

If only I could persuade someone to bring Mr. Potter to me, my proof that I was not an invader. However, although I was within yards of his home, I could not reach him, as no-one would help me, and I remained there, watching the continued destruction and desecration of that fine church, helpless, an anonymous, wounded Irish Republican prisoner looking at death as a traitor.

I was at a loss to know how to save myself. With no access to Mr. Potter, my only hope was to escape. But how? There was no chance of passing through those immense oak doors, barred on the outside, and even if I could have knocked out a window, I was in no physical shape to climb out through it. Besides, there were guards all around the church, looking for anyone who might risk making such an attempt.

CHAPTER 3

We had been there a week or more -- by which time the desecration and destruction had transformed the once-beautiful church into something less than a pig sty -- when the authorities came in, and we were divided up. They separated the sick, which included me, from the others, and told us we were to be transported to a place near Burton, called Barnlake, which had been converted into a hospital.

One hundred and seventeen of us set out, most suffering from the flux, but only one hundred and fourteen of us arrived alive, the others having died on the journey, which was only a few hours from Haverfordwest, Barnlake being located just before the river-crossing to Pembroke.

The weather by this time had broken, and March was coming in like a lion, with severe south-westerly gales and pouring rain. Even so, the journey, and with it the clean, fresh air, was a welcome relief after being locked up in the stinking church, and those that were well enough even removed all their clothes so as to take advantage of the free bath. Cold and covered in filth, I was only partially dressed to start with, and that in the remains of my French uniform, which consisted of torn black breeches with the buttons undone because I could not do them up, a jacket half on, the other half hanging off my shoulder, and nothing else: no shirt, no shoes, my hair matted with my own blood and dirt. My beard had grown too, and was a filthy stubble. Even if I had wanted to, I could not get the breeches off, so all I needed to do was to shake off my jacket, and let the rain do its best.

When my hair was soaked through, which took almost no time at all, the rain being so heavy, I rubbed my hand through it, rinsing out all the foul muck. I think even the lice balked at trying to invade my head, as I was one of the few not infested. I rubbed my hand over those parts of my body I could reach, scraping away with my nails to try to remove what had become almost ingrained, and by the time we arrived at Barnlake, my skin was pink with abrasion, and in some places I had drawn blood, where I had been over-zealous in my attempts to clean myself. Even my fast-growing beard had a thorough cleansing. The only part of me I worried about was my arm, where the rain had softened the cauterized area, and I was afraid it would break through and either start pouring out my blood again, or get infected.

The carts carrying us all, inched along by plodding oxen, lurched and trundled their way over the rough, rock-strewn road, adding even further to my pain. There being so many of us to a wagon, there was no room to lie down, so I sat there with my eyes closed, too worn out to bother to look at the sodden and fog-bound countryside through which we were passing.

I thought of how I should now be back in my comfortable Dublin home, preparing to take part in my next play at the Crow Street Theatre, and tears, blending with my already soaking face, fell unnoticed. Even if I ever got out of this situation alive, my career was over. Never again would I play Romeo or Hotspur, or entertain my audience with a display of fencing. They would be just two of the things I would never be able to do again, ever.

When we arrived, I and others suffering from wounds of various sorts, were separated again from those with the flux for fear that we too might come down with it. If there were any non-officer Irish amongst us, I did not meet them, and as all the officers had been separated from the rest of us before we even got to Haverfordwest, I was among a very rough crowd indeed, and none of them spoke English apart from me. Some, if fit to act in any way at all, behaved like criminals, and their manners were no better than those of animals. No wonder the church had been all but destroyed.

For about an hour we were left outside in the farmyard in the rain, some even collapsing right there into the mud, no longer able to cope with the flux draining the life out of them. Then someone came and inspected all of us, assigning each to certain groups, before leading them away to who knows where. The whole place, a converted farm set in a small depression in the surrounding hill, was almost six inches deep in mud.

As a hospital, it was a sorry place, not even worthy of being considered a hospital at all. There were no beds or wards, only cow barns and stables with straw on the floor. There were no nurses as such, just a few dirty, ill-kempt women, dressed in little more than rags, who did not look as though they knew anything about looking after themselves, let alone the sick and wounded, nor did they seem to be in any way prepared for the arrival of one hundred and fourteen men in various stages of ill health.

Gradually everyone disappeared until I was left by myself, still sitting in the cart, and by this time almost ready to collapse as well, not having recovered sufficiently to be able to cope with what we were being subjected to. I sat there, huddled up, my soaking jacket hanging off one shoulder because I had not been able to pull it round me.

I was at about the end of my ability to stay awake, or conscious, when a man came and led me to a tiny stable that must have been for a donkey by the size of it. He opened the door and ushered me inside, pushing my head down so I did not bang it on the low door frame. At least the floor was above the level of the surrounding mud, and there was a thick layer of clean straw on it, and it was dry, which meant the roof was intact, although water was streaming down the moss-covered stone walls, and there were no windows.

It must have been clear to him that I was in no fit state to try to escape, as only the bottom half of the door was closed, allowing in what was left of the daylight. I sank down onto the straw. After the hard pew of St. Mary's Church, it felt like down itself.

I don't know if it was because I looked and behaved in a manner different from the rest of the prisoners arriving at Barnlake, or if it was because I was the only Irishman, but I was surprised to find I had my stable to myself, my own private accommodation, which was a great relief as long as they did not forget about me, and leave me there to rot.

After all the activity and noise surrounding me for the past week or more, the quiet was strange. There were no footsteps, no-one at all, at least not anywhere near me. There were no cries, no moans, the only sounds being those of the gusting wind rattling the stable door and soughing through the alleyway, the driving rain splattering into the puddles outside, and constant dripping. I lay there on my back, and gazed at the ancient rafters and off to my side where, framed by the open door, the waterlogged clouds, a never-ending convoy of leaden, pearl-edged pillows, drifted past.

The stable was worse, much worse than some of the cow sheds on my father's home farm. The air was dank. The smell of rotting, mouldy straw filled the air, and festoons of generations of spiders' webs hung down from the rafters, and that cold, fine rain continued to drive in from the southwest.

My spirits had reached as low as it was possible for them to get. Even if I had not been a prisoner, the realization that I would no longer be able to do some of the simplest things for myself was enough on its own to send an active and independent young man like me into depression, and I was so weak anyway, I began to cry like a teenage girl, lying there weeping, my shoulders heaving, dwelling on what I could not do, and would never be able to do again, full of self pity.

Apart from no longer being an actor, I would never again be able to do anything that required tying: the strings at the knees of my breeches, a silk scarf around my neck. Nor would I be able to take to the dance-floor with a lady. I could not go game hunting with either a gun or bow and arrow either, or play cricket, wield a knife and fork, or even write properly. Hourly my list grew longer, and by the time someone came to deliver food to me, I was curled up in the straw, shaking, finally overwhelmed by my dire situation, and wishing myself dead.

"Oh my, my! Oh dear." I raised my head. An old woman was standing over me. She was carrying a bowl of something, which she set down on a bench near the door, then came back to me. "Oh dear. Oh dear."

I gazed up at her, still shaking, my eyes so swollen and full of water I could barely see, and she sat herself down in the straw and took me in her arms, rocking me like a baby. "Oh dear. Oh dear," she kept repeating.

I was beyond responding, and lay there, and think that if she had not come at that moment, I might well have succumbed, having given up, my breath coming in short gasps, like that of a dying man.

I think she must have thought so too, because she stroked my head, talking away in soothing tones, like a mother consoling a sick child. "There, there. Not you fret, 'un'." She sat there rocking me back and forth, then went to wrap my jacket round my chest to keep me warm, and saw my arm. "Oh dear. You poor dab. Oh dear. No wonder..."

She stayed with me for an hour or more, until she was sure I was not about to die, then laid me down on the straw, and stood up. "Let me go get you somethin' for that, 'un'. Not you fret now, 'un'. Mrs. Beynon'll take care of it for you. You stay right there now, 'un'. I'll be right back. Not you fret..."

Her voice disappeared into the distance, and I lay there where she left me, unmoving, my breath still coming in deep sobs, and when she returned, I was still lying in the same place. It was as though my body and my spirits had finally collapsed under the strain of the last ten days' horrors, unable to take any more. I was by now too dazed to even think at all.

She sat down behind me and slid her body down so my head and shoulders were in her lap. She had brought a bowl of hot water and a clean rag, and began to clean the soaking stump of my arm, which had bits of fluff and dirt from the jacket sticking to it.

"There, there," she said when I flinched. "Let Mrs. Beynon do this now for you, 'un'. It's a wonder you 'aven't 'ad no infection. You must be of a strong constitution." She was methodical, talking away to me all the time. Then she patted it dry. "There. Now I be goin' to put some of my special ointment on it; make sure you don't get no infection. We'll do this twice a day for you, shall we, 'un'? There now. I'll bind it up with this nice, clean piece of linen, 'un'. It'll keep the dirt out. There we are, 'un'."

All this time I had said nothing, but my shaking gradually stopped, and I began to relax. She remained seated there, and eventually I fell asleep in her arms.

I'm sure Mrs. Beynon saved my life that day, and that without her emotional and physical support I, like so many others there at Barnlake, would have succumbed, and then been tossed into the anonymous trench along with them, and no-one would ever have known what had happened to me. I would have simply vanished, and my parents would have been left forever wondering what became of their only son, something that would have been particularly devastating for both of them, for, after my birth, my mother had been unable to conceive again, leaving me as an only child. It would also have meant the end of that branch of the O'Keeffe line, and the baronetcy that went with it.

"Wot's a proper 'andsome young gent like you doin' 'ere anyway, 'un'?" Mrs. Beynon asked me the next day. "You don' be like the rest of 'em at all. You don't fit."

"What makes you think I'm a gentleman, Mrs. Beynon?"

"Ah, I been aroun' long enough to know one when I sees one, 'un', an' you don' be no peasant like the rest of 'em."

I sighed. "It's a long story, Mrs. Beynon."

She sat down next to me on the straw. "You wants to tell it me, 'un'?"

What had I to lose? And it was good to have a motherly soul on whom to pour out all my sorrows, so I told her, and every now and then she would tut and shake her head, and put a gentle hand on my back.

"And so here I am, Mrs. Beynon, and thanks to you, I'm sure, still alive," I ended, and she took my hand, and squeezed it.

"It's wicked you bein' 'ere in this state, 'un'. 'Ow your dear mother'd worry if she knewd wot 'ad become of 'er son, I dunno. It not be right. Not right at all, 'un'." She got up and left, still shaking her head and muttering to herself.

Mrs. Beynon continued to fuss over and take care of me, and a few days later arrived with the news that Lord Cawdor of Stackpole had decided that those prisoners who could be moved, were to be taken to the prison hulks in Portsmouth.

"Them ol' ships 'as a terrible reputation," she told me. "An' I dunno if a refined young gent like you'd survive, wot with you bein' crippled an' all, 'un'."

"I don't know anything about them Mrs. Beynon. I don't even know what they are."

"I knows someone as was on one once. 'E was supposed to be transported, then wasn't. 'E said as 'ow they be old navy ships moored up by the docks there in

Portsmouth, and 'ow the conditions is terrible, even worse than prisons, and there be many as wot die of the flux and typhoid, 'e said. In daytime, 'e were made to do 'ard labour on the docks, then at night 'e were chained to 'is bunk so as to stop 'im escapin', and 'e said 'Eaven help you if you got into trouble, 'cos you'd be flogged and shackled. No, I can't see you survivin' that, 'un'."

She left after telling me that, but returned a short while later. "'Eaven forgive me for wot I be goin' to do, 'un', but I thinks the Good Lord'll think as 'ow I be doin' wot's right an' just, an' forgive me for it."

"What are you going to do then, Mrs. Beynon?"

She sat down next to me. "I thinks as 'ow you're well enough now, 'un'. Besides, I dunno 'ow soon 'is Lordship plans on sendin' you all to the 'ulks, so I needs to get you outta 'ere soon. I be goin' to make it as 'ow you can escape. Nobody's countin' prisoners 'ere no more any'ow. So many 'as died an' been thrown in trenches, no-one knows for sure who's 'ere, an' who ain't, an' as I be the only one wot's been dealin' with you, nobody's to know if I tells 'em you've died too."

She went on to explain to me how I should leave that night, and gave me directions on how to find my way back to Haverfordwest, where I could find Mr. Potter, and clear my name.

"Mrs. Beynon, are you sure your explanation of my disappearance will be accepted? You've been so kind to me, and I can't leave here fearing that you yourself might be punished for aiding a prisoner escape."

"Not you worry about me, 'un'. I been aroun' a good many years, an' I be a wily ol' woman, an' can play the innocent as well as wot you played your Romeos. Believe me, 'un', no-one's ever goin' to suspect ol' Jemima Beynon'd ever see fit to free a prisoner. I ain't be stupid enough to put my own life an' freedom in danger, so let's not 'ear no more about it... an' it just goes to show as 'ow wot a true gent you be, 'un', that you even thought of me."

She patted my knee. "Now, I don't 'ave no change of clothes for you, 'un', an' in that Frenchie uniform of yours, them's goin' to see you out there on the road in daylight, so you'll 'ave to go by night, an' 'ide by day. It's not far, an' you may do it in one night, but given as 'ow you're not well, I thinks it'll take you two. I'll give you food an' water enough to keep you goin'. I 'as to say you looks a lot better now than wot you was when you got 'ere."

"I don't know how I can thank you for all you've done for me, Mrs. Beynon, but if I come out of this alive and a free man, I'll come back to thank you again." I was silent for a moment, then asked her, "Mrs Beynon, I have one question to ask you. It intrigues me to know why you've kept calling me 'un'. What does it mean?"

She laughed. "Ah that's us down below 'ere, where we speaks only English."

"But I've never heard that word even in English."

"It mean 'oney. It's a term of endearment. I been callin' you, 'oney, 'cept down below 'ere we say, 'un'." She laughed again, and gave me a hug. "So now you knows, 'un'. An' somethin' else I'll tell you too... My but you stinks, 'un'! No doubt first thing your Mr. Potter'll want to do is give you a bath." She gave me a gummy smile, her teeth long-since gone.

I laughed. "Well if that's all that's wrong with me when I arrive in Haverfordwest, I'll count my blessings, Mrs. Beynon."

"Now, I got to tell you too, 'un'. Keep close to the road, if you 'as to get off it. Not you go wanderin' too far. You don't be wanting to come up against them Llangwm folk. They keeps to theirselves, an' don' like strangers. Can even be violent. The other thing is, the 'ole countryside be covered with culm mines, used ones, and them as 'as wot's been abandoned. Watch where you steps, for if you falls into one of 'em, you'll not get out, an' if no-one finds you, you'll end up dyin' in there. The grass grows up all around 'em, so watch it. All right 'un'?"

"What's culm, Mrs. Beynon?"

"It's our local coal. Burns clean. Good stuff, not all smoky like some coal. They says as 'ow that's why the white 'ouses of 'Oney 'Arford, as we calls 'Averfordwest, stays so clean."

That night, just after dark, Mrs. Beynon returned, as promised. She also brought a small jar containing some of the yellow ointment she had been putting on my arm. "That be my marigold ointment," she told me. "An' it'll make sure you don't get no infection 'un', though you seems to be 'ealin' well now anyway. Put it on night and mornin'." She patted me on the back. "Now off you go, 'un', an' good luck."

I put my hand on her shoulder in thanks, and set out on my hike.

CHAPTER 4

It was not that far to Haverfordwest, about eight miles, but for me, in the state I was, the going was slow, especially as I had no shoes, so I kept to the grass verges, long-since worn down to the bare earth by others, and only occasionally stepping on a sharp stone thrown up by horses travelling along the road. There was no moon either, so it was very dark, although the clear sky was ablaze with its billions of stars. I had to take frequent rests too, so by sunrise had not quite reached the village of Freystrop, or about half way.

I left the road, and found myself a sheltered spot in a grove of trees, hoping no-one would come by, especially anyone from Llangwm, but from what else Mrs. Beynon had told me about them, they were mostly involved in fishing and oyster catching, so more likely to stay closer to the Cleddau estuary. Grateful for Mrs. Beynon's warning, I was careful to watch out for the coal mines too, as she had been right; they were dotted around everywhere, hidden traps awaiting the unwary.

It being still only March, there were no leaves on the trees, and the ground was cold and damp, and while making my way into the centre of the grove, I woke a flock of what must have amounted to many hundreds of jackdaws which, having been roosting in the trees, flew up in a huge cloud, clamouring loudly at being disturbed. Early risers themselves, they still resented my even earlier intrusion on their rest, continuing to fly back to their roosts, then off again, time and again, seemingly confused by the upsetting of their daily routine.

I should have liked to have slept, but conditions were not conducive to that at all, as it was necessary to get up and walk around every few minutes just to keep warm, and to loosen up my muscles, which stiffened and ached with the cold.

Later that day, I heard children's voices approaching, and kept as low as I could to the ground, but after coming close enough to my hiding place to convince me they would surely come upon me, they veered off, and went in a different direction. Just before sunset they returned by the same route, so failed to discover me that time too. It would not do for inquisitive children to find me; they would be sure to run home to tell their families they'd seen a one-armed vagabond skulking in the woods, and in no time people would be out looking for me, on the assumption I was up to no good.

After sunset, I removed the bandage from my arm, put some of Mrs. Beynon's ointment on it, then used my teeth to help me bandage it back up again. By dark I was ready to set out once more, if ready could describe how I felt, being cold, tired and still in constant pain.

There were only four miles for me to cover, but first I needed to make a detour around Freystrop as there were quite a few people out and about. Even after I had bypassed the village, though, and returned to the road, I was almost seen by a few men making their way home, and hid behind the hedge while they went by.

Further on I had to leave the road yet again. I don't know where they had been or where they were going, but a procession of small groups of people kept coming down the road, and every time I thought I had seen the last of them, another little knot would come along, so eventually I had to stay off the road altogether. The ground right next to the road being swampy, I had to make a wider detour than I wanted, and then it happened.

Maybe it was because I was so tired, I either did not look, or just did not see where I was going. It being another dark night, with still no moon to light my way, I stepped into space. I had come upon one of those abandoned culm mines. I had no idea how deep they were, but from Mrs. Beynon's description, I assumed they must go way down. I was lucky. This mine appeared to have been abandoned because it was not producing, and was only about five and a half feet deep. Even so, having come across it so unexpectedly, I fell heavily, landing in a pool of water at the bottom.

Given my height, under normal circumstances I would have had no trouble in extricating myself. Now, however, it was a different matter, one arm not up to the task of levering me out.

At first I panicked, and struggled to no purpose. After all, I had no problem seeing out over the top, but after quite a few exhausting minutes, I gave up. I would have sat down at the bottom of the hole to rest after my futile exertion, but there was that small pond of cold water about six inches deep there, so I leaned against the side, and tried to devise a plan, my bare feet almost numb. I did have to get out somehow, or I would die there, just as Mrs. Beynon had warned me.

As I said, it was dark, but tonight again, at least the sky was clear, and when I looked up I could see the black outline of a tree growing next to the pit, with one of its branches hanging out over me. It was difficult to judge distances in the available light, but it appeared to be not that far above me. I reached up, and tried to grab hold of it, but it was too high. It was, however, the only thing likely to help me out of my predicament, but to do that, I had to get a hold of it somehow. After a few jumps, I managed to grab it, and as I landed back on my feet, it bent down with me still clinging onto it.

Even so, I was too far from the edge of the hole, and at this distance from the tree, the branch was too pliant anyway to be of use. I would somehow have to work my hand along it until it was firm, and I could use it to haul myself out. At the same time, I could not let go of it, or it would spring back up, and I would lose it again. I stood there for a few minutes, my arm stretched up, holding onto the branch, and wondering how I was going to achieve the necessary move. Finally, I pulled it down until it was in front of my face, and grabbed it between my teeth, holding on as best I could while I stretched my arm out, reaching up the branch. In the end I managed to gain a further two feet, up to where the branch was firm, and holding onto it at this point, I released the grip with my teeth, spitting out bits of moss and bark. At least I was now in a position where, if my arm was strong enough, I could use it to haul myself out.

I stood there, my arm stretched to its limit, straining at the branch, and standing on the tips of my toes, I tried to work out a strategy as it did not take long for me to realize I still would not be able to get out.

The pit was not that wide, so still grasping hold of the branch, I leaned my back against the one side, and used my feet to walk up other, finally getting them over the rim. The problem then was that, now suspended above the pit, I could not release my hand from the branch without my top half falling back down. I hung there, suspended, and eventually managed to hitch my feet sideways until my rear was on the edge of the pit as well. Then I brought my feet around until all of me was finally lying beside it, next to the tree. At last I could let go of my branch.

For a while I lay there, exhausted, and so close to the edge of the pit, I feared falling back into it again. My arm was trembling with the effort, and I would have given anything to have been able to give it a good rubbing to get the circulation going again, and to calm my quivering muscles. My effort must have taken me well over an hour, and it being almost sunrise by the time I was ready to move on, it was too late to travel any more that night, so I spent another day lying hidden in the undergrowth, afraid and unable to sleep.

Not having slept yet again, and worn out with my efforts of the previous night, my going was even slower that coming night, and by dawn I had gone only another three miles, this time along the road, bringing me to Merlin's Bridge on the outskirts of Haverfordwest. However, I was still too far from Mr. Potter's house on Tower Hill to reach it before daylight, so had to hunker down in a nearby woodland, and wait out yet another day.

I was a bit closer to habitation than was safe, so hoped no-one would pass near me during the daylight hours and, excessively tired even after such a short walk, I did sleep for a while, then spent the rest of the day trying to remove any insignia, buttons or braid that would identify my coat and breeches as being French. In this, as with other tasks, I was beginning to find my teeth most useful as an extra hand, and was fortunate that they, at least, were strong and healthy.

I had long since eaten all the food Mrs. Beynon had given me, so was hungry too, but was careful to follow all her instructions regarding the use of her marigold ointment; an infection at this stage would probably be the end of me.

At last, the days still being short, night fell, but I waited until after eight o'clock, when St. Mary's curfew bell rang to tell all boys it was time for them to go home. Young boys are the worst when it comes to noticing things, and I did not want to be caught by some ten-year-old with nothing better to do than find me. I waited about half an hour after I heard the bell, and set out once more.

Although Shut Street is a rough area, full of hovels, manure heaps and pubs, I decided its inhabitants would be the least likely to take notice of a one-armed, barefooted man dressed in dirty old clothes that were almost in rags. Besides, the street was so badly lit, it would be hard for anyone to even see me at all. I just hoped Mr. Potter would at least recognize me in my altered state. One thing was sure, and that was that no-one would bother to try to rob me.

My steps becoming ever more laboured, and with a steep hill to climb up to St. Thomas's Square, then down another, which was Market Street, it took me about an hour before I was once again within yards of St. Mary's Church. From there it took me only five minutes to arrive at Mr. Potter's front door.

I wondered at first if I should go round to the servants' entrance, but decided I should re-enter the way I had left about three weeks ago. After all, regardless of how

I looked, I was still a gentleman, and had every expectation of being treated like one.

CHAPTER 5

I arrived at Mr. Potter's house to find it in darkness. The downstairs front rooms, forming as they did the library and reading room, were usually brightly lit, with people gathered around, but all was dark tonight, which was not a good sign. I knocked on the door. It was several minutes before it was answered, and then it was opened just a crack by Mrs. Kelly, the housekeeper. "Who is it?" she asked.

"It's Mr. O'Keeffe, Mrs. Kelly."

She opened the door wide, let out a shriek, and made to shut it again quickly.

I put my foot in the door. "Don't be afraid, Mrs. Kelly. I do assure you it's me, and I need to speak to Mr. Potter. I'm in urgent need of his help."

The door opened again slowly, and Mrs. Kelly held her candle up to my face, making a slow inspection of me, accompanied by a look of horror. Her inspection over, she stood there, speechless and in such a state of shock I thought her candle would lean so far over, it would topple out of its socket onto the floor.

"Please, Mrs. Kelly, let me in. If you don't, I think I'm about ready to collapse at your feet."

She opened the door, righted the almost guttering candle, and held it high to light my way. I stumbled over the threshold, and slumped down onto one of the wooden hall chairs. Amidst the pristine cleanliness of the white-painted woodwork, the pale, duck-egg-blue walls, and the gleaming mahogany and silver, I must have looked even more wretched.

Mrs. Kelly finally found her voice. "My dear Mr. O'Keeffe! I don't know what to say. This isn't some acting joke you're putting on for Mr. Potter's sake, is it? For if it is, you're very, very good at what you do." She held the candle above my head, studying me.

I rested my head in my hand, and shook it. "No, Mrs. Kelly. This is no act. I only wish it were."

She put her hand on my muddy shoulder. "Come on young man. Let's get you down into the kitchen. It's the only warm place in the house at the moment, as the master and family are away."

I had started to get up, but sank down again, defeated. "Oh no! I so desperately need his help."

"Well let's see to you first, and we can discuss that after. Come on with you. Down to the kitchen." I clambered to my feet, and she led the way with the candle, muttering and shaking her head, while I followed, but once in the warmth and security of the Potter kitchen, I collapsed onto the slate-flagged floor.

When I came to, Mr. Nash, the physician, was standing over me, and Mrs. Kelly was sitting on a chair next to him, peering down at me, a look of extreme consternation on her face.

Mr. Nash adjusted his spectacles. "Mr. O'Keeffe! My dear man, what on earth has happened to you? I saw you less than a month ago at one of Mr. Potter's dinner parties, and you were in fine shape. Now, I don't know what to say. You've been sorely treated, and Mr. Potter would be horrified if he could see you now, as horrified as both Mrs. Kelly and I are."

I started to get up from the floor, but sat back down. "I..."

Mr. Nash put up his hand. "No explanations yet. We need to take care of you. Poor Mrs. Kelly too nearly fainted when she saw what had happened to your arm. A disaster of the first order for a young man such as yourself. I hope whoever is responsible will be brought to justice... Now, in the meantime, I've taken a look at you while you've been lying there, and while I'm concerned about your arm, although it does appear to be healing, it would seem your main problem otherwise, apart from being dirty, would be exhaustion. With that in mind, therefore, I think the first thing from which you would benefit both mentally and physically, is a nice hot bath. Mrs. Kelly is already heating the water, so once that's done, I'll stay and help you with that. Afterwards, there'll be some hot soup, and then bed, where I expect you to remain for the next three days," He raised his hand again, when I protested about the last bit. "No. I insist. You're doing nothing for three days young man, and Mrs. Kelly will be happy to attend to you. It's too bad the family is away, but it can't be helped. Mrs. Kelly and I will help you as best we can." He slapped his hands on his knees. "How's that hot water coming, Mrs. Kelly?"

"Just a few more minutes, Mr. Nash."

"I can explain..." I started again, but Mr. Nash shook his head, silencing me once more. "No. No explanations tonight, Mr. O'Keeffe. There's plenty of time for that."

I was grateful, as I was not feeling well at all, and could not wait for the opportunity to sleep, a proper sleep, something I had not had since my last night in St. David's.

The kitchen smelled of baking apple pie and roast chicken, and the flames of the candles cast flickers around the walls, as did those from the wide, open fireplace. Mr. Nash helped me to my feet, and I plumped myself down at the huge deal kitchen table, having trouble keeping my head from just falling forward onto it, now from sheer weariness. As it was, my eyes kept closing, and I had to jerk my head up to stop myself from falling asleep right in front of them.

Fortunately the bathtub was brought in and filled before that happened, and Mrs. Kelly retired while Mr. Nash helped me remove my breeches and climb into it, where he washed away all the dirt and grime accumulated since my rainstorm shower on my way to Barnlake almost two weeks previously. He then dried me with a warm, rough towel, and called to Mrs. Kelly to bring me a nightgown. Thus attired, I was sat down at the kitchen table again, and brought the promised soup. Mr. Nash said, "goodnight", and told me he would return in the morning.

Before he left, I said, "I'd appreciate it, Mr. Nash, if you would use your discretion, and not let it be known that I'm here. There are those who would want to seize me and take me away."

He raised his eyebrows, but merely said, "Of course. You have my word."

I don't remember eating the soup, or afterwards being led up to the same bedroom I had occupied just weeks ago. Even so, despite my exhaustion, my night was beset with nightmares, and I did not fall into a proper sleep until the early hours of the morning, after which I slept till noon. That afternoon, both Mr. Nash and Mrs. Kelly sat at my bedside and listened to my story.

Both knew, of course, I was telling the truth, but at the same time, Mr. Nash had some concerns, not only for me, but for Mrs. Kelly as well.

"This is a small town, Mr. O'Keeffe, and if it were discovered that Mrs. Kelly, a fellow citizen of Ireland, were harbouring what the authorities still believe to be an Irish Republican invader and killer of one His Majesty's officers, she too would be indicted, which I'm sure would be the last thing you would want. I'd been hoping you could stay here until Mr. Potter returned, at which time, with his particular influence, he could make sure you were exonerated, but his return is still weeks away, as he won't be back until mid June, and for Mrs. Kelly to keep you hidden all that time would be well-nigh impossible. Your physical state now making you particularly noticeable too, it would be easy for someone to come to the conclusion that you're the missing fugitive, especially with the real killer being, I'm sure, only too anxious to have you caught and tried not only for treason, but for the murder he committed."

"But I don't think they'll even notice I'm missing at Barnlake. There were so many dying of the flux there, they'd stopped counting, and Mrs. Beynon said she'd tell them I was dead."

"It's not a risk we can ask Mrs. Kelly to take, Mr. O'Keeffe. You understand, I'm sure."

I nodded. Mr. Nash was telling me that I could not stay, and would have to leave the protection of the Potter home, once more setting out on the road, still a wanted fugitive, in constant fear of being recaptured. Even the thought of having to set out yet again so soon made me weary, and I laid my head back on the pillow.

I had assumed my arrival at Mr. Potter's would be the solution to all my problems, well, not all -- there was no bringing my arm back -- but it was not to be. Although I might not be a prisoner at this moment, I stood every chance of being one again very soon if I could not get my name cleared, or find my way back to Ireland. I could even end up dying in those terrible prison hulks Mrs. Beynon had described to me. It was of little consolation to know I would be exonerated posthumously.

"Of course, I understand. The last thing I'd want on my conscience would be getting Mrs. Kelly into any trouble. I'll leave as soon as possible, and try to get back to Ireland without getting caught." I think my desperation must have shown, as Mrs. Kelly put her hand on mine, and squeezed it.

"I know you're of age, and perhaps it's none of my business," Mr. Nash said, "but is there no way in which your father could be of help to you? As a baronet, surely he must have sufficient influence to have access to the right people, and get this matter dealt with?"

"Yes, under normal circumstances he'd most certainly be able to do as you suggest. However, he and my mother have been away on a grand tour since the end of December, and aren't expected to return until the end of May. They're probably in Italy, but where, I don't know. Of course, if I'd had the opportunity, which I haven't had until now, and if they'd been at home in Ireland, I *would* have looked to my father for help, and would still do so, but unfortunately, it's not possible."

Mr. Nash stood up. "This has been altogether a most unfortunate combination of circumstances from beginning to end, and it's certainly landed you in a dire situation all round. I don't know what to say or do, other than offer you my sincerest sympathy, young man, and I only wish I myself could be of help, but you need someone with the influence of Mr. Potter or your father to help you in this particular situation, and unfortunately, neither of them is here." He shook his head. "A most unfortunate situation indeed."

"Yes, and I do understand it puts Mrs. Kelly in an awkward situation as well, and that, I can't allow..." I tried to sound optimistic. "I should be well enough to leave in about three days, don't you think? I'll need some clothes though. All my own were taken, along with all my money."

"I have some savings, Mr. O'Keeffe," said Mrs. Kelly. "I know you to be a young man of honour, and will see I'm repaid as soon as you're able. I'll let Mr. Nash have sufficient money to get the tailor to run you up some clothes. I think it wiser that Mr. Nash sees to that, as it would look rather strange for me to go into one of our tailors in town and order a suit of clothes for a man. That would most certainly raise eyebrows and set tongues wagging."

Mr. Nash nodded. "A sensible suggestion, Mrs. Kelly. Get up and stand up for me, will you, Mr. O'Keeffe. Let's take your measurements. You're an unusually tall young man too, which unfortunately makes you stand out in the crowd even without your other problem. I just hope we can get your clothes made up for you in good time. The tailor I'm thinking of is a hard worker though, and efficient, as well as being excellent at what he does, so we should have you looking like a gentleman again in no time."

I climbed out of bed, and stood up.

"Mrs. Kelly, do you have a measure please?"

Mrs. Kelly went off and returned with the necessary tape, and Mr. Nash took my measurements. Three days later

70

he returned with a heavy wool coat in a rich dark blue with a high black-velvet collar, a silk waistcoat, a white linen shirt, silk scarf, breeches, stockings and a fine pair of boots in the latest fashion, with cuffs at the top, and tassels. To top it all, I had a smart hat, also in the latest fashion. I tried them on, and Mrs. Kelly was brought in to inspect me.

"It's a fine, handsome young man you are, to be sure, Mr. O'Keeffe." She leaned forward and tucked the empty sleeve of my wool coat into the pocket, patted it in place, then stood back. "There. That's better."

I smiled. "At least no-one can mistake me for an invader now."

"No," Mr. Nash agreed. "The only people who will recognize you now, I think, will be those who most definitely will be out looking for you, Mrs. Beynon's assurances notwithstanding. And for that reason, you need to get out of the country as soon as possible, although I'm not satisfied you're quite ready to leave yet. Give it an extra three days, and I think you'll be up to the trip. You should take the stage, which leaves at ten o'clock in the morning from Castle Square. It goes right through to Aberystwyth, but stops off in Fishguard on the way."

"What if I were to sail from Haverfordwest instead? Would that not make more sense than going all the way to Fishguard now?"

Mr. Nash shook his head. "I think not. It's far more likely for the sheriff's deputies to be round and about the quay area in Haverfordwest than in Fishguard, looking for smugglers and the like. You're more in danger of being spotted here. I should add too, that you should try to get on the coach as soon as possible, and not be seen standing around in the square. The less chance you have of anyone noticing you, the better."

I nodded, beginning to feel altogether defeated before I had even set out on my next journey.

CHAPTER 6

Three days later I set out from Tower Hill at about half past nine, with some bread, cheese and an apple in my pocket, and enough money to pay for the stage, the crossing to Ireland, and one night's stay at an inn in Fishguard, if necessary. Fishguard was only fifteen miles away, so, all being well, I should have arrived at my destination by mid afternoon at the latest, even taking into account the stage's stopover at *The Harp* inn in Letterston.

By the time I arrived in the square, it was busy with people going about their business. The weather being fine, and spring on its way, the ladies were already discarding their winter clothes and stepping out in their spring finery, sporting their colourful dainty bonnets and hats, hoping, no doubt, the wind would not rise and carry them away. Children were running around playing with their coloured tops, and young men paraded on their horses, raising their hats to the young ladies. It all looked so normal, but even though I blended in reasonably well with everyone else, I nevertheless felt as though all eyes were on me, not, alas, for the same reasons as in the past, but because they were recognizing me as a fugitive from justice.

The coach was there already, waiting outside the Castle Inn, and trunks and other luggage, including the mail were being loaded up. I was the first passenger to appear, so having paid my fare, climbed aboard and sat down next to the window, now safely out of sight.

I was glad I did not have too far to go as the seats were not that comfortable, the leather cracked and worn, buttons missing, and lumpy where the horsehair stuffing had clumped together, bits of which poked out in places where the stitching had broken. However, they were at least clean, and the coach had been washed, so one could look out of the windows without the view being interrupted by spattered mud and a layer of dust.

I had not been sitting long before a plump, elderly woman made her appearance at the entrance. She was being assisted aboard from behind, but needed some help from within too, so I went over to her and held out my hand. She grabbed hold of it, and with me heaving, and her pulling, she eventually emerged inside, almost popping through the door like a too fat mouse out of its hole.

"Ah! Thank you young man. These old bones. Old age doesn't come alone, does it?" She looked up at me. "But then, you wouldn't know yet, would you?... A long way to go," she added. She plumped herself down opposite me, and I could almost hear her bones sighing with relief. She was all muslin and lace, a whole froth of it, and looked like a large and exotic confection sitting there, taking up almost half of that side of the coach.

No sooner seated, she launched into a full description of why she had been in Haverfordwest, and why she was going all the way to Aberystwyth. This was interspersed with explanatory descriptions of everything and everyone she felt I should know about, so I sat with my fine new hat sitting on my lap, offering polite smiles, and hoping I was giving appropriate nods and sympathetic shakes of my head as my mind was wandering, being in no way interested in hearing every detail about how Aunt Letitia's pug dog had eaten too much, and had suffered greatly thereby.

I was saved, albeit temporarily, from this monologue by the arrival of a young woman in her early twenties, accompanied by a girl of about sixteen, and another of about five. I rose again to help them on board, but this time received cold looks that told me to mind my own business, so I remained standing, all politeness, until they too had seated themselves, all on the same side as the old lady, making it rather crowded, and leaving me alone on my side. I began to wonder if there was something the matter with me that they felt it necessary to avoid sitting near me.

We set off a short while after and, as I said, it was a fine day, but a cool north-easterly wind was rising. There were fewer people on the road than I was expecting, and only one carriage passed us going towards Haverfordwest. My six days' rest and good food had given me back some of my strength, and had boosted my spirits, and when not being obliged to listen to the old lady's travails along with all those of her family and acquaintances, I took time to look at the countryside out of the open window. I even started to enjoy the fresh air and my new sense of freedom, although I would not be able to relax until I was on board a ship headed for Ireland, and out of sight of the Pembrokeshire coast.

"Look Nanny. That man there has only one arm. Why has he got only one arm, Nanny?" I had been aware of the child's stare every since we had started out, and I looked across and smiled at her.

"Don't point, child. It's rude to point." Nanny looked at me, glaring as though it was my fault the child had seen fit to comment.

I smiled again; after all, she was a very attractive-looking nanny, and I started to say something, although what, I can't remember, but she tossed her head and looked the other way, leaving me in mid sentence, so I went back to looking out of the window. I did not dare to even glance at the sixteen-year-old to see what her reaction might have been to the snub I had received. I would not have done that anyway, as it was obvious from her closed bonnet, she was not yet out in society, and no gentleman would be so rude as to try to attract her attention.

Sitting there though, with nothing else to occupy my mind, I began to wonder why the nanny had treated me with such obvious distaste. After all, I looked at my most presentable. Her reaction to me had not been at all what I was used to from young women; young women always blushed and returned my smile, always. What was wrong?

My head jerked up in an involuntary movement. It was as though someone had poured a bucket of ice-water over me. Now I was sure I knew why she had turned away. She had to have found the lopsided me repellent, and could not bear to look at me, let alone sit next to me.

Ever since my disastrous encounter with the murderer, the last thing on my mind had been how, if at all, it would affect my relationship with women. Now though, as I stared out of the window during a respite from the old lady's monologue, what the young woman opposite me had indicated by her actions, devastated me; she had told me I was no longer attractive.

My somewhat upbeat attitude thus far on my journey died, a candle snuffed out, leaving only a thin trail of smoke, vanishing along with my self esteem. The thought that young ladies, hitherto always delighted to be seen in my company, might recoil from me now, shattered my image of myself, and instead of sitting up proudly, I sank back, shrinking into my seat, trying to become as unnoticeable as possible, my self-confidence crushed in an instant. This was a whole new experience for me, a realization for which I was unprepared, and a feeling of emptiness surged through my gut.

I did not have time to dwell on this further though, as it was then that three men on horseback rushed out at us from behind some trees. We were about three miles out of Haverfordwest at the time, and approaching the ford crossing the Western Cleddau river. All were holding pistols and shouting at the coachman to stop. The coachman, with one of the highwaymen aiming his pistol at him, reined in the horses, while his guard, sitting next to him, was rendered helpless by a second man, also holding a pistol.

The door of the coach was opened by the third man. He checked out the occupants, and seeing I was the only man, and therefore the only one likely to cause him trouble if I were armed, which I was not, of course, waved his pistol at me.

"Out! Now!" he shouted when I hesitated.

I climbed out. "And where do you think you're going, eh, my fine young dandy?"

The child started to cry, and he yelled at the nanny. "Keep that child quiet; you hear? Or I'll send the bogy man after her... And take off all your jewellery. If you don't, I'll come in and rip it off you...You too, old woman." At which the child cried some more, and I could hear the nanny trying to soothe her.

Meanwhile, he made me back up against the side of the coach, and holding his pistol on me with his one hand, checked to see if I was carrying any weapons with the other. Finding none, he turned out my pockets, tossing my bread, cheese and apple onto the ground. "What? No money? A young gentleman like you doesn't travel without money, so where is it then?"

I had hidden it in the sole of my boot.

"I said where is it?" he repeated when I said nothing. He had hold of my silk scarf, pulling me towards him, his face inches from mine, and smelling of stale ale.

"It's because of people like you that I don't ever carry money with me. I've got nothing, I assure you. You've already searched me, so take your hands off me." I raised my hand to push him away, and he whacked it with his pistol.

"Don't you get clever with me, Paddy."

The stage was carrying the mail, most of which would end up in Aberystwyth, many miles to the north, and one of the other highwaymen was going through it and the trunks belonging to everyone else on board, ripping open bags, and prising open the trunks, tossing the contents out onto the road, looking for anything worth taking. The second man stood there, keeping an eye out for anyone coming from either direction, as well as keeping guard over the coachman and his own guard, who had been relieved of his weapon, having been made to toss it down onto the ground.

The third man still had his attention focussed on me. "You're not leaving here without giving me something for my efforts. I think I'll have that nice wool coat of yours. Yes, I'll look a right gentleman in that."

"You'll never look a gent..." I started, my temper flaring.

He raised his pistol as though to hit me with it again. "I told you, Paddy, not to get clever with me. Take that coat off. Now."

It had been stupid of me to let my temper get the better of me when faced with a man armed with a pistol, so I started to undo the buttons, but was too slow for his liking. The coat being new, the buttonholes were still stiff and unyielding, and Mrs. Kelly's help had been required to even get them done up this morning.

"Heh! Let me do it. We'll be here all day otherwise." He shoved my hand out of the way, and shouted to the man sorting through the mail to hold his pistol on me while he relieved me of my coat. Finding the buttons stiff as well, he simply ripped them away, and pulled my coat off. Then he did the same to my beautiful waistcoat, and took that too, as well as my silk scarf.

"Shall we leave him the shirt on his back, boys?" he shouted to the other two.

They decided they would. However, because I had, as he claimed, been rude to him, he decided to punish me. "You're young and strong enough," he announced. "You can walk the rest of the way, wherever it is you're going. Do you good," he added, and after they had taken everything of value, they sent the coach on its way without me, after which they gathered together whatever they had gleaned from their holdup, which seemed to be very little after all.

I watched them disappear into the woods, leaving me standing in the middle of the road in my shirt, boots and breeches. The contents of the trunks and mail bags lay spread all around me, and those things light enough to be lifted by the brisk wind, were already being whisked down the road to land either in the muddy ditches or festooned from the still bare hawthorn branches of the hedges. The scene looked as though an enormous bird of prey had torn apart some equally enormous feathered quarry, the impression being strengthened by the many feathers flying from the various hats and bonnets previously so carefully packed in their dainty bandboxes, and now cart-wheeling down the road, their fragile ribbons trailing along, ripping as they went.

I stood there in the midst of the rumpled, tangled heap of fine muslin dresses, petticoats, silk shawls, pelisses, panniers, newspapers, letters and ripped packages. I still had ten miles to go, and a one-armed man walking along the highway in such a state of undress in this cold weather, looked nothing if not conspicuous.

Even if no-one were to pass me, as soon as the coach reached Letterston, only a few miles distant, a hue and cry would be raised, and men would be gathered together to search for the thieves, and they would find me, for sure. Word would also come out, of course, that a one-armed man was one of the passengers, and had been left behind. Maybe they would conclude, moreover, that I was not only the escaped criminal, but also one of the gang, not left behind as a punishment, but because they had a horse waiting for me in the woods, and had escaped with them. For whatever reason, I did not dare pass through Letterston now, for no matter what happened, I would be the centre of attention and questioned closely, and I so dreaded being taken prisoner again, and sent to rot in those prison hulks, or hanged, I decided to take no risks, and to get off the road as soon as possible.

This meant I would have to walk over the heather-covered hills instead, something I was not in a fit state to do despite my renewed strength. Even so, once I had forded the river, I did leave the road, intending to stay as close to it as possible.

Almost immediately, however, I had to move further into the moors than I intended, my way being blocked by some impassable terrain which I had to circumnavigate. To add to my woes, as so often happens when the sun is too bright too early, it began to rain. It was that fine, penetrating, wind-driven rain that, without the protection of my heavy wool coat and waistcoat, quickly had me chilled to the bone and brought back the memory of that terrible ride to Barnlake that day. My fine hat too, had been left on the coach, so that was gone as well, leaving me with nothing to protect my head either from the cold and wet.

The going was difficult, the area being covered with many boulders and huge clumps of impenetrable gorse, interspersed with equally formidable carpets of ancient heather, whose stiff branches did their utmost to impede any progress. Before long my new breeches were ripped, and my new boots covered with deep scratches, their beautiful tassels clotted with mud. My linen shirt clung to my skin, soaking and almost transparent, except where it too was spattered with mud. To think that only a few hours previously I had looked the perfect gentleman, striding out from Mr. Potter's Tower Hill home!

Forced to make many more detours, I eventually lost my bearings, and had no idea in which direction I was going, the sky giving no indication as to where the sun might be behind the solid grey mass of cloud. The rain was now almost horizontal, driven into my back by the wind, and I took shelter under a rock waiting in vain for it to end, and when darkness fell, I had no idea where Fishguard might be, and was lost on the wild Pembrokeshire moors.

I spent the night on the wet ground, shivering with the cold, and at dawn a slight glow low in the sky gave me some idea of where the sun was rising, letting me know in which direction I should head. I trudged on, basing my steps on that glow. It soon disappeared into the overhanging pall of dark grey sky, however, and I was as lost as I had ever been, as without any sign of the sun at all after that, it was impossible to tell where I was going. I might even have been going round in circles. With a low-lying fog covering the countryside as well, there was no point even in climbing a hill to look for the sea. I was hungry now too, having just my apple which I had retrieved from the road, where the highwayman had tossed it. My bread and cheese had really been too dirty to be picked up, but I had done so anyway, just in case, but was not hungry enough yet to take the trouble to remove all the accumulated grit and dirt from them. My spirits, sinking ever since the young lady's rebuff, sank even further, and I wondered if I was ever going to reach Fishguard, always so close, yet never attainable, like a mirage.

Another night passed, and the following morning the storm had abated. It was now bright and clear again, and when I climbed a small hill, could even see Fishguard not that far away. Another hour or so, and I would be there, providing I did not have to make too many more detours along the way, and at least I still had my money safely tucked in my boots. I even persuaded myself that, once in Fishguard, no-one would take any notice of me, Fishguard being a fishing and ship-building port, used to all sorts of characters passing through. I doubted too that I could possibly be so high on the authorities' list of wanted men, that they would be keeping any sort of lookout for me at the harbour, although in my own mind I was becoming almost paranoid in the belief that everyone was out to capture me, especially with the attack on the coach added to the list of possible reasons for wanting me in custody.

I walked for about an hour, but between lack of sleep and lack of food -- I still could not face the dirty bread and cheese -- was soon exhausted, so lay down in the heather for a brief rest.

It was then that I was confronted by the formidable Miss Saunders.

CHAPTER 7

The bolt on the upper stable door was being drawn back, and the door pushed open.

"Heh! You! I've brought you some supper. Come and get it."

I stood up and walked up to the door. A young servant girl stood there, holding up a bowl of something steaming in one hand, and a mug of ale in the other. She barely reached the top of the lower door. I reached out my hands to retrieve them, taking hold of the hot bowl in my left hand, and waiting for her to release the mug of ale into my right. When she continued to stand there, I looked at her, and there was the mug, still in her hand, waiting for me to reach out and take it. I had forgotten; I could have sworn I had hold of that mug. I could even feel it in my hand. This sensation kept happening to me these days, and it was disconcerting.

"I was tempted to spit in it," she was telling me. "But I didn't. You don't deserve to be given anything, you don't."

I went to set down the bowl, and came back for the ale. I saw no point in hurling abuse at her in return, reducing myself to her level; I was too proud for that, so instead I smiled down at her. "Your consideration is greatly appreciated... What's your name?"

"Gwenda."

"Gwenda? That's a pretty name. Well, thank you Gwenda."

She seemed flummoxed by my response, and went away muttering to herself.

I went back to my meal, and sat down in the straw to eat it. It was lamb hot-pot with vegetables, and tasted wonderful, whether she had spat in it, or not. David, the head groom, had brought me a coat earlier on, and for the first time in three days, I began to feel something approaching warm both inside and out, and my spirits began their long climb yet again. As Mr. Pope said, "Hope springs eternal in the human breast".

That night it rained heavily once more, and it was soon clear the roof of the stable was not in the best shape. There was no way I could avoid its constant dripping, as depending on the gusts of wind driving it, the rain would change direction, causing the streams of water to shift around. As a result, by the morning I was soaked yet again.

Gwenda brought me my breakfast of hot gruel, accompanied by another mug of ale. This time I remembered I needed to collect them one at a time. This time too, she said nothing, but gave me a bemused look, as though she did not quite know what to make of me. I smiled at her again, but said nothing other than, "Thank you", and off she went.

Gwenda was the only person I saw in the following days, when she brought me my two meals a day. I spent most of my time sleeping, and remembering to use Mrs. Beynon's ointment, which felt as though it was doing its duty in that what was left of my arm was becoming less painful.

I don't know how many days I had been there, but as they went by, Gwenda started bringing me little extras, for which I continued to give her my most gracious thanks. She even started blushing when I smiled at her, and I think she had begun to quite enjoy her duty of being my bearer of food. At least she did not seem to be repelled by the sight of me, although that was most likely because she was not tall enough to see over the top of the door, so had not noticed.

One evening, after she had brought me a late snack, she shut the stable door, but did not bolt it. I could only think she had left it undone on purpose, especially as it was already dark, and a prime time for me to look to escape. If she had done so, there was one thing she had not thought of, and that was that when my clothes were taken away to be laundered, my muddy boots had been taken as well, and along with them, my money. Although my clothes had been returned, my boots had not, no doubt with the specific intention of deterring me from trying to escape. The result was that I could not run away for two reasons: one being that I could not walk to Fishguard in my bare feet, which still had not recovered from that trek across the moor at gunpoint, and the other that, even if I did, I had no money with which to pay anyone to take me to Ireland. The result was that, when morning came, and with it Gwenda and my gruel, I was still there.

It then became obvious she had indeed left the door unlocked on purpose, because when I appeared, she jumped, almost spilling my breakfast over herself. She looked at me with a puzzled expression.

I took the bowl from her. "Gwenda. I know what you did, and I want you to know how much I appreciate your thoughtfulness. It was very kind of you, but I couldn't run away, because without my boots, and without money, I can go nowhere, I'm afraid."

To my consternation, she started to cry. "Don't worry, Gwenda. I'm sure I'll find a way of freeing myself somehow. Go now, before you're missed -- can't have cook berating you, can we? Oh, and don't forget to bolt the door."

She picked up her apron and wiped her eyes, then turned and fled back to the house, and must have refused to bring me my food anymore, as I did not see her again.

Another week or so passed; I had lost track of time, and during this period I still saw neither Miss Saunders nor her father, nor yet anyone else other than the servant delegated to replace Gwenda.

The darkness, the loneliness and not knowing what was going to happen to me were wearing me down, filling me with despair, until I wondered how long it would be before I would lose my senses altogether, especially as an old and jolly Irish drinking song seemed to have invaded my brain, going round and round in it like a windmill, and so at odds with my state of mind.

It was called, in Gaelic, "Preab san Ol -- In Praise of Drinking", and is usually sung by those who dislike the wealthy, although in our family we used to like to sing it anyway. I would often break into song when I was happy. Happy was not a word I could in any way use to describe myself now though, so why a jolly Irish drinking song would have taken up residence in my head was a mystery. Maybe it was because I associated it with my family and home, my brain reminding me of how homesick I was. I did not need reminding; all it did was to depress me even further, and it seemed as though the only way to exorcise it would be to sing it out loud, and get it out of my system that way.

By the position of the shaft of sunlight coming in through the stable door, I could tell it was late afternoon, and it was then that I stood up and started singing Preab san Ol in Gaelic. There was something about the old stable that added to the quality of my voice, and I threw all my passion into my singing.

It is sung with verve and vigour, and I started out well. As I progressed though, and became affected by the nostalgia it evoked, I slowed down, and by the time I ended the last verse, my voice was choking with emotion, not on account of the words, but by the simple act of singing something that reminded me of happy times with my family.

To my amazement I heard a chorus of applause from outside the door, which was then opened, and David's head appeared over the lower half. Gathered behind him were all the stable boys.

"You have the voice of an angel, I'll say that for you."

I turned away.

"Would you care to sing us some more?"

"No. Not now."

"Well, later perhaps. Let me know, and I'll gather some more of the servants to listen to you."

He shut the door again, and once more I was alone in the dark. True, I had little pride left by now, but I made no offer to sing again, and the song gradually faded away, so perhaps my exorcism had worked after all.

To keep my brain alert I began to recite speeches from Shakespeare to myself, although I kept my voice low, not wanting to attract any further attention. It was the more sombre speeches that kept coming to mind, and one evening I sat the there in the darkness, my head in my hand, and recited Macbeth:

"To-morrow, and to-morrow, and to-morrow,
Creeps in this petty pace from day to day
To the last syllable of recorded time,
And all our yesterdays have lighted fools
The way to dusty death. Out, out, brief candle!
Life's but a walking shadow, a poor player
That struts and frets his hour upon the stage
And then is heard no more: 'tis a tale
Told by an idiot, full of sound and fury,
Signifying nothing."

After that, I stopped reciting anything, and just sat and wondered how long I was going to remain incarcerated.

Then, one morning, David came to take me out of the stable. It happened to be another of those bright, sunny mornings, and I had been in the dark for so long, the brilliance was unbearable, and for a while I could not keep my eyes open.

"Right. It's off to Haverfordwest for you. Mr. Saunders has business there today, and prefers to use the carriage, rather than ride, as it looks like a rain storm might be on the way, so you're to go along too."

He handed me my boots. The money was gone, and I not only wondered who came into that small windfall, but realized this was a disaster for me because, even if I did escape, without money I could not get to Ireland unless I worked my passage, and what captain would hire a one-armed crew member? I could not handle cargo, haul in or raise a sail, or pull in a lobster trap or a fishing net. I was useless, and now had no hope at all.

The carriage was standing there in the yard already. It was a handsome carriage, similar to one my father owned, and was painted in the blue and gold livery colours of the Saunders family, with their crest on the side. It was drawn by four superb Cleveland Bays. The family obviously had money, as had most of the English landowner gentry in the area, something I had found out during my stay with Mr. Potter, and which had no doubt led the French to believe the poor local Welsh population would side with them when they invaded.

I was to ride up front with the coachman, and once seated, my hand was tied with a leather thong to the rail next to me. The carriage was then driven round to the entrance of the mansion, and within seconds Mr. Saunders strode out. His daughter, I noticed, was watching from a window. He glanced up at me briefly, then climbed aboard. The footman closed the door, took up his stance at the rear along with the other footman, and we set off for Haverfordwest.

We drove down a long, rhododendron-lined avenue before entering the main road, and before long it started to rain heavily. The coachman was well prepared in his liveried greatcoat with two over-capes to keep out the wet. I was not, so once again was soon soaked, the water dripping down off my bare head, and down my shirt, and all the time I was wondering how I was ever going to escape, or now if there was even any point in trying, having no money. There was still the thought of the prison hulks, however. Anything had to be better than ending up in one of them. I tested the strength of the leather thong, but it was tough, and breaking it was out of the question. The rain too, was wetting it, giving it a limp, slimy feel, and seeming to make it even stronger.

The coachman was staring straight ahead, ignoring me.

"Beautiful horses," I said.

"Yes, Mr. Saunders knows a good horse when he sees one." As head man in charge of all the stable hands, including David, he had adopted a style of speech akin to that of his master, to show how superior he was to his underlings. In that, he was a bit like my father's coachman, arrogant, and probably not very nice to work for. His livery was immaculate, and his coachman's wig and cocked hat sat perfectly on his head. His features though, gave him away. They were coarse and peasant-like, and showed every sign of an overindulgence of rich food and porter, as did his size in general; there was not much room left for me on the seat.

"All in great condition too," I added.

"David is proud of his horses and takes good care of them." He did not deign to look at me, but addressed me while still looking straight ahead.

"I can see that. My father breeds racehorses, and races them every year on the Curragh. I was hoping to get home in time to see the June races as he has a special horse he's been training for this year, sired by one of his own original Arab stallions."

"Yes, and I've been to the moon -- twice." His arrogant voice was brittle with sarcasm, and he refused to talk to me after that, so we continued the trip in silence.

We had been travelling for about an hour, with the storm picking up force, when Mr. Saunders called out for the coachman to stop at *The Harp* in Letterston. An ostler came out to hold the horses, while Mr. Saunders, the coachman and the two footmen disappeared inside, leaving me sitting in the driving rain. Still only early April, there was no warmth in the air, and I shivered until my teeth chattered against one another, my arm covered in goose bumps.

The ostler looked up at me and said something in Welsh. I shook my head. "Don't understand." We remained there in silence for the half hour it took before everyone reappeared, during which time I looked to see if there was any possible way I could free my hand, the prospect of wandering around Pembrokeshire penniless being preferable to that of dying in the prison hulks. David had done an excellent job of making sure I was secure, however, and I gave up, and we were on our way once more.

We had gone just a couple of miles before we came to a ravine where we needed to ford the Western Cleddau, and which I recognized. Just the other side of the river was where the highwaymen had robbed me of my clothes, and where I had set off over the moors on my way to Fishguard. The steep sides of the ravine had been the cause of my getting lost when I had had to find my way around them, and lost my bearings. At that time the river was easily fordable, even for pedestrians, having stepping stones leading from one side to the other. Now though, because of the heavy rain, along with the effect of another recent storm, it was not only swollen and dangerous looking, but many feet wider. Given the option, I would never have attempted to cross it in its present state.

It was clear the coachman was of the same opinion, for he stopped and dismounted, and I could hear him telling Mr. Saunders he thought it too dangerous to attempt to cross. I did not hear the squire's reply, but after a few minutes, the coachman returned, climbed aboard and sat down. He muttered, "damnable fool", and urged the horses into what was now truly a raging torrent, with dangerous branches sweeping along, carried by the current.

I too thought it madness. Mr. Saunders's business in Haverfordwest must be of pressing urgency for him to even attempt it, and I hoped he did not consider me to be the cause of that urgency. That I might be, made me even more nervous. Maybe he had even received word that I was a dangerous criminal, and wanted to be rid of me as soon as possible.

As the coachman urged the horses into the maelstrom, I even began to wonder whether my life was going to end soon anyway, whether it be in the hulks or even sooner, in this river. We had gone barely twenty feet when the lead horse lost its footing and went down. The river tried to wash it away, and within seconds, all four horses were a writhing mass of screaming and shrilly whinnying bodies, their heads bobbing up, then disappearing under the water, the whites of their eyes showing their terror. It was horrifying to see the poor, magnificent animals fighting for their lives. The coachman was shouting, but there was nothing he could do; with all four horses churning around in the river, the reins were useless. There were a couple of loud cracks, the carriage lurched, and the river slewed it around so it was facing downstream and at right angles to the horses, the shafts having snapped off like twigs.

A huge tree trunk appeared from round the bend, and came surging towards us, crashing into the rear of the carriage, splintering it, and creating a hole through which the water poured, slewing the carriage around yet again, the added weight of the water turning it on its side and hurling the coachman and the two footmen headlong into the river. Swept away, they were soon out of sight, their cries lost in the roar of the river and the screaming of the one remaining horse that still had not drowned. I wished it would hurry up and succumb, so ending its agony. Being a lover of animals, especially horses, it was a terrible thing for me to have to witness. The whole scene was as though from the mind of some demented artist, bent on depicting a moving tableau out of Hell itself, with me, the only survivor -- Mr. Saunders surely having drowned inside the carriage -- trapped, and waiting only for the river to rise so high that I too would drown.

The carriage, weighed down with water, and with the horses still harnessed to it, ground its way some yards further downstream into even deeper water before lodging itself on the riverbed, while my body, pulled by the river, but unable to go anywhere, lay stretched out on the surface like a piece of river grass. The horses were all dead now, their bodies no longer visible. Apart from the roaring of the river, there was silence, the only objects remaining visible being just me and a few inches of the side of the carriage sticking out of the water, mid stream.

My own life had been saved thus far by being tied to the rail on the side of the carriage still above water level. If it had rolled to the other side instead, I would have drowned almost at once. Minutes passed, the current roaring past me carrying away my body heat along with it, and it was clear I could die of cold just as well as drown if I failed to free myself. I looked off to my side. I was at least twenty feet from the shore, but I had to set myself free somehow, before the river rose any further.

There was nothing sharp against which I could scrape the thong and cut it through. It was shrinking too, and although David had tied it as loosely as he dared, now it was tightening to the extent that, embedded in my wrist, its pressure was causing my hand to go numb.

Normally this was quite a busy road, but this was a real Pembrokeshire storm, and others had wisely stayed at home, so nobody came by at all. I needed to free myself soon though, as the river was still rising, and my rail fast disappearing. If it rose much higher, there would be no way of keeping my head above it, and I would drown. There was only one weapon left to me, my teeth, and I set about gnawing through the leather strap, like a rat. At least it had softened in the water, and the first quarter inch was quite easy, but then the last part became almost impossible as my jaw ached with the effort, and my arm ached with holding it above the water.

The river continued to rise, and soon I was gnawing under water, stopping frequently to come up for air. It was exhausting, but the will to live kept me working at it until a mighty, wrist-wrenching tug freed me, and within an instant the river was sweeping me downstream.

I am a strong swimmer, or used to be, and for the most part kept my head above water, although I could not help swallowing mouthfuls of the silt-laden river when eddies dragged me under.

I don't know how far the river had carried me, when my shirt snagged on an overhanging branch, bringing to a sudden stop my headlong race down what was now a roaring cataract. Once again my body was flat out on the surface, straining to join the fast flowing waters, but now I was only a couple of feet away from the riverbank, and I prayed my linen shirt would not rip and send me careening off once more.

I took hold of the branch, and hiked myself towards the shore, landing in a sort of backwater, away from the main flow, and reached out towards the bank, grabbing hold of ferns, normally above the river, but now all but submerged. The waterlogged and crumbling earth scraped against my chest, and lying flat on my stomach, I hitched myself forward to safety, digging my elbow into the ground to act as an anchor, lurching along like some lumbering seal heading along the shore.

Once out of reach of the river, at least for the moment, I lay there getting my breath back, almost buried in a tangle of dripping grasses, ferns and undergrowth, but then needed to start gnawing again, the thong having tightened so much around my wrist, my hand was starting to turn blue. It was quite a few minutes before I was finally rid of it, and the blood started to flow freely again.

After all the emotional intensity and the physical energy expended over the last half hour or so, there was time now to consider that I was free again, and safe for the time being, lying on the sodden river bank. I rolled over onto my back, and looked up at the bare and dripping trees, beyond which the sky, still divesting itself of its seemingly bottomless well of water, remained a solid pewter grey.

What should I do now? What *could* I do now? Exhausted yet again, not to mention penniless, here I was, this time lying in a steep gorge in the pouring rain, with the ground, ferns, undergrowth, moss, everything around me dripping and saturated, the crowns of the trees above me swaying in the wind. Knowing I could not afford to lose any more of my body heat, however, I needed to move, and fast, before I was too cold to get going at all, and before the river rose to where I was lying.

I pulled myself to my feet, and began to work my way back through the undergrowth towards the Fishguard to Haverfordwest road, following the river which, having already overflowed its banks, threatened to inundate the whole area at any moment. It was not as far as I expected, and on reaching the point where the carriage had overturned, was amazed to see Mr. Saunders standing on the no longer visible side of the coach, up to his ankles in water. He must have found an air pocket, and had then been able to crawl out and hold on without losing his grip. He was already having trouble keeping his balance though, and it was obvious the water would not have to rise much further, before he too would be swept away.

I looked at him standing there, and was faced with a choice. Here I was, on the Fishguard side of the river, free, with no-one around to recapture me, and there was my captor, Mr. Saunders, facing certain death in the middle of the river. I turned away, determined to think only of myself, and to head once more towards my elusive destination, Fishguard.

Mr. Saunders did not cry out or beg me to save him. Perhaps he assumed I would not make such an attempt anyway. I took about twenty steps, the last five of which found me going slower and slower until I came to a stop. What was I about to do? I, Connell O'Keeffe, an honourable gentleman, was about to let a man drown, without making any attempt to save him, and to my mind, not to try made me little less than a murderer myself. He was not an evil man. Arrogant he may be, but he had not mistreated me, and had made sure I had been well fed, even if he had kept me locked in solitary confinement in a dark stable for nearly three weeks. Well, perhaps that could well be considered mistreating me, although presumably, in holding me in the belief that I was a wanted criminal, and with the intention of turning me in to the authorities, he had thought he was doing what was right, not out of any thought of revenge, which was something that could not be said of his demonic daughter.

Visualizing her standing there at the window, that look of hatred still ruining what might otherwise be a beautiful face, and watching me being carted off to be hanged, or to rot in the prison hulks, made me think of the terrible vengeance of which a woman can be capable, but that was beside the point. This was her father, and I wondered for an instant if it *had* been the daughter standing there now on the carriage roof, would I have tried to save her? It was a question I dared not answer, and fortunately did not have to.

If I were to rescue him, it would be easy for me to then continue with my escape as soon as he was safely on land, he being a man well into his middle age, and old enough to be my father and, by the look of him, not in the best physical shape. There would be no way in which he could catch me, and he was not carrying any arms.

If I were going to try to help him though, it would have to be soon, and how could I help him anyway? There was a twenty-foot cascade of raging river between us. I had to make the effort at least, and I turned around and walked back to the edge of the river. He still had not called out and begged me to save him, and I respected him for that.

I looked about me. Off to one side was a small side-stream, equally swollen and swift running, but still fordable, and beyond that, over a fence, a field already submerged in about two inches of water, with a cowshed at the far end of it. Farmers quite often keep useful items handy in such sheds. It saves them from having to return to the farm if a fence needs mending or a gate fixing. With luck I might find something I could turn into a lifeline. With no other option available, and if I did want to try to save him, then I would have to get to the shed. I signalled my intention to Mr. Saunders, and set off.

The stream was quite narrow, but now quite deep, and I was up to my waist at the deepest part. Then there was the fence, or hedge to negotiate. It was one of those

Pembrokeshire laid fences, and the broken stems poked up their sharp edges, acting as a deterrent to animals trying to get out, or now to me to get in. By the time I was sloshing my way through the field I was covered with scratches inflicted by the ubiquitous brambles stretching their long canes everywhere through the hedge.

The door to the cowshed opened easily, and I had been right; there were all sorts of bits and pieces in there. "Ah! Yes!" I exclaimed out loud. A ball of heavy twine lay on a shelf right next to the door. "Now I need something heavy to attach to it." There was not much light, and at first I could find nothing of a suitable weight. Everything was either too flimsy or too heavy. Then I found an iron gin-trap. It was almost too heavy, but with luck I could heave it the necessary twenty feet. It would have to do though, as I could find nothing else more suitable.

It was impossible to carry both the ball of twine and the trap in one hand, and at the same time negotiate my way back to the river's edge, so I locked my teeth into the twine, and hooked the spike and chain attached to the trap into my breeches, letting the trap dangle from my side, and carried them that way, leaving my hand free. It took a good twenty minutes to get back to the river's edge, by which time Mr. Saunders was almost up to his knees in water, and the river several feet wider.

My task now was to attach the twine to the trap. At last it was secure, and after measuring out about thirty feet of it from the roll, I swung the trap a few times before launching it in the direction of the carriage. The first three attempts failed, and I had to haul it back each time, using my foot to stand on the line to stop it from slipping away from me as I dragged it back. Then, at the fourth try, it almost hit Mr. Saunders on the head, but he was able to catch it.

I unwound some more twine, and shouted to him to haul it towards him until he had a double length to attach to the trap, so adding extra strength to the line. I then fed the ball round a smooth sapling, giving me some control, as the only way I could pull him to shore was to walk backwards and tow him in. After that I shouted to Mr. Saunders to jump into the river. The pull on my arm was immense, and I was glad I had wrapped the twine around the tree, or I think I would not have been able to hold on to him. In another few minutes, he was safely back on land, lying on the wet ground, his legs still in the water. It was a few moments more before he was able to stand.

I walked up to him. He held out his hand, and I shook it. That was all. It was all that was needed, or expected.

"A bad business. A very bad business. Three good men lost. A very bad business." Mr. Saunders turned his back on the scene of the disaster, and set off down the road back towards Fishguard. After he had gone about fifty yards he turned round. "Come on then," he called out, then resumed his walk towards his home. A few more yards and he turned again, and seeing me standing there, hesitating, said: "I'm a man of honour. You saved my life. I can't in good conscience turn you over to the authorities now. You're welcome to come home with me if you wish, or you can run away. It's your choice. I can't prevent you, nor would I even want to try after what you've just done for me." He turned and began walking away again.

I caught up with him, and we walked side by side in silence. I kept telling myself I could still escape at any time now if I wanted to. As he said, there was no way he could prevent me, being unarmed. I did not run away, though, knowing I could trust him. Such men do not go back on their word; it's a matter of honour, and a gentleman's honour is sacrosanct.

The rain stopped, and the sun came out. Soon the countryside was steaming, and seemingly the whole of Nature glittered with pregnant raindrops, each reflecting its own tiny image of the welcome sun. In another hour we were back at *The Harp*, and he headed inside. After a few seconds he appeared again. "Come on in then."

Conspicuous as I was, looking like the filthy victim of a shipwreck -- although he looked little better than I now -- and still some miles from Fishguard, my chances were better with him than trying to make it to the port on my own and without any money, so I followed him, and he invited me to sit down with him. He was still in shock. Gone was the arrogance, and I almost felt sorry for him. He had a right to be subdued. It was at his behest his coachman had followed his master's orders, and gone to his death. It was at his behest he had also caused the death of two young, healthy footmen, and also, I was sure was in his mind, he had lost four very valuable horses, not to mention his carriage. It had been a disastrous trip from every point of view. That he had also failed in his mission to deliver me up to the authorities, I imagined was the least of his regrets.

He ordered two mugs of ale, and I sat in silence, water oozing out of my breeches and dripping onto the floor. Mr. Saunders sat opposite me, looking down, hands wrapped around his mug, drumming his thumbs against the pewter. At this time of day we were the only customers, and the only sounds came from the ticking of an oak long-case clock in the corner and someone singing in the kitchen just beyond where we sat. Finally he sighed and lifted his head, looking me in the face for the first time.

He was a stout man with a florid complexion. His eyes were faded blue, his once blonde hair turning a straw-tinged grey, receding from his temples. Like most men now, he had given up powder and wigs since the new powder tax had come in, but still wore his hair long, and tied at the nape of his neck.

"So," he said at last. "And who *are* you? I suppose I should at least know the name of the man who saved my life."

I thought before answering. My judgment had already told me this was a man I could trust, a man who would keep his word and his council. I had to hope I was correct, and further judged that I had nothing more to lose.

"My name is Connell O'Keeffe, first son of Sir Connell O'Keeffe, of Dunleary, loyal subject of His Majesty King George III."

Mr. Saunders's head whipped up in amazement, and he stared at me, then nodded. "And you're telling the truth, I can see that." He stroked the side of his mug, studying it as though it were a fine work of art. "Would you care to explain yourself, Sir?"

And I did.

"Why didn't you explain yourself earlier?" he asked when I had finished my saga.

"Because I didn't think you were of a mind to listen to, or even believe, anything I might have to say." I gave him a wry smile. "Besides, you didn't give me the opportunity."

He nodded. "You're right there, on all counts." A brief smile appeared, then vanished. "I'm not looking to excuse myself, but my daughter's loss, which I believe was explained to you by David, has affected us all greatly. I fear I've wrongly indulged her notions about finding the killer of her beloved fiancé, and have allowed my common sense to be overridden by my efforts to help her overcome her grief. For my own behaviour towards you, I apologise, and you would indeed have had every right to challenge me over it, although it would have been a brave move indeed, considering your own loss, a terrible thing to have happened to you."

I said nothing. There was not much I could say, and after a short silence he continued. "You will come home with me, will you? We need to see about getting you absolved from this indictment. I have some influence, but this gentleman at whose home you were staying during your time in Haverfordwest -- how influential is he? Would the authorities be willing to believe him if he were to vouch for your being at his home all the time leading up to the French landing?"

I had not mentioned Mr. Potter by name when telling him my story, but now I did, and it turned out he knew him well. "Oh well then," he said. "If Mr. Potter can vouch for you, then there can be no doubt you had nothing to do with it at all, and as both he and I can attest to your good character, then the authorities would be hard-pressed to come up with a reason why you should suddenly decide to go into a field and arbitrarily kill one of His Majesty's officers while making your way home to Ireland. The idea is absurd. That you were dressed in a French uniform also shows someone went to great lengths to set you up as the murderer." He paused. "I assume you would remember the killer if you were to see him?"

"It's a face I'll never forget."

Mr. Saunders nodded, and finished off his ale. "I imagine not." He stood up. "Well, we'd better get going. We don't want to be out in the dark, and the days are still short. I'll see if they have a couple of saddle horses here for us to hire." He called the serving girl and asked her to find out, but it was the innkeeper who returned, full of apologies.

"I'm so sorry, Mr. Saunders, Sir, but all we have here at the moment are carriage horses, and you would not want them -- not broken to the saddle. If you'd like to wait over till tomorrow though, I'm expecting one saddle horse back tonight... Others would have been here earlier but for the river being impassable."

Mr. Saunders shook his head. "No, I need to get home, or my wife will be wondering what has become of me." He stood up. "We'd better get going then, O'Keeffe. At least it's stopped raining." He headed for the door, then turned back. "Just a minute." The innkeeper was still in the room, and Mr. Saunders drew him aside, and whispered something to him before returning and heading once more for the door. "I know him well," he told me, "and asked him not to mention you were with me, just in case that murderer is out looking for you. I doubt the authorities are. They're too busy preparing for another invasion to bother about one prisoner who has slipped away. That killer though, he probably won't rest easy until he finds you, or is convinced you've escaped back to Ireland." He stopped again. "Come to think of it, we have to get you back to my place safely, and you do look highly conspicuous. We need to do something to disguise you somehow." He turned round and headed back inside. "Come back in," he said.

I followed him, and once again he had a whispered conversation with the landlord, at the end of which he beckoned to me, and we were taken into a back room, the landlord's private apartment, where his wife was busy cooking.

"Martha, we need to find some clothes for this young man, something that will make him unrecognizable. Have you any suggestions?"

Martha put down the ladle she was using to stir a pot, put the lid on, and turned to look at me, wiping her hands in her apron. I think my unusually tall stature and my features, along with my fine boots, covered with mud though they were, told her I was a gentleman, and she smiled and curtsied.

"Well," she said, coming closer and looking up at me. "You're really too tall for a woman, but I think that would be the best even so. It's the only way we can disguise your disfigurement, which is most noticeable when you're dressed as a man. Let me see what I can find. I'm fairly tall myself, so I'll see what I can do."

An hour later, the several weeks' growth of my beard had been removed, and I was dressed in several heavy wool petticoats topped with a dog-tooth check, black-and-white skirt, a blouse, and the all-important huge Welsh shawl which, when wrapped around my shoulders, hid whatever was, or was not beneath. A white bonnet with a frilly edge was tied over my head, and a beaver hat placed on top of that. My hair, loose about my face, peeped out from under my bonnet, giving me, I suppose, a somewhat feminine look as well. The skirt was too short to hide my boots, but it was decided that everything was so muddy that before we had gone very far, there would be no telling what I was wearing on my feet.

Martha stood back and surveyed me. She seemed pleased with her handiwork, as did her husband and Mr. Saunders.

The latter patted me on the back. "Now all you'll have to do is to remember to keep your mouth closed. The pitch and timbre of your voice are anything but ladylike."

He thanked the innkeeper and his wife, promised to return the clothes as soon as possible, and headed once more for the door, as did I, almost falling on my face, when I forgot to hoist my skirts as I went over the step. They all laughed.

"Pick your feet up, O'Keeffe," said Mr. Saunders.

And so we set out for Mr. Saunders's home, an ill-assorted couple, with the 'wife' a good six inches taller than her 'husband'. The few moments of jollity, however, soon descended into depression as we both contemplated the tragedy that had taken place just a few hours before.

"Thomas, my coachman, was a good man," Mr. Saunders lamented as we walked along. "And he has a wife and two children... Of course I'll see to it that they're well taken care of. Billy and Ted, my footmen, were only about your age, and not married. I don't even know their families, although I think they came from down below somewhere -- Tenby, I think."

I said nothing. There was no doubt he had indirectly contributed to all three deaths, and I could not bring myself to console him on that score by saying it had been unavoidable. However, when questions were asked, as they surely would be, I could say truthfully I had not heard Mr. Saunders order the coachman to proceed. Those questions though, when they were asked -- would I myself come under scrutiny again? Should I accept Mr. Saunders's offer to stay at his home until Mr. Potter's return, or should I try yet again to leave the country before that would happen? Trudging through the ankle-deep mud of the lanes leading to his mansion, it was something I would have to think about later as my mind was too weary now for rational decision-making, although there was one question I did need to ask:

"Mr. Saunders, Sir, what about your daughter? I'm sure she won't be pleased at all with the idea of my having gone from sleeping in one of your stables for the last three weeks, to sleeping in one of your beds tonight, or indeed any night."

"Don't worry about Miss Saunders, O'Keeffe. Headstrong she may be, and there's no doubt we shall both be on the receiving end of her wrath, although when she hears the truth, I can't see how she can continue to consider you as one of the enemy. I think you'll find her bark worse than her bite, however, even if her bark is considerably louder, and longer too, alas, than that of most young ladies of her class." He gave a wan smile, and shook his head.

"It's all my fault for spoiling her. As the doting father, I just can't help myself. Just you wait and see. When you have a daughter, see how you will treat her too."

The idea of getting married, let alone having children, was farthest from my thoughts at this moment, so I said nothing, and we continued our walk back to his home tucked away in the north Pembrokeshire countryside, although exactly where it was located, I had not yet discovered.

Too much had happened, and too much still lay between us for us to carry on any casual conversation, although anything that was said, was cordial. For most of the time though, we walked in silence, each deep into our own, no doubt widely disparate thoughts.

I am not sure how long we had been walking, but the sun was getting low in the sky, and Mr. Saunders was showing signs of the strain of the day's events. He was also not used to exercise, and was having to stop often to take rests, his breathing becoming laboured, especially when we had to climb hills, of which there were many.

"Mr. Saunders, Sir, come onto my left side and put your arm round my waist. I'll put my own arm round you and help you along." And that is what we did for the next couple of miles, the sun sliding quickly now towards the horizon, our shadows stretching many yards behind us.

We were at the entrance to the estate when he came to a final stop, and for the first time I saw the name of the property. It was *Carregowen*.

He shook his head. "Only about another half mile, but I can go no further, O'Keeffe. I'm going to have to ask you to go ahead and fetch help; it's right at the end of this drive. I wouldn't blame you if you chose now to flee, although dressed as you are..." He leaned his back against a tree. "Anyway, I'm going to have to trust you won't abandon me out here. Go to the servants' entrance for now. They'll probably be in the middle of their dinner at this time, but it can't be helped. Get David to hitch up the pony to the gig, and tell him where to find me. There's no need for you to return. You're exhausted too. Tell Metcalf, the butler, he has my instructions to feed you."

I picked up my skirts, now weighed down with mud, and went as fast as I could, arriving in the stable yard just as darkness was falling. It was empty as Mr. Saunders expected it would be, everyone being at supper, and I made my way to the servants' entrance and rang the bell. I heard it clang from somewhere below, and waited. After a few minutes the door opened, and a man in livery stood there. He looked me up and down with obvious distaste. "Yes?"

Forgetting I was dressed as a woman, I commanded in my usual voice, "I need to see David. It's urgent."

The man, the butler no doubt, frowned at me. His dinner was going cold, and he was not pleased. "You can tell *me* whatever it is you want him for. He's eating his dinner. Who are you anyway? Your voice..." Realizing I was a man, he began to close the door in a hurry.

For the second time in the space of just under a month -- at least I think that's what it was; I was losing track of time -- I put my foot in the door, and decided to assert my superior rank as a gentleman.

"You. What's your name?"

He pulled in his chin, raising himself to his full height. "I'm Mr. Metcalf, Mr. Saunders's butler. And who, I might ask, are you?"

I did not answer his question. "Metcalf." I specifically left off the "Mr". "Get David here, *now*, or I'll see to it that when Mr. Saunders is rescued from his current dilemma, you'll be out of here on your ear." My arrogant tone was not one I would ever normally choose to use on anyone, servant or otherwise, but this was an emergency, and there was no time to be wasted discussing my credentials.

The door was opened. "David. You're needed here. Now."

By the time the groom arrived at the door, I had pulled off my beaver hat. My lace-edged bonnet had gone into a knot, and as I could not untie it, I pulled it back off my head, so it was now sitting on my neck, like a ridiculous frilly scarf. I must have looked like a character in one of John O'Keeffe's comedies, although nobody, including me, was laughing.

"You!" David shouted. "What's happened. Why...?"

I put up my hand. "There's no time to explain. Mr. Saunders wants you to hitch up the pony and gig, and fetch him. He's about a half mile down the road."

The butler meanwhile, had crept off, and came back holding a pistol, which he aimed at my stomach. "Stay where you are. Explain. What's going on here?"

I ignored him. "David, go now and do as Mr. Saunders has asked. Metcalf here can hold me as hostage if he wants until you get back. Hurry though. He's exhausted, and needs your help."

The butler nodded his approval of the plan, and David grabbed his coat and set off for the stable. Some minutes later, I heard the pony cantering down the road. I, meanwhile, was still standing in the doorway. Metcalf, confused by my tone of voice and the way I spoke, stood there also, his pistol still pointing at my stomach.

"Why don't you let me in?" I suggested. "You have the pistol, so I'm not going anywhere. Besides, Mr. Saunders said for you to provide me with some food, and I could certainly do with it, not having had anything to eat since breakfast."

The butler raised the corner of his lip, ignoring my request. "My own dinner is going cold, and I'm not standing around holding a gun on you, either inside the house or out, for whatever time it takes for Mr. Saunders and his groom to return. You can stay in one of the stables. In fact, now, from David's reaction to you, I'm beginning to wonder if you're not the one who was there these last weeks." He turned and called out, "Gwenda. Come here and bring a candle with you, girl."

Gwenda appeared. "Hold that candle up to this person's face and tell me if you recognize it."

Gwenda approached, holding the candle high, then let out a shriek, almost dropping it.

"I gather you recognize him then," said the butler.

Gwenda nodded.

"Right, off you go."

He prodded me with the pistol, and motioned me towards the stables, where I soon found myself locked back where I had started just over eight hours ago. A short while later Gwenda appeared with a bowl of soup, some bread, and some ale. I had come full circle.

It was less than half an hour later that I heard the pony returning, and a few minutes after that David came to open the stable door. "Mr. Saunders says you're to be brought to the house." He let me out, and as we walked he said Mr. Saunders had told him everything. "I'm all befuddled," he said, shaking his head. "So much to take in. A disastrous accident all round. Damn but they were valuable horses too, and the mare was with foal as well."

I suppose, as groom, he would feel that loss even more so than that of the humans who were drowned. Grooms, I know, become very fond of their charges, and often think of them as their pets. He must have been greatly grieved as to what had happened to four fine animals.

"He told you about me too, then, did he?"

"Yes, Sir. Mr. Saunders knows he can trust me not to say anything. I should give you a warning though. The rest of the staff may not be so loyal, so it's best not to reveal anything more about yourself than necessary, although with you now suddenly going from the stable to the family quarters, there's certainly going to be a considerable amount of speculation amongst the rest of the servants as to who and what you are, Sir. You may rest assured though, they'll find out nothing from me."

"Thank you David."

We had reached the house, and he delivered me to the front door, where I was greeted by a bemused Metcalf for the second time in the space of an hour, although perhaps 'greeted' is not the right word, as it was obvious he was still rankled by my ordering him about earlier.

I held out my hand. "No hard feelings, I hope, Metcalf. I'm afraid I had to be demanding for Mr. Saunders's sake."

He took my hand, but the handshake came with no additional smile. "I understand, Sir. This way Sir." He led me up to an elegant chamber. "Dinner will be at eight o'clock, Sir. In the meantime, I'll send up a tub and hot water, so you can take a bath. I'll see to it that you're provided with suitable attire as well... Will that be all Sir?"

"For now, I think so. I'm so tired, I hardly know what I want."

"Yes Sir. Oh, and Mr. Saunders has also asked me to provide you with someone to act as your personal valet during the time you're here. I'll send him up shortly. His name is Morgan."

It seemed as though lately I was finding myself in dire need of being cleaned up, and now was no exception. I was covered with mud, slime and greenery, and am sure must have left a considerable layer of silt at the bottom of the bathtub. Once again, however, it was good to look and feel respectable, and by the time I was expected to make my way to the family dining salon, I looked a gentleman yet again, Morgan's help being greatly appreciated in enabling me to achieve this. I walked down the grand staircase, hoping that this time, there would never be any further calamity to reduce me to looking anything but a gentleman.

Despite knowing Mr. Saunders was now on my side, and in a sense acting as my guardian, it was with great trepidation that I entered the salon. I had not seen his daughter -- except at the window earlier in the day -- since she had brought her father to see me in the stable that day, and had no idea how she would receive me now, nor had I met Mrs. Saunders. Clean I might be, and looking the part, but was now so tired after the day's exertions, I would have much preferred to have collapsed onto my comfortable and clean bed, where I would no doubt have fallen asleep immediately. That was not to be, however. I had to find the strength to face the fearsome Miss Saunders and her mother who, for all I knew, might be equally intimidating.

I was ushered into the large salon by a stone-faced footman in livery, at which Mr. Saunders rose and greeted me, then introduced me to his wife.

"My dear, I should like you to meet Mr. Connell O'Keeffe, first son of Sir Connell O'Keeffe of Dunleary, Ireland, and loyal subject of His Majesty, King George III."

I bowed my most elegant bow, and Mrs. Saunders held out her hand. "Oh Mr. O'Keeffe! How can we ever repay you for bringing Mr. Saunders home safely to us? He's told us all about you, and your courage and concern are all the more remarkable considering the possible consequences to you, and given that you could well have chosen to make your escape instead."

I bowed again, and smiled at her. "I like to think I made the right choice, Ma'am."

Mr. Saunders then introduced me to his daughter, Miss Saunders. "Katherine, my dear, I think we need to introduce you properly to the gentleman whom, three weeks ago, you treated in a most unwelcome fashion as, to my regret, did I also."

I bowed. "Miss Saunders," and ventured to give her a smile, which was returned with an expression no less malevolent than when I first saw her out there on the moors.

Raising her head in disdain, and ignoring me, she turned to her father. "What proof have you, Father, that this man here is who he says he is? How do you know he's not just another lying Paddy? Why would any law-abiding man, especially a gentleman as he claims to be -- My! My! The son of a baronet no less..." She waved a sarcastic hand in my direction. "Why would the son of an Irish baronet be wandering around the Pembrokeshire moors, almost naked, his arm recently severed? Ridiculous! He *has* to have been one of the invaders. How else would he have been wounded, if not by one of our own brave militia? It makes no sense, and I don't believe a word of it. Think father. You have no proof whatsoever that he's telling the truth. None. *Of course* he was one of those Irish Republican invaders! How you can possibly believe otherwise, I cannot understand."

I stood there, not knowing which way to turn, or what to do. I had never been in such an awkward social situation in my life, and felt like fleeing, not just to escape the authorities, but to escape from this formidable young woman, the like of which I had never ever encountered before.

She was banging her fist on the table. "And I refuse to sit at table and dine with such an imposter. Saving your life was nothing to him. He did it only to serve his own ends, and to ingratiate himself with you." She stood up, almost knocking into me. "And *you*, my father, have fallen for it." She put her hands to her head. "I can't believe it. I just can't believe it." She folded her arms in defiance, and marched over to the window, looking out into the darkness.

"My dear, I've already explained to you why you found Mr. O'Keeffe as you did, and he's behaved in a thoroughly gentlemanly fashion throughout his ordeal. If he hadn't, then I, your father, would not be alive to talk to you now. He could just as easily have left me to drown."

She swung round and laughed. It was not a pleasant laugh, but one of scorn. "Just look at yourself, Father. You're behaving exactly as he's planned. You've become his protector, a much safer option for him than trying to make his own way out of the country. You're being made a fool of. Well, he won't make a fool of me." And she marched out of the room.

Mr. Saunders sighed. "I do apologise, Mr. O'Keeffe. My daughter has been under a great strain as I told you. Please forgive her. She being my only daughter, I'm afraid, as I explained to you earlier also, I'm guilty of spoiling her as well."

The need to think of self-preservation had finally arrived. "There's no chance Miss Saunders will betray me to the authorities, I suppose?"

"No. I may spoil my daughter, Mr. O'Keeffe, but she knows the limits, and being disloyal to her family is not something she'd even consider."

"I'm glad to hear it."

"Come, Mr. O'Keeffe." Mrs. Saunders patted the chair to her side. "Come sit here next to me." To my great relief, unlike her daughter in every way, except in her handsome features, she was pleasant, friendly and considerate, even taking it upon herself, in a natural and unobtrusive way, motherly almost, to make sure my food was such that I was not faced with the insurmountable task of carving the large slice of rare roast beef that sat on my plate -- a consideration for which I was most grateful. It was the first real meal I had had since leaving the care of Mrs. Kelly, and I ate every last crumb, including a large slice of apple pie that followed the beef, vegetables, potato and gravy, all washed down with some excellent port.

The talk over dinner was, of course, about the day's tragedy, and Mrs. Saunders plied me with question after question, wanting to know how I managed to save her husband and bring him home. I answered as best I could, but was well aware of, and bothered by the empty chair at the table. Would Miss Saunders remain loyal to her family? I could only hope so. Also, would my time spent in the household be made intolerable for all by her continued hostile attitude towards me? What would happen if it were?

Mr. Saunders might be my protector for now, but my situation was still not one in which I could feel sufficiently safe to relax. I think I sighed out loud, but if I did, it went unremarked.

After dinner, Mrs. Saunders excused herself, and retired to the drawing room, leaving Mr. Saunders and me to finish off the last of the port.

Mr. Saunders leaned back in his chair, fingering his glass. "I'm afraid I haven't yet been able to think through every detail you told me of your recent trials, but there is one thing. Given your father's position in society, is there no way you could solicit his help in getting you out of the horrendous situation in which you find yourself? Surely, a word to the right authorities...?"

It was of course, what Mr. Nash had wanted to know as well, so I repeated my explanation regarding my parents being abroad somewhere, but I did not know where.

He nodded. "Ah yes, I see. Most unfortunate. Most unfortunate."

Both of us being exhausted, our conversation languished, and we were soon saying goodnight and retiring to our chambers.

As promised, my new manservant, Morgan, was there to help me, which was just as well, as the combination of the day's events followed by the large meal and several generous glasses of port made it so that, left to myself, I most likely would have awoken the next morning on the bed still fully dressed, including boots. I do not even remember Morgan undressing me.

CHAPTER 8

When I finally appeared for breakfast the following morning, I was alone, the rest of the family having already eaten and gone about their business. I was relieved, as I did not feel in the mood for polite conversation right then, nor had I wanted to come face to face with Miss Saunders.

The Saunders family ate well, something attested to by Mr. Saunders's girth, and the quality and quantity of what was served at breakfast was no different to what was served at dinner. I helped myself to some veal pie, lambs' kidneys and some delicious pork sausages along with potatoes mashed in cream and butter. This I washed down with coffee of an excellence to rival some of that served at the best coffee houses in Dublin. I was replete, and returned for a while to my chamber, feeling somewhat ashamed of myself for having overeaten. Still, for someone who, apart from the dinner the night before, had not eaten a decent meal for weeks, I forgave myself, but nevertheless lay down on the bed for a while to allow myself to digest it. I also warned myself to be careful, or I should soon be as rotund as my host.

After a while I got up and made my way down to the stables to see David, and to commiserate with him over the loss of the horses as well as the loss of the head of the stable staff, the coachman. He seemed genuinely glad to see me, and was almost in tears, certainly more because of the loss of the horses than of his overbearing and arrogant superior - - not, I am sure, that he would have wished the man dead.

"What do you think Mr. Saunders will..." I began.

"David. Would you please saddle up my horse for me. It's such a beautiful morning, and I feel like taking a turn around the estate." Miss Saunders had marched up to where David and I were in conversation, and acted as though I was not there. I gave a polite bow anyway, but she ignored me. "I'd like to try out the new saddle too, please David."

"Yes, Miss Saunders. Right away." David went off, leaving me standing there, but not for long. She may find me repulsive to look at, and believe me to be a traitor on top of that, but no woman was going to insult me quite so blatantly. I gave a quick nodding bow, turned on my heel, and walked off, leaving her no chance to be any more rude than she had already been.

I went to look at the other remaining horses, and found the four empty stables shocking, bringing yesterday's tragedy all back to me. A few minutes later, Miss Saunders swept past me, and I was sure she rode as close to me as she could without actually knocking me over, her aim, I assumed, being to let me know she had no intention of talking to me, or of having anything to do with me.

She was certainly succeeding in making me feel unwelcome, and I wondered if it was going to be possible even to spend the time here, waiting for Mr. Potter's return. My stay, if I did decide to remain, was not going to be a pleasant one; that was obvious.

The rest of the day did prove most awkward and embarrassing for me, with Miss Saunders refusing to eat at table with me, and looking the other way whenever we happened to meet. Even so, she was the daughter of my host, and I felt obliged to continue to behave like a gentleman, even if she could not bring herself to behave like a lady.

The following morning we happened to arrive at breakfast at the same time. I gave her a slight bow, and stood back to allow her to enter the salon ahead of me. She swept past me without acknowledging my presence, but if she thought I was going to retire and come back later after she was finished, she was mistaken. I followed her into the room, standing aside to allow her to select what she wanted from the sideboard, before going to help myself. She said nothing, so neither did I. Maybe she was hoping I would try to make polite conversation, so she could take satisfaction in not answering me, but I refused to give her that pleasure. I picked up my plate and deliberately set it down opposite her, before going back to help myself to coffee. I sat down and ate my breakfast, which I finished before she finished hers, so I stood up, bowed, and left the room. Despite being convinced she found me repellent to look at, and that that was one reason why she refused to even look at me, I still had some self-respect, even if my pride in my person was gone; two could play at this game.

I have always loved horses, and as Mr. Saunders owned some handsome saddle horses, I went down to the stables again later that morning to see them as well as to see David, who, of course, was still in mourning for the lost carriage horses, and would continue to be so for a long time. We sat together on the mounting block, and he was glad to have my sympathetic ear. It helped me too as Mr. Saunders was off, seeing to the aftermath of the disaster, and Mrs. Saunders was holding a morning coffee and embroidery session with some of her friends, leaving me with no-one to talk to.

"Hard to replace horses like that, and that young mare too, with foal. I could weep for them. Such a tragic death too. Their suffering, I can hardly bring myself to contemplate it."

I listened and nodded my head. I could have given him a vivid description of their deaths, but saw no reason to add further to his agony. He was content to simply have me listen. We had not been there long when Miss Saunders appeared. Of course we both jumped to our feet, and I bowed as I had done the day before.

"Good morning David," she said, flouncing past me, brushing against me as though I were not there.

As soon as she was out of earshot David looked at me. "If looks could kill..." he commented.

"I'd be long-since dead," I replied.

She reached the stable where her own horse was kept, turned, and for the first time addressed me.

"If I had my way, you wouldn't be here at all, and it's only because I respect my father that you *are* still here."

I bowed in response, and said nothing. What could I say? It seemed that nothing I did, however, pleased her.

"I don't expect or want your hypocritical bows, trying to make a fool of me the way you are of my father. Believe me, if I could kill you, I would."

I started to walk towards her.

"Stay away from me, Paddy. I don't want you near me. In fact, stay away from the stables altogether. I don't want you here. Go! Now! Get out of my sight."

By this time I was within three feet of her. "Miss Saunders," I said quietly. "Feel as you will about me, but please don't castigate me in front of the staff. It's highly improper, and your father would be most upset if he knew. I know you don't believe me to be who I say I am, and right now I can't prove who I am, but as soon as I'm exonerated, you *will* know, and at that time, I'm sure you'll regret how you've behaved towards me."

While I was speaking, she turned her back on me and went into the stable, ignoring me. I walked away and returned to the house, the prospect of enduring an extended period in such an atmosphere not a happy one. It was such a shame as she was a vibrant and beautiful woman.

I did suggest to Mr. Saunders at dinner that night that perhaps it would be more comfortable for them as a family if I were to eat my meals in my own apartments, but he would have none of it.

"Indeed not, Mr. O'Keeffe. My daughter is a grown woman, and this is one instance where I'll not give in to her whims. Her behaviour is unacceptable, and if any inconvenience is to be had, then it shall be she who suffers it."

After dinner, Mrs. Saunders took her leave as usual and disappeared to the drawing room, leaving Mr. Saunders and me to ourselves and a bottle of port. I had not been very hungry this evening, and had failed to eat all my dinner, and had even felt so warm that I was sweating, despite there being a chill in the air. I was about half way through my glass, when I realized I really was not feeling well at all, the room starting to sway around me. I was telling Mr.

Saunders about my acting career at the time, and halted in mid sentence.

He looked at me. "Mr. O'Keeffe. I fear the trials of recent weeks have caught up with you at last. Your colour is not good at all, and you're clearly unwell. I think a good night's sleep is what you need. Why don't you go right now? Don't let me detain you here."

"Thank you, Sir. I think you may be right, so if you'll please excuse me." I stood up, took two steps, and crashed to the floor.

CHAPTER 9

I opened my eyes to see Miss Saunders looking down at me. I was in my own bed in my own chamber and, convinced she had come to kill me, my first thought was to try to escape, but then I saw her expression was one of concern, not hate.

"Welcome back, Mr. O'Keeffe." She was even smiling at me. Confused, my conviction now was that I was dreaming. I tried to concentrate.

"Mr. O'Keeffe," she was saying. "I apologise. I was wrong. You were indeed telling the truth. I know that now. I'm afraid my loss has made me bitter. Forgive me."

I think I smiled, convinced I was still dreaming, but then the dream faded away.

She was still there when I woke up again, but now she was sitting over by the window, working at some embroidery. This time my mind was clear.

She must have felt me looking at her, because she put down her work and came over. "Ah there you are Mr. O'Keeffe. How are you now?"

"I don't know. How am I?"

"I know how you *have* been. You've been very ill. We were afraid we were going to lose you."

"Afraid? Isn't that what you wanted?"

She laughed. "I was wrong, very wrong."

"Oh? *I* know you were wrong, but how do *you* know you were wrong, very wrong?"

"Because of everything you've been telling us these past three days while you were taken over by your fever. It's obvious your experiences were real, and that everything you'd told my father was the truth. My father even insisted I come to listen to you."

I was not sure which shocked me more, the time I had been unaware of what was going on, or the knowledge that I had obviously been saying a great deal during that time.

"Nothing self-incriminating, then?"

"Not at all. On the contrary, it was the very opposite. What you said, or quite often shrieked, caused me to alter my opinion of you. Your terror was very real."

I was feeling sleepy again, and confused by her startling change in attitude towards me. "That's a relief. Too bad I had to almost die though, to get you to change your mind."

I think she replied, but I didn't hear her, and gather I then went into a deep, but natural sleep for almost eight hours.

This time when I woke she was still there, reading on this occasion.

"What happened to the embroidery then?"

She laid the book down on the window ledge, came over and stood over me, looking down. This time she was not smiling.

"What's wrong? Am I out of favour again already?"

She shook her head. "No."

"Why that look then?"

"I'm just studying you. I haven't really looked at you before."

"True. Not a bad verdict, I hope."

"No, not too bad, I suppose."

I had been prepared to accept that she had changed her mind about me, but being now most self-conscious about how I looked, especially to women, her comment took me aback, and I assumed she was letting me know she did not like what she saw. My face must have reflected that.

"Don't look so downcast."

"I'm afraid I'm finding your attitude confusing. First you are only too anxious to have me carted off to languish in the hulks, and to be hanged, then suddenly I wake to find you all full of light-hearted pleasantries. Now you're already being critical again. How do I know that you won't just as easily revert to your former opinion of me?"

She laughed. "No, I assure you that won't happen now I'm convinced of your innocence, and I was only teasing you anyway."

That she was now on my side was a good thing, but being on my side still had not prevented her from finding me repellent to look at. Perhaps she *had* simply been teasing, as she said, but having become so sensitive about my disfigurement, it was not a subject about which I could accept much teasing, at least, not yet. That, presumably, was something I should have to learn to do.

"I'm happy to hear it, but all the same, you're going to have to give me time to adjust to the new you, given the transformation."

"You should know," she informed me. "I do have a temper, so the new me, as you call it, may get cross with you, but it won't mean that I hate you again. You wait and see."

"I'll do that. In the meantime I'll hold my judgment of you. I don't want to let myself be off my guard, only to be vilified again. It was not something I enjoyed."

"I know. I'm sorry."

"Your apology is being held in abeyance for the time being. I'll let you know when it's accepted, agreed?"

She nodded. "Agreed." She clapped her hands as though dismissing everything that had gone before, the matter closed, forgotten, and flopped herself down on the bed beside me. "So, Mr. O'Keeffe, tell me all about your acting career. It must be wonderful to be an actor. I think that would have been something I'd have loved to do. Do you think I'd have been any good as an actress? A friend and I used to put on little plays for my parents when we were young, although I'm sure we must have bored them. How old were you when you started? Did your parents mind you becoming an actor? There's always been that opinion, somehow, that actors are not respectable people... Oh! Is your arm hurting you? Mrs. Jenkins said she'd be coming to visit you again today. She's a herbalist, and has been coming to see you twice daily, putting marigold ointment on it. Mr. Richards, the physician, has been coming twice a day too. He was very worried about you... You still haven't told me about your acting career."

"I think that maybe because you haven't given me a chance, Miss Saunders."

"You're very stoic about it all. I'm sure your arm must be hurting you."

Her sudden reversal of attitude was confusing me. I could not tell how genuine it was, and didn't know how to deal with it. "Is this sympathy I'm receiving now? I seem to remember you showed me none at all when you forced me to walk barefoot all the way here. In fact, all you did was to tell me to hurry up as you could not wait all day, when it was obvious I was on the verge of collapse at the time."

"O dear. I did, didn't I?" She giggled. "Now, tell me about..."

Perhaps being still unwell made me irritable, but her airy change in behaviour towards me, not to mention the giggle, were altogether too casual for me to ignore it.

"*O dear*! Is *that* all you have to say? I can't believe you can so easily forget all the things you did and said to me -- the way you behaved towards me! How can you brush them off so easily? How am I supposed to react to this new you? One minute you're trying to kill me, or threatening to, wanting me to hang, insulting me, locking me in a stable in the dark for as long as it pleased you. Now you're all caring, all lightness and cheeriness, asking me about my acting career, as though nothing bad ever happened between us. If you were a man, I'd challenge you for what you did to me."

She tossed her head. "My! That was quite a speech! And as for fighting a duel with me, a lot of good you'd be."

I swallowed. "And this is the new you? How could you say that?"

"I was just telling the truth."

"And just because it's the truth doesn't mean you have to say it. Don't you *ever* think before you open your mouth, Miss Saunders? *Ever* think about other people's feelings? Are you that selfish? That apology of yours is still in abeyance, if you want to know."

"Are you trying to pick a quarrel with me, Mr. O'Keeffe? Because if you are, I'm always game for a spat. Spats are stimulating."

"Not to me, they're not. I don't like confrontation, especially with a woman."

"Why not with a woman?"

"Because, as a man, I'm at a disadvantage. I can't say to you what I'd say to another man."

"Why ever not? That's ridiculous."

"Can we stop this please? You appear to expect me to forgive you and forget everything, just as though it never happened, but I can't do that, at least, not yet. It seems our attitudes and characters are very, very different. Your temper is quick to rise and seemingly forgotten in an instant, regardless of whatever you said and did while it lasted. I'm much slower to anger, but once roused, mine lasts much longer. When I have a row with someone, it destroys something in the relationship, and I find it hard to feel the same about that person again, and your behaviour towards me was altogether too outrageous for me to dismiss it just like that."

"Are you saying you can never forgive me then? *Never* accept my apology?"

"No, not never, but it will take me time. There's a lot to forgive here, and no matter what you say, I'm still not convinced you won't just as easily switch back to your former opinion of me. You're mercurial, if nothing else."

"Well, I had reason, I thought, to behave towards you as I did. I was furious with you, convinced as I was that you were one of those who killed my dear Richard." She hesitated, and sighed. "It was so very sad, especially as so few of our own people were killed in the invasion. Why did *he* have to be one of them?"

This was precisely why I did not like having confrontations with women. She had played a very feminine trump card here, effectively silencing me. Whether calculated, or not, I didn't know, but either way, it had the desired effect. How could I possibly say anything further?

"The invasion has had a sad ending for you too, Mr. O'Keeffe," she added. "Very sad, and you weren't even a part of it." Her eyes welled up with tears -- tears, yet another feminine trump card, although I had to assume they were on Richard's account, not mine.

To my great relief there was a knock at the door, and Mr. Saunders and the physician entered.

"Ah! Still taking care of our patient then, Miss Saunders." Mr. Richards, about the same age as Mr. Saunders, strode up and looked at me. "Well, young man. I'm glad to see you're finally out of danger of being carried out of here feet first."

"All thanks to your fine care, I understand, Sir."

"Ah, not altogether. Miss Saunders here has scarcely left your side, and without her timely warnings and ministrations, we might well have lost you. And there's Mrs. Jenkins too. Without her marigold ointment... although I understand a small pot of that was found amongst your clothes as well."

"Yes, I'm sure that's what saved me last time."

"Well, I see you're well on the way to recovery now, so won't be back to see you unless something untoward happens, although I can't imagine there being any problems. Just don't go swimming in the river again, for that's where I'm sure you picked up this fever. Stay out of the stables too." He smiled, obviously aware of how I first came to be at the Saunders's mansion. "We can't guarantee to rescue you again, young man. If, like a cat, you have nine lives, from what I hear, you must already be reaching your limit."

I was up and about soon after, and being treated like a member of the family by everyone this time, even the servants, and thoughts and fears of the authorities, and what might happen if they were to discover me, receded into the background of my mind.

"I see our daughter has transferred her focus on finding McCaffrey's killer to attending to you, O'Keeffe. Both Mrs. Saunders and I are relieved, I must say. Having one's daughter wandering around the countryside carrying a musket, and being of a mind to use it, is not something to be easily tolerated."

I felt like pointing out that he, her father, *had* tolerated it, and surely could have restrained his daughter if he had had a mind to. Ordering her to stop did not appear to have entered his thoughts any more than restraining her in any other way had. It was obvious she did and said what she wished, her parents having no control, so at least it was a relief to me too to have her on my side now, instead of against me.

Her attentions though, were a mixed blessing, as they say, the price of her new approval of me being a constant concern for my welfare, which while not so alarming as having her intent on killing me, nevertheless presented its own difficulties.

A woman of moderation Miss Saunders was not. Everything she did, I was to discover, was done with almost obsessive zeal, and that now included fussing over me. "Let me help you with this... You shouldn't be trying to do that... Let me show you a way to do this... No, leave it. I'll do it for you...No, you can't do that..."

And so it went on until I began to tire of her constant, solicitous attention, and telling me what I could, or could not do. I was a man who had spent my life in vigorous pursuits, and in striving to achieve excellence in whatever it was I was doing. I had been independent, and used to doing things in my own time and in my own way, rarely needing, or having to ask for help or permission to do what I wanted. Now though, no matter how well-intentioned her efforts on my behalf may be, they were a constant reminder to me that I was no longer totally independent, and I resented it. Having become extra sensitive about my deformity as well, I was convinced she found me repellent to look at even while she continued to fuss over me, reinforcing my new-found shortcomings. This all added guilt to my feelings as well, as I knew I was becoming irritable with her, when she herself was guilty of nothing more than being concerned for my welfare.

Whether because of this, or not, I was beginning to feel stifled too. Despite everyone's kindness towards me, I was in desperate need of getting away from them. Since arriving here, I had not been more than several hundred yards away from the mansion. I needed to get away on my own, somewhere where I could take stock of, and come to terms with my situation, somewhere where I was not simply gazing up at the embroidered canopy above my bed.

"Not that I'm complaining about being around your beautiful home," I said to Miss Saunders one day, "but I'd like to go out somewhere, so I need to borrow a horse for a ride around, please..."

"You've been told not to go near the stables, Mr. O'Keeffe. You don't want to pick up another infection. You know what Mr..."

I held up my hand. "Please. Enough. Anyway, I don't have to go *into* the stables to be able to ride. All I'm asking is to have a horse for a few hours."

"No, but... Besides, how can you ride...?"

I put up my hand again, interrupting her. "I know what you're going to say, but I can handle a horse very well, thank you."

"I really don't think... How about we take a ride in the curricle instead?"

I ignored the 'we'. "I'd much rather I went on horseback, thank you. That way I can go places I couldn't go in a curricle. So... a horse then, please, Miss Saunders, if you don't mind?"

This woman certainly knew how to irk me. How did my simple request to borrow a horse lead to this? I was amazed to hear myself, Connell O'Keeffe, pleading with a woman to be allowed to go out on his own on horseback. This was ridiculous, and could not continue, or I would be a laughing stock even among the servants if they were to hear her arguing with me like this. Gentlewomen with whom I had always been associated with in the past would never dream of standing up to a man at all, especially in such a forceful manner -- it would have been considered most unladylike, and I wondered at the way in which she had been raised to be so argumentative, independent-minded and contrary. I had never met a woman like her before, at least, not one that was supposed to be a lady. I was at a loss to know how to deal with her, and stared at her in amazement.

She still had not finished her harangue however. "Well. I'll discuss it with Father. We'll need to see what he says. How do we know how good a horseman you are, anyway? And what's this 'I'? If you go anywhere, I'm coming with you, just in case you get into trouble, and need help. What if you...?"

Slow to anger I had said I was, but now I was either going to fly into a temper with this shrew of a woman, or take a deep breath. Not having the stomach for any more aggravation, I took the deep breath. "Believe me, Miss Saunders; as I've already told you, I'm an expert horseman. My father owns a stud farm, where I rode even the most difficult of horses. Need I say more? And much as I appreciate your attention to my welfare, I need to be on my own for a while... to get away."

"You're not thinking of leaving us, are you? Not now."

"No, not at all. I simply need some time on my own. You understand that, don't you? After all, you yourself spent time on your own, wandering around the moors."

"That was different. You're no longer..."

I think the look on my face prevented her from finishing that sentence, which was just as well. I could not believe I was having this argument. Nothing like this had ever happened to me before, unless perhaps when I was seven years old, and had a set-to with one of my female cousins -- a silly, bickering tiff.

I did prevail in the end, and on the first suitable day, set off alone. Soon I was off the estate and following well-worn tracks made by both humans and animals. It was such a relief to be out in the fresh, open countryside, free at least from Miss Saunders's suffocating attentions, if not from that sword of Damocles hanging over my head. I would never be free until the true killer was found, and I was exonerated. Still, I was grateful that for a few hours I would not have my new protector, Miss Saunders, nagging me, and for the first time in a long while now, could do as I wanted.

There were sheep and black cattle everywhere, and being spring, the young lambs were making their appearance. The day was sunny and, unusually, without a wind, and the ground emitted a warm, earthy smell. I noticed adders here and there too, lying curled up on the trail in the sunshine, recently out of their winter hibernation. Fortunately, the horse was much quicker at noticing them than I, so avoided getting bitten. Not a pleasant snake, its poison being quite potent and easily capable of killing a small terrier, or even a bigger dog, or child.

My intention had been to stay out all day, so had prevailed upon cook to provide me with some cheese, cold ham and bread. I wandered along sheep tracks through the heather, the gorse, and the tall rafts of green bracken ferns, breathing in the smells of the countryside, very much as I was used to doing around my father's estate in Ireland. Eventually I found a large rock, and wrapped the horse's reins around a small hawthorn tree, bent over like an old man, and grown that way by being perpetually buffeted by the prevailing south-west gales.

The rock was warm in the sun, and I sat there on the ground, my back against it, and enjoyed the welcome heat. I was quite high up, the sea glittering in the distance, a lugger, some fishing boats and a brig dotting its surface. Above me, a pair of circling buzzards emitted their mournful cry, and all around ewes were calling for their errant lambs, and lost lambs cried out for their mothers. Somewhere in amongst the rocks some ravens with their deep, throaty croaks, were playing aerial-acrobatic games with one another. Pembrokeshire, although wild, was beautiful.

I ate my bread, ham and cheese, then leaned my head back against the rock and shut my eyes. I felt more relaxed than I had felt in a long time, fell asleep, and was woken by my hand itching. I reached across to scratch it; the itch was right there in the valley between my thumb and index finger, and felt as though a mosquito had bitten me. Of course my hand was not there, and because I could not scratch it, it went on itching, a reminder that although I may get my freedom and be fully exonerated, one thing could never be put to rights and be perfect again.

That last thought marred my otherwise pleasant day, but I tried to set it aside, for one thing was sure, and that was that this was a problem about which I could do nothing at all, now or ever. I sat there, watching the sun slide across the sky, and the sheep wander around the hillside. Off in the distance was a small, whitewashed cottage, but there seemed to be little activity there, although later in the afternoon a woman came out and shook something, then returned inside. The door was open, just as all the cottages seemed to have their doors wide open, regardless of the season. Far above me some clouds were taking on a familiar formation, like the bars on the sea-green skin of a fresh-caught mackerel. "Mackerel sky, soon wet or long dry," I recited to myself. Getting to know Pembrokeshire as I was, the former was the most likely.

The sun was well into the western sky when I set off back to *Carregowen*, and as I descended from the crag, down towards the woods, a huge cloud of chattering jackdaws assembled, blackening the sky as they came in from every direction, circling, ready to land on their favourite group of trees to roost for the night. Later -- it was almost dark now -- a family of badgers crossed my path, leaving their sett for a night of snuffling around in the earth.

By the time I reached the stable yard a full moon was rising over the eastern horizon. My day had been as perfect as it could be under the circumstances, and I was basking in my new sense of calm, determined not to allow my irritation with Miss Saunders's well-intentioned ministrations to get the better of me. I was preparing to dismount, and was surprised to see her walking towards me. What was she doing at the stables so late in the evening, I wondered. I smiled down at her.

"Mr. O'Keeffe! Where have you been? We've been out of our minds with worry about you. Why didn't you let us know where you were going? I've been out looking for you. Do you realize how long you've been gone? It's well over eight hours! I've been imagining you, fallen off your horse, and lying in the heather somewhere, unable to move. What if something had happened? We wouldn't know where to look for you. In future you must let us know..."

"Are you looking to ruin my peaceful and pleasant day, Miss Saunders? If you are, then you're well over three quarters of the way there already. I've just arrived here feeling more at peace with my life than I have in ages. Now you've more than succeeded in spoiling it."

I dismounted, handed my horse to the waiting stable boy, and marched off into the house, going straight to my chamber, leaving her standing there. In my whole life, only my mother had ever chastised me in such a manner, or had ever asked me where I was going, and when I was coming back, and even she had not done that for at least seven years or more. My pleasant day forgotten, once back in my chamber, I paced about the room, angry at what I felt had been an unwarranted intrusion into my private life -- in front of the servants too! My time was my own. What right had this woman to reprimand me, a grown man, for failing to tell her where I was going, and when to expect me back? It was none of her business. And even if she thought it were, any genteel woman would refrain from saying so -- and yes, she had ruined my day.

I wished the fresh air had not given me such an appetite, as I had no desire to face her again at dinner, but my stomach won out, and within the hour we found ourselves sitting across from each other at the table, me still filled with indignation. That I should have been so irritated after having so enjoyed my day, put me even more out of humour. I was the last to arrive at table, and out of politeness nodded briefly to everyone, but other than that, could not even bring myself to look at her.

Good manners, however, dictated I could not display my bad mood to my host and hostess, so, on their enquiring how my day had gone, I described with as good grace as I could muster, my whole trip. The telling did help raise my spirits, and by the time Mr. Saunders and I were left alone to our bottle of port, I was once again almost back to the place I had been when I had first arrived back at the stable a couple of hours before.

The large dinner, followed by the port, mellowed me even further, and I followed Mr. Saunders into the drawing room, where Mrs. Saunders and her daughter pressed the two us to take part in a few rubbers of bridge.

I had hoped to sit quietly on my own and read a book, and so avoid having to face Miss Saunders and whatever she would manage to say that would remind me yet again of things I did not need reminding of. I was beginning to think she even enjoyed baiting me and, if so, she had certainly been successful in getting me to rise to it. She had riled me sufficiently to have me even snap at her!

I shook my head at the invitation, annoyed now even with Mr. Saunders for failing to raise his daughter as a gentlewoman should be raised -- demure, modest and submissive-- so as to know her place and role in society.

"I'm sorry, I don't have any money with which to lay any stakes."

"That's no problem, O'Keeffe. The stakes are minimal, and I think I can afford to help you out just this once," Mr. Saunders laughed.

"I'm not in the habit of borrowing money, Sir. It goes against my principles." Saying this reminded me I still owed Mrs. Kelly money, but she would have to wait a bit longer for me to repay her.

"Oh come along, O'Keeffe, we're talking less than a shilling here at the most."

"Yes, do join us, Mr. O'Keeffe." Mrs. Saunders, in her sweet, natural way encouraged me.

I relented, and smiled at her. "Very well, but just this once I'll agree to borrow money. I suppose it would seem churlish of me to refuse."

Mr. Saunders slapped me on the back. "There. That's more like it. Besides, you're doing me a favour. I like to play cards, but without you to make up the four, I shouldn't be able to."

A servant set up the card table, and Mrs. Sanders and her daughter sat down.

Miss Saunders looked up at me, and catching my eye, smiled and indicated where she wanted me to sit. "You *will* be my partner, won't you Mr. O'Keeffe?" Her smile was open and genuine. It was as though nothing ill-natured had passed between us at all, or if it had, it was over and done with, forgotten, nothing more dire, it would seem, than one of those 'stimulating spats' in which she claimed to delight. How could I remain sullen, when she obviously held no malice towards me whatsoever, or expected me to hold any towards her either? I relented, returned her smile, and all was well.

"Of course. I'd be delighted."

Was it this lady's intentions to keep me on my toes emotionally? It would seem so, and it was not a state in which I liked, or was used to being held. She was full of surprises, and never knowing what to expect from her next, I was finding her company stressful.

Another thing I had forgotten though, when accepting Mr. Saunders's offer, was that playing cards one-handed is almost impossible, and within minutes mine had fallen onto the floor. My composure still fragile, it was with great restraint that I refrained from losing it now, bending down to retrieve them. I was expecting some comment from Miss Saunders any second too, and was convinced it would push me over the edge and I would lose it altogether, but to my great relief she remained silent, and the rubber continued.

After dropping some of my cards on two further occasions, I was closer to simply giving up than losing my temper, but instead of doing either, tried laying them out on my lap, under the table, where only I could see them. It helped, but was not entirely satisfactory. Without any comment Miss Saunders then rang the bell, and asked the footman to bring me a small tray to put on my lap, so I could lay out my cards on that.

"That was a good idea of yours, Miss Saunders." I was not above being magnanimous now, and complimented her after this improvement proved to work well for me.

"I'm always full of good ideas, Mr. O'Keeffe," she smiled.

I nodded. "So it would appear."

She and I won our rubbers, and I was able to return Mr. Saunders's loan, and went to bed richer by sixpence.

After that day I went out regularly, riding on my own. Refusing, on principle, to bow to Miss Saunders's command that I should let her know where I was going, and when I was coming back, I set off each time, merely telling

David, "I'll see you later then, David," to which he would answer, "Right you are, Sir." I had won that battle at least, because Miss Saunders refrained from making any comment as a result.

I wondered about the sense of triumph I seemed to be experiencing over having won a battle with Miss Saunders. That I should even have had such a battle with a woman was a source of continued amazement to me, and was winning it *that* important to me? Of course it was. After all, no man should allow himself to be dictated to by a woman. I had heard of petticoat government, and it certainly was not something to which I would ever allow myself to be subjected. It was a matter of principle... Wasn't it?

I had by now established my favourite haunts and routes, and as a result was no longer feeling hemmed in and stifled, so when one day at breakfast, Miss Saunders asked if she might accompany me if I planned on going out riding that day, I felt inclined to agree to it. There was that battle with her that I had won, so could now again afford to be magnanimous. I smiled. "I don't see why not."

We went, and finding that she refrained for the most part from dictating to me, I agreed that on Saturdays we should always go out together. Because it suited me I began to allow her to choose the routes too, so as to not encroach on my own paths, about which I felt oddly possessive. They were mine, and I wanted to keep them that way, to protect what little privacy I had. As she had a favourite route she liked to take, this meant that every Saturday we always passed through the same clearing, at about the same time.

By now I had graduated to a more spirited animal from the one I had been allowed to start with, and this pleased me. A horse was something, at least, over which I had sole control, and as Mr. Saunders, like my father, knew a good horse, I was more than happy with the mount that became 'mine'.

"You know," I told Miss Saunders one morning as we rode side by side along the path, "In America, some people ride using their left hand only, like the Indians, so I've trained this horse to neck rein, as they call it."

"Show me, then. I'd like to see a demonstration." So when we arrived at the clearing where there was some space, I showed her.

"I can even make it do a full passage sideways. Look. I can make it rear on command too." And I made the horse stand on its hind legs. I was so pleased to be able to show her there was at least something at which I was still proficient, and not fumbling around as I so often seemed to be doing in her presence, always humiliating myself. For some reason I found myself wanting to impress her, although I could not think why. I always felt uncomfortable in her company and, considering her to be a domineering shrew, did not even like her that much. I suppose it was my man's natural instinct to want to impress a woman, regardless.

Being at the same place at the same time on Saturdays turned out not to be the best idea, for as we were coming home on our third outing together, both our horses shied suddenly. Neither of us lost control of our animals, but before we could recover, found ourselves faced by two men on foot, armed with pistols.

"Right, Miss Saunders, you leave. Now!"

"I'm not going anywhere. How dare you!"

The one waved his pistol at her. "I said leave, we have no quarrel with you, so go."

"No, I won't. And don't point that pistol at me like that."

The two men were so busy concentrating on Miss Saunders and her customary refusal to obey, they did not notice me, even though it was me they wanted. I was close to them, and took a risk. I performed my trick of making my horse rear, and without warning it stood up on its hind legs, its front legs striking out, kicking one of the men in the back, knocking him down. I then ran it straight into the other man, taking him by surprise, and knocking him to the ground as well, his pistol flying off into the bushes.

"Go!" I shouted to Miss Saunders. "Go! I'm right behind you."

Without hesitating she set her horse into a gallop, and we raced away, going flat out until we were safely out of range, when we brought the horses to a stop, allowing them to regain their breath, and us, our composure.

I looked across at her, prepared to offer a smile, albeit a wry one, but the look on her face stopped me.

"That has to be the stupidest thing you've ever done, Mr. Connell O'Keeffe! You could have fallen off. And they could have shot and killed you." She glared at me. "Stupid!"

I turned my horse away, my face reddening with anger. "Well I didn't, and they didn't."

She followed me. "You were just lucky. Didn't you think?"

"Didn't *you*? They could just as well have shot *you*, you being your usual stubborn self."

"Don't be ridiculous. Of course they wouldn't have shot me. I'm a woman. You shouldn't..."

I sighed, and looked away. It had been a shock to both of us, and I forced myself to believe this was her way of coping with it. Whatever the reason, I was no longer willing to face up to her, and although she continued to nag me for the rest of the way home, reminding me how fortunate it was that I had not been alone, I refused to be drawn in further, and remained silent.

Although I would not admit it to her, of course, I was well aware too that had she not behaved in her usual contradictory way by refusing to accede to the men's orders and leave, I would surely have been recaptured; she *had* saved me. I did not want to admit this even to myself, and being beholden to a woman, especially this one, infuriated me; it was I, not she, who should be the protector. Throwing me off balance by her vacillating attitude as usual, I was confused and resentful, my stomach in a nervous knot, more as a result of her tirade than on account of our encounter with the would-be kidnappers.

Once home, she rushed in to recount our tale to Mr. Saunders. "And you should have seen Mr. O'Keeffe make his horse rear up and knock the men over," she told her father, her voice full of excitement. She clapped her hands. "He was magnificent. Such an amazing trick! He really is an expert horseman, Father." She looked at me with pride.

I'm sure my amazement must have been obvious, and I stood there, not knowing what to say. If nothing else, it seemed I at least finally had a reason to look good in her eyes, which was, I supposed, something for which to be grateful, and it appeared her blunt statements of what she saw as the truth went both ways, one minute being harsh, the next, singing my praises. She was an honest, if outspoken person, it seemed. Yet again she had managed to throw me off balance, and as usual I didn't know where I was with her. She had me riding an emotional see-saw, and it was so very wearing, and I pitied the man who would be unlucky enough to ever become her husband.

"The fact still remains..." Mr. Saunders brought me out of my reverie. "Someone is out looking for you, and fully expected to be able to capture you alive, presumably to deliver you to the authorities. How did they know where to find you out on your ride, and how did they know you are living here? They even called you by name, Katherine. Someone here must have betrayed you, and I find that highly upsetting." He flipped his coat tails, and stood, hands behind his back, shaking his head. "One of my own servants? But who? This is most disturbing as it makes me suspicious of all my staff, except David, of course. David would never be disloyal, nor Metcalf." He went to the window and looked out over the lawn as though this would tell him what he needed to know. "I'm going through everyone in my mind, but can think of no-one who would dare. Besides, I've noticed how well the staff have taken to you, O'Keeffe, and I can't imagine any one of them wanting to betray you."

"Are you sure about Metcalf?" I asked. "He wasn't happy with the way I spoke to him the night I came for help for you... I had to order him, and he didn't like that at all. Maybe he bears a grudge against me, although I did apologise to him for the way I spoke to him."

"No, Metcalf wouldn't let me down. In fact, none of my upper level staff would have betrayed you, I'm sure of it. It must be one of the under-servants -- someone who couldn't help gossiping. I'll talk to Mrs. Dewhurst, the housekeeper. Maybe she can find out. She can be quite terrifying to the staff. She terrifies me at times too. Whoever it was though, it means someone knows you're here, and I fear now for your safety. It's a shame, but until Mr. Potter returns home and we can get this matter sorted out, you're going to have to keep within the grounds of the estate, or if you do go beyond it, then we'll need to know exactly where you're going, and someone will have to accompany you, as a guard."

"I don't like to put you in this position, Mr. Saunders. Maybe I should just try to get back to Ireland. Perhaps someone could escort me to Fishguard, and see to it that I get safely on a boat."

Mr. Saunders shook his head. "People can be bribed, and the people looking for you now are after reward money, I'm sure, although discrete enquiries on my part have not revealed any indication that the authorities are even looking for you, let alone offering a reward. Whoever tried to capture you though, must think you're worth something to them. Even if I were to have someone escort you to Fishguard, they'd probably follow you, and bribe any captain to hand you over once you boarded. It's not a risk we can take. Besides, it won't do to spend the rest of your life with this matter not settled. You need to be able to leave this country a free man. No. I can't keep you here against your will, but I strongly urge you to remain here, even though your movements will be more restricted now."

My solitary rides had proven to have such a calming effect on my spirits, the thought of now being confined once more, forced to be accompanied everywhere I went, my chamber the only place secure from Miss Saunders, sent them plummeting. Was I never to be freed from this trap into which I had fallen all those weeks ago? Was I never again to be my own man? As it was, I could feel my character changing, almost as though I were becoming another person. The necessity to have to ask for help to perform tasks I had always done for myself was enough in itself to force me to change in some respects, and I tried hard not to let it make me bitter about my loss. My solitary rides had helped me cope, giving me time to enjoy something I *could* do without any help from anyone, but this other problem still hanging over me would have to be resolved soon, or I could see myself descending into a morose and bad-tempered man no-one would find good company.

"Of course I'll follow your advice, Sir. I know you have my best interests in mind, and I appreciate that."

I excused myself, and went to my chamber, again needing solitude. Once there I caught a glimpse of myself in the long mirror standing in the corner, and not liking what I saw, angrily flipped it round to face the other way. I had enough reminders without having to look at myself as well. I threw myself down on the bed, and lay there, gazing up at the carefree stags bounding across the embroidered canopy above me, and fearing I may never recover any of my old self.

A couple of hours later Morgan came to tell me I was needed in the drawing room. I arrived to find Mrs. Dewhurst had just entered, accompanied by a weeping Gwenda. They both curtsied to me, and I sat down.

"Come, Gwenda. Explain to Mr. Saunders and Mr. O'Keeffe what you did. Come along child. Stop that snivelling, and speak up." Mrs. Dewhurst was at her terrifying best.

Between sobs, Gwenda explained. "It was my day off, so I went home to see my family in Scleddau. They wanted to know how I was, and how I was enjoying working at the big house, and I didn't think, and told them how I'd taken food to a strange, one-armed man, who was being kept locked in the stable. Then I told them how I'd seen him being tied to the carriage, and when I'd asked one of the stable boys where he was going, he told me he was being taken to Haverfordwest to be handed over to the authorities. Everyone thought it was such an exciting story, especially my two brothers, who kept asking me more and more questions about Mr. O'Keeffe. Of course I didn't know your name then though, Sir."

"And were you able to tell them why the authorities might be interested in having Mr. O'Keeffe delivered to them?" Mr. Saunders asked her.

"No. I didn't know. I still don't know, so I couldn't tell them. All I told them was I saw him tied to the carriage, and I'd overheard one of the stable boys saying he'd escaped and was going back to jail." She started weeping again. "I didn't know they were going to try to catch you and take you to the sheriff, Sir." She looked at me. "I'm so sorry, Mr. O'Keeffe. I like you. I didn't know what they were going to do, I swear. I don't even know how they found out where to find you. They must have started nosing around right after I told them. They must have decided too that there might be some money in it for them, so made a plan to capture you. If I'd known, I'd have warned you. I would Sir. I truly would have."

Her tears were such that Mrs. Dewhurst had to offer up her own kerchief, and while *I* did not know how to answer the poor girl, Mrs. Dewhurst did, as she had plenty to say.

"See child! Look what you've done with your gossiping," she berated Gwenda. "You could have cost Miss Saunders and Mr. O'Keeffe their lives!"

Gwenda continued her weeping. "I'm so sorry."

"Well, for all we know, your brothers might be out there seriously injured as a result of their venture. For their sakes, I hope they're not, but they threatened Miss Saunders and Mr. O'Keeffe with guns, Gwenda. With guns!"

Gwenda wept some more.

"Well, you're lucky I don't fire you on the spot," Mr. Saunders told her. "Let this be a lesson to you not to gossip, putting people's lives at risk. Now, go home, make sure your brothers aren't hurt, and warn them that should they attempt anything further, or encourage anyone else to act in a similar fashion, then they'll be the ones in jail. Not only that, but I'll make a point of seeing to it that they're transported to that penal colony in New South Wales, or Australia, or whatever they call it now, permanently. Do you understand?"

"Yes, Mr. Saunders, Sir. Thank you Sir."

"Right. Go. And I want you back here to work by breakfast time the day after tomorrow. Is that understood?"

"Yes, Mr. Saunders, Sir. Thank you Sir."

"Right. Take her away Mrs. Dewhurst."

Mrs. Dewhurst put her hand on Gwenda's back, ushering her out of the room.

Gwenda looked over her shoulder as she was being marched through the door. "I'm so sorry, Mr. O'Keeffe. I really like you. I think you're such a nice man, I..." The door was shut, the end of what else she might have had to say in my favour, lost.

They were gone, and there was silence for a minute or so. "What do you think, O'Keeffe? Is it possible the brothers spread the word too?" Mr. Saunders asked.

"If they were in it for a possible reward, I think it unlikely they would have let anyone else in on it, don't you?"

"Yes, I agree." Mr. Saunders sighed. "Well, let's hope we have no more incidences. Even so, as long as you decide to remain here, you're not to go out anywhere without an armed guard, please. Is that understood?"

"Yes, Sir."

After that, wherever we went, or wherever I went on my own, one of David's staff, a big, swarthy man, the estate's blacksmith, was right there, and he carried a musket and a pistol. It had a severe effect on my self-esteem though, knowing I was no longer capable of defending either myself, or a lady accompanying me. Me! Big, strong, Connell O'Keeffe, needing a bodyguard! It made me feel such a weakling, and it depressed me -- and yes, it was all changing my personality.

After our mistake of always going the same route every Saturday, we naturally decided to vary it, although still going in the opposite direction from my solitary rides, and a few weeks later rode until we came in sight of Carreg Wasted, on Pen Caer, the point at which the French invaders climbed the cliffs after leaving the ships that had transported them here.

We decided to go closer, which meant crossing the St. David's to Fishguard road. Somewhere behind us, but keeping a discrete distance, was our armed guard. Once on the road, I looked about me, and realized we were at the spot at which I was waylaid by the murderer and his friend. I reined in my horse.

Miss Saunders stopped. "What's the matter Mr. O'Keeffe? Are you all right? You're not ill again are you? You don't look well at all. You've gone very pale. I'm sure you're not well. We should go home at once. You've not caught a fever again, have you?"

I shook my head. "No, it's not that."

"What then? Tell me. What's the matter? You look quite ill. Do get off your horse now, before you fall off." She jumped off her horse and came towards me.

"This is where..." I could not get the words out as my voice had gone hoarse. "Where I..."

She had her hand on my horse's bridle, looking up at me. "Oh no! Oh Mr. O'Keeffe! You're saying this is the place? I'd never have brought us here if I'd known. We must leave at once."

"No... I think I need to get this over with. I've had nightmares about this spot. Now we're here, I need to lay the demon to rest... return to the spot where it happened..."

"I really don't think..."

"Please Miss Saunders. I do appreciate your concern, but you need to allow me to get over this in my own way. You don't... can't understand."

She let go of my horse. "Oh, all right. If you must then, although I don't see how it can possibly do any good reliving what happened that day. I'm sure it will upset you beyond, and make you ill. You already look so pale."

In no mood to have one of her so-called 'spats' over this, I ignored her comments, and looked at the gate through which I had been dragged that day. I had to do it. I could not walk away from it now, or it would haunt me forever.

"I need to go in there, into that field." I dismounted and dropped the reins over a fence post, then walked to the gate and opened it.

She hung back, standing next to her horse, watching me.

"You can come with me if you want to... it'll be easier for me if you do," I added. It was the closest I could come to asking her for help. A short while ago, I would not have admitted to myself, let alone to her, that I needed her support. Even if I had, I would not have asked her for it, as a matter of principle. As I said, though, I was changing.

She tied up her horse, and we went into the field together. My stomach muscles had tightened into a cramping knot, afraid I would actually see the remains of my arm still lying on the ground, but of course it was long gone, and there was nothing to indicate any violence had ever occurred there. The field, the scene of such a brutal act, was tranquil, the only sounds being those of the birds claiming their territories with their spring songs and the occasional bleating of contented sheep.

After about thirty yards, I stopped. "It was here."

"You're shaking," she said, as though I would be unaware of it.

I did not answer. It was hard enough not to repeat the cry that had echoed throughout the countryside that terrible day. I coughed. "... go now." I fled back to the gate, and leaned against it.

"It's all right, Connell." She had used my Christian name! "It's all right," she repeated. "You've done what you needed to do. I hope you can let it rest now." Her tone was gentle, kind even.

At that moment, despite my opinion of her, I found myself wanting her to touch me, to hold me and take away my lonely emptiness, but she didn't, and the moment passed.

I nodded, and went back to my horse. "While I'm here, I need to go back to where it all started too. I have to go to where the murder took place... I need to do that... Need to..." I repeated. "Then I can let it go, I think."

She sighed. "If you must." For once she did not argue with me, and I was grateful for it.

We continued up the road to the field with the style. It was only about a half mile, but seemed much further. During that time I said nothing, trying to compose myself. It was hard, as the panic kept rising, my stomach still tightening with that gnawing pain of fear.

Once at the style, Miss Saunders dismounted and tied her horse to a tree, the same one that I had used that day. She then took the reins of my horse and tied it to the tree too, while I made my way towards the style. I thought to help her over it, but she passed me and was up and over before I could do anything, and was already striding up the field. She turned.

"Where did it all happen then? If you insist on reliving this, then we might as well relive everything, and I mean everything, although the worst part must surely be over."

I pointed up the field, "That's where the officer was killed. Up there."

"What sort of uniforms were they each wearing?"

"They were both in the same uniform."

"What? Both men in the *same* uniform?"

"Yes." I described it as best as I could, and could see her eyes widening.

"That was Richard's uniform too! The Cardigan Militia. You say they were both wearing the same uniform? I know you said you saw one officer kill another, but they were both in the Cardigan Militia then?"

"If you say the uniform I described was that of an officer of the Cardigan Militia, then yes."

"So you're saying an officer of the Cardigan Militia was killed by one of his fellow officers, and not by one of the invaders?"

I nodded. "I'll take you to the spot where it happened if you like." I hoped I sounded in control, and the horror of that day, still coursing through me, was not noticeable, but she was too surprised by my information to notice anyway.

"Yes, please do. I'm intrigued myself now."

We walked up the field. There must have been sheep there until very recently because the grass was clipped short. "It's hard to tell exactly, but I think it was around here."

"And whereabouts were you when you had your duel with the killer?" She was peering down at the ground.

I pointed back towards the hedge next to the road. "Down there. What are you looking for?"

"Nothing really, I suppose. What would there be to find, unless one of his jacket buttons was cut off when he was killed?"

"I shouldn't think you'd see it. I'm not even sure if we're on the exact spot."

She straightened up. "No, it's a bit like looking for a needle in a haystack, isn't it?"

I was ready to leave. Now I had revisited the spot, I could not wait to get away from it, but she seemed intent on trying to find some clue. I stood there waiting for her to finish her search, and looked down at the short turf. How anyone could hope to find anything as small as a uniform button in such an area, or why anyone would even want to try, was beyond me.

"Yes, I agree it *is* like looking for a needle in a haystack. Definitely." I straightened my back. "Let's go now. I'm ready to get away from here."

As I spoke, something caught my eye. The sun was reflecting on it, and it flashed, and I bent down to take a closer look. As I bent down, my shadow fell on it, and I lost it, but when I moved back, there it was again, down in the short turf. Except for the sun's rays lighting it up at that moment, and at that angle, it must surely have remained hidden forever. Sure it was nothing important, I nevertheless leaned over and plucked it out from the depths of the tuft of grass, and held it up. It was a gold ring. "Oh look! I've found a ring. A gold ring."

She rushed over. "Oh have you? How exciting! Let me see."

I handed it to her, and she screamed. Her face blanched so much I thought she was going to faint, and I put out my hand to steady her. "What? What is it?"

She was breathing so heavily she could barely speak. "It's Richard's!... It's my betrothal ring to Richard!" She sat down heavily, and began to weep. "It's Richard's," she repeated.

I sat down next to her on the grass. "You're saying the man I saw being murdered was your fiancé, Richard?"

"It has to have been. How else would his ring be here, right on this spot?"

We sat in the field, neither knowing what to say, the implications of my find being overwhelming. Afterwards, we rode home in silence, both of us with our thoughts in a turmoil, my own horror of returning to the dreadful scene of my mutilation almost overshadowed by my finding of McCaffrey's ring, and for Katherine, the realization that her fiancé had not been killed by one of the invaders at all. He had been murdered by one of his own fellow officers, the same officer, moreover, who had crippled me.

Strangers until a few weeks ago, and both of us convinced since then that we had nothing in common, she and I were now linked, both incapacitated in our own way, both our lives ruined by the same man.

CHAPTER 10

"As soon as Colonel Stevens arrives back, we must tell him of your discovery, and have him start an investigation." Mr. Saunders was pacing back and forth the full length of the drawing room, hands behind his back, his face even redder than usual. He was so incensed, it seemed almost as though his body was expanding, and at any moment his waistcoat buttons would fly off with the strain.

"Outrageous! Outrageous! That McCaffrey should have been simply murdered, not even killed in battle -- and by a fellow officer at that. It's outrageous! And why? That's what I want to know. Why? What cause would the murderer have? What cause could he *possibly* have? McCaffrey was such a mild-mannered man. He wouldn't have offended anyone. He was the nicest man you could hope to meet."

"Who is Colonel Stevens?" I asked during a pause in which Mr. Saunders had been obliged to stop to regain his breath.

"Ah yes. You wouldn't know, of course. He's a close friend of the family, and a colonel with the Cardigan Militia. A fine, upstanding man he is too, and a close friend of McCaffrey's as well," Mr. Saunders explained. "Both of them spent so many happy hours here together with us, and after his friend's death, he could scarcely bring himself to visit, so overwhelming were his memories. He told us it was almost a relief for his regiment to be sent to England for a number of months. 'It will give me time to come to terms with my dear friend's death', he told us. I dread to think of his reaction when he finds out he's been living in the same camp with Richard's murderer. I'm sure he'll have to be restrained from killing him with his bare hands when he's found."

Mr. Saunders, more red-faced than ever, was forced to pause again. This time he plumped himself down in a chair, his waistcoat pulling ever harder at its restraining buttons, and I waited, almost transfixed, for the series of small explosions with which they would all finally release their hold. I think Mr. Saunders himself must have recognized the imminent danger to his waistcoat as he excused himself and, bending over, liberated each button from its hole. I felt almost as relieved as he must have done.

"Father, we need to start our investigation now, not wait until they come back. Do you even know when they'll be back? We can't wait. I want this man brought to justice. We can't simply sit around waiting until they return. Besides, Connell here needs justice too. This man has wounded both of us."

"Connell?" Mr. Saunders turned to look at his daughter, eyebrows raised. "Connell? Since when, such familiarity?"

"Oh Father! All this formality! We've been brought together by this double tragedy. He no longer feels like a

'Mr. O'Keeffe' to me, and I've told him to call me Katherine too."

"I'm not at all sure about this, and I'm not sure either that your mother and I should be allowing you two young people to be wandering around the countryside without a chaperone. It's most improper. I'll be taken to task over it by some of the wagging tongues hereabouts, no doubt about it."

"I care nothing for the wagging tongues as you call them, Father. Why should we care? We know we can be trusted to behave in a proper manner, and surely you and Mother can trust us. Besides, we *are* chaperoned now by Connell's bodyguard, Davies. Also, we're getting way off the point here -- our common purpose."

Her declaration struck a sensitive nerve yet again. What she had *not* said, was that *of course* we could be trusted, because she could not possibly be in any way tempted to behave in an improper manner with me, even given the opportunity. After all, she was repelled by my body. I knew it, just as I knew no women found me attractive now, or ever would again. Me, a lopsided figure to be remarked upon and pointed at by five-year-old children was all I saw myself as now, and the fear of being pushed away and rejected meant I too could be trusted, as this knowledge about myself was more than sufficient to inhibit me from ever trying to court her or any woman again. That was yet another aspect of my life the murderer had destroyed, one of the most important aspects, and that depressed me more than anything else. I went over to the window and stood gazing out at nothing in particular, my own private anguish an ever-present weight bearing down on me.

"Oh well, my dear. As usual I suppose I'll let you have your own way," Mr. Saunders was saying. "Such a headstrong young daughter I've raised, Mr. O'Keeffe, or should I too call you Connell now?"

"Connell, Father asked you a question. How can you stand there daydreaming at a time like this?"

I turned, and gave him a cheerful smile. "I'm sorry, Sir. Yes, Connell will be most acceptable."

"Well, now. Back to this sad affair then. Connell, first of all, what do your parents know of all this? When did you last write to them? Oh yes, I remember now. You told me; they're on a grand tour and out of communication until the end of May, and as they left home in late December, they know nothing at all about any of this, and there's nothing to be gained by writing to them in Dunleary at this time."

"That's correct, Sir. I have to say, though, that while I could certainly have done with my father's help, as far as my mother is concerned, I think that to inform her by letter about what happened to me would be most distressing for her. I'd sooner be able to present myself to her in person. It'll be shocking enough for her when that happens as she's sure to be severely overcome, but at least she'll be able to see I'm well otherwise -- assuming I *am* exonerated, of course, and I *do* get to see her again."

"Nonsense! Of course you'll be exonerated, and of course you'll see her again. But given what you've just said, my own opinion is that it would be kinder to forewarn her. Anyway, it's your decision. You know your parents best... Now, Katherine, regarding the return of the Cardiganshire Militia, I'll find out when that is, but the reason I think we should wait until they do return is that we don't want to let the murderer know what we've discovered. If he knew we had found out he's a member of the regiment, even though we don't yet know who he is, he's likely to abscond and we'll never find him. Once we have them back here we can go about our search in a methodical manner with Colonel Stevens's help and without tipping our hand in advance, as it were."

I nodded. "Yes, I agree with your father, Katherine."

Katherine threw up her hands. "It's so frustrating. I want to *do* something. Now! I want to find this beast; I want to kill him myself. I'd do it too if I met him and had my musket with me."

"Having been on the receiving end of your wrath and your musket, I believe you would too. I can see I have to count myself lucky."

"Yes, my dear daughter. See where your hotheadedness might have led you. You could have killed Connell."

Katherine shrugged. Presumably, that she *hadn't* killed me was all that mattered. "Well, at least I could write to Colonel Stevens, and let him know what we know. Maybe he has some idea as to who it might be."

"I'm going to say 'no' as well regarding writing to him. Leave everything until they're all safely back here. We don't want anything to let the murderer slip away from us, and Colonel Stevens would find it hard not to start investigations right away. He will, as I've already said, be as incensed as we are when he finds out the true cause of McCaffrey's death. So you see, my dear, we can be sure he'll do his utmost to help us in our investigations when the time comes."

"Well, the waiting is going to be interminable. I do so hope they're due back home soon, and I'll need to be doing something to occupy me until they do, or I'll go out of my mind thinking of this monster going about his life, carefree, sure in his own mind he has nothing to worry about, because he's set up Connell so perfectly to pay for his crime. It's wicked! Intolerable! Poor Connell! Here he is with his life in jeopardy, his career in ruins and his ability to function normally so severely affected." She clenched her fists. "I swear I could so easily kill the man myself. We need to be able to do *something*."

Mrs. Saunders had been sitting quietly throughout this whole exchange, her head bent over what looked to me to be an impossibly difficult crocheted shawl she worked at constantly. At least, I think it was crochet. As a man, I'm not too well acquainted with the feminine arts. Now she spoke up. "There are so many things for you to be doing, my dear," she said. "You've been working on that same piece of embroidery for the past year or more. Maybe this would be a good time for you to settle down and complete it. It will keep your mind and your fingers occupied."

Katherine turned to face her mother. "Embroidery! Embroidery! At this time! Mother! How can you even suggest such a thing? I can no more think of doing embroidery than, than..." She paced about the room, picking up an ornament here, then setting it down, rearranging flowers in a vase, stopping to look out of the window, fiddling with the long, tapestry bell-pull. Finally she came to a stop. "It makes me so angry to think how my loss drove me to go out there on the moors on my own to try to hunt down Richard's killer. I know it was a ridiculous thing for me to have done, but I was so distraught, and it *is* a relief now to finally know what did happen to him, and to know even where his killer is, and that we're all set to apprehend him -- a great relief. It was, of course, a shock to find his ring, but I'm glad now." She became pensive and looked at me. "How strange, Connell, that you should be the one I found out on the moors, and that you should not only be the one to have witnessed Richard's death, and then to have found his ring, but to have yourself suffered at the hands of the same man. So strange."

"Fate plays strange tricks sometimes."

"Well, now that there's nothing more we can do to hasten his capture at this moment, and it appears we still have several weeks remaining before the Militia returns, I need, as I said, to be doing something to fill the time." She plumped herself down on a chair. "I'd like to do something constructive too. I want to achieve something worthwhile, and please, Mother, don't suggest embroidery or drawing likenesses. I don't have the patience for either, and I'm no good at them anyway; I find them boring... Oh I could kill him for what he did to us!"

Although I said nothing, in this I had to agree with Katherine -- as far as the embroidery and the likenesses were concerned, that is. The last occupation I could see her involved in at this time was embroidery. Indeed, the last time I had seen her with a needle in her hand was when she was keeping watch over me when I had come down with that river fever, and she did not look the sort to sit down and draw likenesses. I envisioned her, temper flaring, paper, crayons and paints being tossed into the air in exasperation, and smiled to myself at the image.

Having no wish for Katherine to shoot down any of my own ideas about how she should fill her time -- although, when I thought about it, I did not have any to shoot down anyway -- I decided to say nothing. Instead, I went over and looked out of the window again, this time watching some rabbits nibbling away at the lawn.

"Connell, have you no suggestions as to what we can do? Stop gazing out of the window, just daydreaming. I can't believe you're so calm about it all. Don't you feel you want to kill this man?"

I turned around. I was damned if I did say something, and damned if I did not. "I'm not sure it's up to me to make suggestions about what you should do. Besides,

I don't know you well enough to know what sort of things you like to do. As for killing the man, if I were to continue to let what he did to me eat away at me, I'd be causing no-one any suffering but myself, and if he were to know that, then I'm sure I should be giving him even more pleasure than I've already provided him with."

"Oh, you're useless! So calm! You drive me crazy. Don't you ever lose your temper, Connell? Get mad about anything?"

"Yes. I do, but I choose my battles. As I told you before, I don't like confrontation. I save losing my temper for when it's something I care about deeply. I'm not the sort to fly off the handle at every minor irritation."

I wished I could have explained to her that my seeming expression of calm was not calm at all; it was futility. If she were able to read my thoughts, she would understand that what he did to me *did* eat away at my soul, all day, every day, and that even as I had spoken, I knew that despite the suffering it did cause me, this was exactly what I spent my waking hours doing; I couldn't help it.

"And you don't care deeply about *this*?" Her voice was reaching a crescendo, the idea of achieving something worthwhile seemingly forgotten already.

"Of course I do, and if I were to meet him face to face, I certainly wouldn't be able to vouch for what I might do. My storming around here and now, however, would achieve nothing other than to upset everyone, including myself."

"Oh, you're useless!"

"So you already said, and if you want to see me lose my temper, just keep this up, and I might well just do that."

She laughed. "You know something, Connell? I'd like to see that. I must see what I can do." There was a silence. "I know. I've thought of something worthwhile, something constructive, something you and I can achieve together, Connell, something that'll keep our minds off what is to come, and help you at the same time. I can help you retrain yourself. Yes! Definitely! You need retraining."

"*Retraining?*" Mr. Saunders and I spoke at once.

"Yes. I'll take you in hand, and we'll get you to practise using your left hand more. I remember you remarked a while ago that everyone was fussing over you too much, making you lazy and dependent. So, I have decided: no more help from anyone, only instruction and help with how to help yourself -- exercises too. I think we should even withdraw the services of Morgan for a while and see how you get on now without him."

Despite the merits of the suggestion, I cringed at the prospect, and sighed. "Fair enough, I suppose, regarding what you choose to call 'retraining'," I agreed with no enthusiasm at all. "Although I think the correct word is 'therapy', but please don't take Morgan away. It's only with his help that I appear at breakfast each day in a state fit to be seen."

"All right. You can keep Morgan, but you need practice. You need to improve your coordination. Yes, you definitely need to improve your dexterity with your left hand. To look at you, I sometimes..."

I sighed. She was off again on one of her tirades, and I needed to stop her before she made me lose my composure, and snap at her. "Generous of you, I'm sure, regarding Morgan. Regarding using my left hand, however, I assure you it's always done very efficiently whatever I asked it to do."

"Well, all I can say is, is that you must have..."

I interrupted her again. "What was it you asked me a short while ago? Do I ever lose my temper? Do you realize what you're saying to me? How much do you expect me to take? Or are you deliberately trying to bait me? Are you following up on your threat to see what you could do make me lose my temper? I assure you that, contrary to your expectations, it's not an experience you'd enjoy."

I was right in that. Those who knew me before all this had happened, were well aware that Connell O'Keeffe in a temper was a man to be avoided, and maybe in time I would be that Connell O'Keeffe again. Now though, as I said to start with, I was resigned and weary. I just did not have the spirit to fly into rages. Not now. Not yet.

It was as though she had not heard me, or at least, had not been listening. "I can think up all sorts of things we can do to help you be as good with your left hand as you were with your right, and we should start as soon as possible. Now that's constructive, isn't it? Together we can achieve something important, necessary even... Are you sure, Father, that we should not allow Colonel Stevens to start his investigation? You *will* find out when they'll be returning, won't you?"

"Yes, my dear, on both counts." Mr. Saunders had been sitting, observing the verbal exchange between his daughter and me, and from the slight upward turn of his mouth, appeared to be finding it quite amusing, but I was no longer amused, if I ever was. As I said before, she was not like any woman I had ever known, and I still did not know how to deal with her, which, on top of everything else, I found most disconcerting, especially as I was beginning to find myself willing to agree to almost anything to get her to stop nagging me. I was even starting to understand why her father was as he was with her -- anything for the sake of peace. Perhaps that was what he was finding so amusing. As regards all the so-called ideas she had for her therapy project, I had no concept of what she had in mind, but was nevertheless quite alarmed at the enthusiasm with which she went about embracing them, whatever they were to be.

I had reason to be alarmed as it turned out. I went from being fussed over by a far-from gentle and demure female to begin with, to being treated as a trainee in the militia, browbeaten by an overbearing sergeant. If all this did not end soon, I should likely go out of my mind altogether. I had always considered myself to be a strong character, but I no longer felt like the old me, my character changing. It would, I was sure, take very little now to send me over the edge, and Katherine Saunders could well be the person to achieve this.

Almost immediately I found myself out on the front lawn playing ball, which Katherine had determined was good for my coordination. However, for this 'exercise', as she called it, she had found an old football, a very misshapen and ancient pig's bladder that she had had someone re-inflate. This would have been all right, had she expected me to kick it, but she did not; she expected me to catch it.

"Nobody can catch a football with one hand," I complained. "It's too big. Here, you try it," and I kicked it at her. "There," I said, triumphant, when she failed to catch it. "You can't even catch it with both hands, so how can you expect me to catch it with one?"

"You're a man. You're supposed to be able to catch it."

"No, I'm not supposed to catch it. It's a football. I'm supposed to kick it."

"We're not using it to play football." She threw the ball towards me again, and I put out my hand to try to catch it between my hand and my body. It didn't work, and it went wobbling off down the lawn, and after about a half hour of frustration and being nagged my patience ran out.

"That's it. I've had enough. I'm not going to stand here bickering with you like this. I'm going." And I started back towards the house.

"Connell. Come back. Surely you're not the sort to give up so easily."

I continued walking.

"All right. I do have another ball here -- a small one. Are you willing to try with that?"

With great reluctance I returned to the lawn, and she threw it to me. I missed, and it too rolled away, this time into the shrubbery. I went to retrieve it, having to crawl through a pricklier-than-usual holly bush to find it. Things were not looking good for my therapeutic endeavours.

"Now throw it back to me."

I did, but it went wide of her, and then she had to run after it.

"There. Now this is something we can practise. We'll have you throwing straight in no time, I'm sure, Connell, even catching it."

Her enthusiasm for her new project aimed at helping me was such that I found it hard not to be petulant and reveal how her endeavours were serving only to cause me intense frustration, anxiety and anger. How could I share any of my true feelings with her, a woman? If only there were a man in whom I *could* confide -- one who had received a similar injury. It would have helped so much to talk over my feelings and experiences with a man who had gone through what I was going through. Finding such a man, though, out here in the wilds of north Pembrokeshire, was not likely to happen, so I would have to continue to try to come to terms with my problem on my own, something I found debilitating, and even overwhelming on those frightening occasions when I would experience the vivid, waking dream that I was reliving the horror in that dreadful field.

Katherine was right though in what she said. I knew that. After all, it was obvious I needed to practise, but I also knew that if we kept this up, she ran the risk of being witness to my temper at its worst, and I didn't want that.

I sighed. "No doubt you'll have me doing everything perfectly in time, but even so I think you're going to have to bear with me in the meantime if I do show my frustration sometimes. You try catching this with your left hand, and see how you do." I threw it towards her, once again sending it far wide of her.

"If you threw it where I had some chance of catching it, I'd be willing to try."

I had to laugh. "All right. Well you throw it to me left-handed then. See how *you* do with that... There. See. You're just as bad as I am."

"Yes, but with me it doesn't matter. I have..."

"I thought we'd gone from bickering to bantering."

"You're the one bickering. Me? I'm just telling the truth."

"So you've said... but we've been through all this before, and..."

Our session continued, and she did not censure me anymore, for which I was grateful, and we parted, our relationship, such as it was, intact, our tempers under control.

Katherine's therapy continued unabated, her enthusiasm matched only by my lack of it, and each day I dreaded it, and each day it only reinforced the reality of what that killer had done to me. How much more could I take? And Katherine, determined as she was that I learn to do everything perfectly, frequently lost her temper with me. Of a fiery temperament at the best of times, her anxiety about catching McCaffrey's murderer brought her temper very near the surface, and as we now spent so much time together, I was the obvious object on which to release that frustration and anxiety, and the tension continued to rise.

It was not as though I was deliberately trying to thwart her efforts, but her constant nagging, or encouragement as she believed it to be, along with everything else, was wearing me down, the same thoughts forever milling around in my mind about all I had lost: my independence, my pride in my looks, my career, my attractiveness to women, my ability to do things I used to take for granted. Having to ask for help with simple tasks was so detrimental to my self esteem I felt emasculated, no longer the natural leader, humiliated, and it hurt. Even something as simple as putting butter on my bread was no longer possible, and while I was slow to lose my temper with people, I found my temper easily aroused by pure frustration, although this was usually at times when no-one else was around to witness it other than long-suffering Morgan. What I would have done without him, I don't know. That killer, that monster, had succeeded more than he knew; he had brought me crashing down, and at times, I almost wished he *had* killed me.

CHAPTER 11

Although the Saunders family had my best interests at heart, were concerned for my welfare, and showed me every kindness, I began to long for the time when Mr. Potter would be back home, have me exonerated, and I could leave and go home to Ireland. Apart from my anxiety to get away from Katherine's well-intentioned efforts on my behalf, it was no good my denying it to myself, but should the authorities decide to make a point of coming after me, it would be no difficult task for them to find me and cart me off to jail to await trial in Haverfordwest, or to rot on those prison hulks.

There were days when these fears of indictment weighed on my mind in addition to everything else, and at these times I needed more than anything to be on my own, and find a place where I could hide away from everyone, so fearful was I of being seen to be out of control of my emotions. Even this though was impossible with my guard, Davies, close by, although, to give him his due, he did try to keep as far away as was feasible without destroying his purpose.

After one bad day, when both Katherine and I had been on edge, our tempers short, I wandered off by myself, and found a hideaway behind a large rock about a half mile from the house. Katherine came looking for me though, and no doubt told by my guard where to find me, came upon me and, to my utmost embarrassment, found me in tears. I turned away, hurriedly wiping away the evidence with the back of my hand, but it was too late.

"Oh Connell! What's the matter?" She plopped herself down next to me, acting in her usual natural, uninhibited way.

"Nothing. Nothing at all," I repeated. How could I possibly reveal to her my despair? A man should face these things like a man, not blubber like a girl, and I felt ashamed that she should have caught me this way. Yet it was all too much for one person, even a man, to bear alone, and I wished again, as I so often did, that there was a man I could talk to who would understand my particular anguish of knowing I would never again know the love of a woman, feel her touch, her warmth? But there *was* no such person.

"Nothing's the matter," I repeated again.

"Nothing? There has to be *something* wrong."

"No, it's nothing," and afraid she was going to start nagging me, I seized on the first thing that came to mind. "I know you're trying to help me, but I'd be glad if you'd give up your ideas about all this therapy. It's making it worse, rather than better, so please... No more of your therapeutic efforts on my behalf. I'm a pretty resourceful man. I shall, in time, relearn skills, but I need to do it at my own pace.

170

Can you understand that?" I looked at her. "Couldn't you find another focus for your energies, perhaps?"

"*That's* what all this is about! *This* is what's made you cry? Me trying to help you? I can't believe it! That's ridiculous!"

"I wasn't crying. I... I got something in my eye, that's all, and it was watering. Anyway, I've decided. No more therapy. All right?"

She stood up. "Right. So be it. No more therapy. Stand up and let me see your eye. Perhaps I can help you remove whatever's in it."

I stood up and smiled. "No, it's fine now, thank you. Whatever it was, is gone."

"Shall we go for a walk then? It's a beautiful evening."

"Why not?"

So we went for a walk, and no more was said about the matter, but then, at dinner time, she made some comment about the way I was attacking my food. Perhaps it was nothing much at all, but I shot up in my chair, shoving it backwards so that it fell over. "Enough!" I shouted. "I've had enough! That's it!" And I stormed out of the dining room. As I reached the door, I heard Katherine's voice.

"It seems our Connell does have a temper after all."

After my noisy departure from the dining table, she confounded me yet again by even seeming to respect me for having stormed out.

"I should make you lose your temper more often, Connell," she informed me, when we met over breakfast the next morning. "It brings a fire to you, and I like that."

"Is that so? Well, if you counted that as me losing my temper, you have misjudged me. That 'fire' you refer to was but a mere spark. As I said before, me being in a real temper would not be something you would want to witness."

She shrugged. "Oh Connell! You're useless. Why do you take it to heart so? Don't you like me teasing you?"

"There's a difference between teasing someone and goading them with the intent of making them lose their temper. I'm happy to be teased any time about most things, but you seem to make a point of striking a raw nerve."

"I wouldn't be so mean, Connell, as to really goad you about something which I knew would hurt you. If you think about it, I think you'll realize you were being oversensitive."

"Perhaps you too, if you think about it, will realize that I'm not yet ready to be teased about this. It's only a short time since it happened, and still all too new to me, and although I'm doing my best to come to terms with it, and although I try not to show it, I'm finding it difficult to cope with, not just physically, but mentally as well. So you're wrong," I snapped. "If *you* think about it, you'll realize you have indeed goaded me about something which *does* hurt -- quite unmercifully too. At least, that's the way it has seemed to me."

I had not meant to say all this, but it was too late now. It was there, out in the open. Surely now she would have no respect at all for me for being so unmanly, and admitting to my mental state like that. Once again though, I misread her.

She got up, and came to me. "My dear Connell. You're right, of course. I haven't understood you well enough to see that the impression you give to everyone of learning to cope very well with what's happened to you, is just that, an impression, and that you've been making the effort to hide your true feelings from us. I'm so sorry if I've been hurtful. I would wish though, that you'd be more open.

There's no shame in *expressing* your fear and sorrow. It doesn't make you less of a man. Pretending to be what you're not, is asking for people to accept you falsely, and you can't then blame them for not seeing what you're trying so hard to hide."

I nodded, but being unable to find a reply, said nothing. Katherine was indeed a most unusual woman, I was discovering, and she was drawing out of me a side I did not even know existed.

One night I lay awake thinking about it. I cleared my head of my prejudices against domineering women in general, and thought about her, in particular. The thing was, she was a very intelligent woman, and when I allowed myself to be open-minded enough to put myself in her shoes, could see how frustrating it must be for her to live in a man's world, where women in her class of society were treated as fragile creatures, whose only purpose in life was to do embroidery, play the piano, draw and paint, and produce endless children, and to know that, if, like Katherine, they *were* intelligent or knowledgeable, then they must on no account show it, especially to men. It was a woman's role I myself had never questioned, but how would *I* like it? I asked myself. Yes, Katherine did break all the rules governing a gentlewoman. She was nothing if not opinionated, determined to be heard, and forthright in what she said, frequently way too forthright. But she was so full of life, full of ideas, so enthusiastic, and she had to be frustrated with the feminine role demanded of her, often being forced to submit to men less intelligent than herself.

And she was right, believing it to be the manly thing to do, I *had* tried to give the outward impression to everyone that I was coping very well with everything -- taking it all in my stride even. Apart from opening the door slightly to my soul to her on this occasion, I had not told anyone about my inner desperation. Those things I had agonized about to myself alone, so how would she have known that her teasing would hurt? Not knowing the depth of my despair, and still not fully knowing it, she had a right, perhaps, to consider me as being oversensitive.

I was guilty too of refusing to go along with her ideas, even sensible ones like the therapy, because, to my mind, it meant I was submitting to a woman. I had never submitted to any woman except my mother, but when I thought about it, my behaviour did not make sense, even though I was behaving like other men. Men did not submit to women; it just was not done, and left them open to ridicule by their peers if they did. Those women who tried to get their ideas accepted were considered domineering shrews, unless they resorted to wile, and this meant flattering a man into thinking that her ideas were really his own. Katherine was too proud to do that, and I told myself that, by rights, I should respect her for it.

By dawn, I still knew I would have great difficulty in opening up my soul completely to Katherine. Why should I anyway? We weren't married, or even courting. Even so, I had nevertheless made the decision to make our relationship less prickly by not always balking, on principle, every time she tried to dominate me. This did not mean having to submit to her every whim, but when her ideas were better than mine, then what was wrong with letting her have her way? I asked myself. Nothing except my own pride, came the answer.

"My dear, what with all the recent events, we haven't had the pleasure of hearing you play."

We were all sitting in the drawing room after dinner. The days were getting longer, but it was already becoming dark, and there was a lively fire in the enormous fireplace, and candles flickered from every corner of the room. The atmosphere was warm and welcoming, and cosy too, despite the great size of the salon.

"Would you care to entertain us with a few songs, my dear?" Mr. Saunders asked his wife, then looked at me. "My wife has a beautiful singing voice, Connell, and plays the pianoforte as well as anyone I know."

"Then I join your husband, Ma'am, in asking you to please play for us. Would you?"

Mrs. Saunders smiled, and went over to the instrument. Her husband was right. She played beautifully, and also had a soothing, melodious voice that was a pleasure to listen to. Maybe one of the reasons her daughter refrained from such pursuits, I thought, including doing embroidery, was that her mother was so talented in these areas, Katherine felt it not worth the effort to try to compete.

I sat comfortably off to one side of the fireplace, my elbow resting on the arm of my chair, legs stretched out, my head on my hand, gazing into the embers. My mind wandered as I looked at the clear, clean glow of the coal, and was reminded of Mrs. Beynon, and her description of culm. This must be culm burning here too. Mrs. Saunders's gentle voice, the fire and the candlelight made me relax more than I had done for a long time. That, together with a generous helping of port at dinner, made me doze off, and I was woken by my hand slipping, and my head jerking forwards.

I looked up, fearful I had been seen. I would have hated to have anyone think I had been bored by Mrs. Saunders's singing, which I was not at all. It was just the unusual feeling of having set aside my problems for the moment that had caught me off my guard. I hoped I had not missed too many songs, but if anyone had noticed, they showed no signs of it, for which I was grateful.

"Do you sing at all, Connell? I'd be delighted if you could join me in a duet."

I was still feeling sleepy, and remembered I had not sung since that awful night in the stable. For a moment even the thought of singing made me flinch. "Don't be stupid, Connell," I told myself. "You can't not ever sing again because of that night."

"Connell?" Katherine called over to me. "Have you gone into a trance, or something?"

I stood up. "Oh no. I'm sorry. What would you like us to sing, Mrs. Saunders?" She chose an Irish melody. "Ah yes. That one I know. Are you trying to make me homesick, Ma'am?" I laughed.

We sang together, and the manner in which our voices blended made us a perfect duo. When we finished, we smiled at each other. It was the first time since my arrival that I had felt any sort of true rapport with Mrs. Saunders, and it felt good to feel so close, as though our spirits had come together as well as our voices.

There was applause at the end. "My, my, Connell," said Mrs. Saunders. "You have a beautiful voice, and that is something with which you'll be able to entertain everyone for the rest of your life. Now, let us hear some more of you."

"David said you had a voice like an angel. He was right," Mr. Saunders commented.

"What! And you never said anything, Father!"

"I'm sorry, my dear, what with one thing and another..."

"I think we should listen to you sing on your own, Connell," said Mrs. Saunders. "I should be happy to accompany you."

I bowed. "You're all very generous in your praise, at least you and Mr. Saunders are..." I looked at Katherine, and grinned. "Am I in need of remedial instruction here too?"

"No, of course not. I was just wishing Father had let us know about your talent sooner. We've been deprived of a true pleasure."

I gave her a bow, then sang some songs for them, and for the first in a long time, found something, apart from riding a horse, in which I *could* be self-confident, and not feel unworthy and useless. I was even enjoying myself.

Despite my demand for no more of Katherine's therapy sessions, she was still encouraging me to make the effort to help myself, and writing was an area in which she decided I needed practice.

The first thing I found, of course, was that moving my quill while trying to keep the paper still, was impossible, and I happened to be looking around my chamber for something heavy with which to hold the paper down, when Morgan came in to see if I needed any help with anything.

"Ah yes, Morgan. The very man! Do you suppose you could find me a weight of some sort with which to stop my writing paper from slipping?"

He came over to study the problem, and I illustrated it.

"I think maybe I can solve that. I'll be back in a few minutes, Sir."

A short while later he returned with a heavy brass weight. "Cook says she doesn't use this very often, so you can borrow it for a while."

"Excellent! Thank you Morgan."

He watched while I tried out my new paper weight. "All those words, Sir. To be able to write and read them..."

"You can't read and write, Morgan?"

"No, Sir. Where my family live, it was too far to go to any of the classes being held by Miss Morris. I regret it too. I should very much have liked to learn."

I thought, and gave Morgan my broadest smile. "Ah! Morgan. Now *I* have an idea. What say we ask Miss Saunders to give you some training in reading and writing? I'm sure she'd be only too delighted to have such a willing pupil."

Morgan's eyes opened wide. "You think so, Sir? You really think so?"

"I'll talk to her today about it. I should warn you though: she's a very dedicated teacher, and you'd have to be committed to learning. Would you be?"

"Oh yes, Sir! I've always wanted to read, in particular."

"Excellent!" Morgan must have been somewhat surprised to discover I was as enthusiastic about his learning to read as he was. He went off, excited at the prospect, and I sat down to attempt to relearn how to write, delighted to have found a new and even willing victim of Katherine's dedication to training. My sigh this time, was one of great relief.

Not long after, Morgan, now in full training, came to me bearing a present. "Here you are, Sir." He held out a piece of beautifully-carved and polished oak, with another intricately-carved strip across the top.

I took it. "It's beautiful, Morgan, but what is it?"

"Well, Sir, the carpenter and the blacksmith and I got together, and came up with something to stop your writing paper from sliding around when you try to write on it. Look, Sir, I'll show you... May I?" He took a piece of one of my horribly-blotched efforts.

"Yes, please, do."

He raised the narrow, carved piece at the end, slid the top end of the paper between it and the board, so the rest of the sheet was lying on the board, then let it go. He then held it upside down, and the paper remained exactly where he had clamped it. He then turned the board around so I could see where the blacksmith had created a strong spring to hold the two pieces of board firmly together.

"Ingenious, Morgan. Thank you so very much." I tried it out, and it worked perfectly. That writing board is one of my most treasured possessions. The only thing it could not do was improve my writing. However, Katherine, her enthusiasm now successfully transferred to her new pupil, had softened her approach and was no longer behaving like a drill sergeant, so in the spirit of my new determination to accede to her wishes where they made sense to me, I continued my efforts.

CHAPTER 12

One morning I was woken by the sound of Mr. Saunders out on the front lawn, calling one of his dogs, and when I came down to breakfast, found him in a state of great consternation. Neither Mrs. Saunders nor Katherine had yet made their appearance, both having a tendency to be late risers. That was something else in which Katherine and I differed too.

"It's my best hound," Mr. Saunders told me. "He's disappeared. I know he's liable to go off on his own every now and then, but he always comes home. Last night he didn't, and I've only just found out about it. Baker told me first thing this morning. It seems he stayed up until the early hours, waiting for him, but he hasn't shown, and I've been out myself calling for him. It's most upsetting. I'd hate to lose him. I've sent a couple of the footmen out to see if they can find him, but he could be anywhere. These hounds can go miles once they get a scent in their nostrils."

"Perhaps I could go out on horseback and search for him."

"That would be very kind of you, but I can't let you go too far afield today. Davies is busy shoeing horses this morning, and I can't spare anyone else to accompany you."

"Well, it should be all right as long as I don't wander outside the estate. Besides, no-one else seems to have taken an interest in me since Gwenda's brothers' efforts to kidnap me failed."

"True. Well, yes, I'd like to take you up..."

"Good morning everyone." Katherine breezed in. "My! Why the long faces?"

Mr. Saunders explained about the missing hound.

"Oh no! He's such a lovely dog too. Well, Connell and I shall go out and look for him right after breakfast, won't we, Connell?"

I had hoped to go on my own, but could not refuse. "Yes, I was just arranging to do that."

"I think that rather than going on horseback," Mr. Saunders suggested, "you should take the pony and gig, just in case the dog is injured and you need to carry him back, although I do hope that's not the case."

We set off after breakfast, as arranged, taking the pony and gig. "Your father has forbidden us to go beyond the edges of the estate," I told her, "So perhaps the best thing for us to do would be to go out to the perimeter, then make a circuit around the edge. I've noticed on my ramblings that some sort of path has been cleared around the estate, and I think the gig would go over it all right. What do you think?"

"A good idea. That should take us most of the day, unless we find Bounder first."

"Bounder? That's his name?"

The weather was fine, and spring now well on its way. The mansion was more or less at the centre of the Carregowen estate, and we set out, heading straight for the boundary. As we travelled further away from the house, so the land turned rougher and very similar to the area in which Katherine had first found me. She knew her way around much better than I did, having been brought up there, so knew of a wider path we could take out to the perimeter. We took that, eventually coming to the boundary.

Here we decided to head in a clockwise direction, and Katherine had been right. It would probably take us all day to complete the circle, some of it being quite difficult terrain. There was no sign of the lost hound at all, and around mid day we stopped and ate the lunch cook had prepared for us. We were in a valley here, surrounded by lichen-covered trees, mostly aspens and withies, and quite boggy in areas, and as the day was quite warm, the gnats soon found us, along with a few horse flies. We ate up, and were soon on our way again.

Given the position of the sun, it was about three o'clock when we both heard that familiar half bark, half howl of a hound.

"That's Bounder!" Katherine turned her head, trying to locate the source of his cries. Here, we were quite high up, the land dropping away steeply in areas, with a couple of small cottages about a mile away down in the valley.

She pointed. "The sound is coming from over there." I had brought the pony to a stop, but before I could say anything, she had leapt out and was running through the heather.

"Wait! Wait for me, Katherine." I could not follow in the gig because it was too rough, and I could find nothing for the moment to which I could attach the horse. Katherine, of course, being Katherine, did not wait for me, and was soon out of sight over a hummock.

There were no trees nearby, but I finally found a large rock. I raised one corner of it, then pushed the end of the reins under it with my foot, before letting it drop back into place. Unless the horse were frightened by something, then it should be still there when we returned.

I set off after Katherine, calling her as I went, but without receiving any reply. I could still hear the hound though, which must have heard her and was now half yelping, half howling even more loudly. I followed the sound and almost tripped over her. She was lying on the ground, unconscious.

She was lying face downwards, and I tried to turn her over, but could do nothing without risking doing even more damage. She must have tripped and fallen, and in her fall, hit her head against a rock, as there was blood on her forehead.

"Katherine! Katherine!"

Bounder was barking and yelping continuously now, but he would have to wait; I needed to see to Katherine. I ran back to the gig, and found a bottle of water we had brought with us, then carried it back to where she still lay. I intended wiping some of it on her forehead in the hope of rousing her. I held the bottle between my knees, and got the top off, but then found there was no way of holding it so as to pour some water into my hand as I had intended. It seemed there was nothing I could do to help her; I would simply have to wait there and hope she would come around soon. Going all the way back to the mansion to get help was impossible too, as it would be night by the time we arrived back here, and I could not possibly leave her alone all that time, especially in the dark.

Frustrated, I set the bottle down in the heather, where I hoped it would stay upright, then sat down next to her and worked my hand under her forehead, keeping it between her head and the rock she had hit.

"Please Katherine. Please be all right. I don't want anything to happen to you. Please wake up." I kept up my talking for several minutes, and then she stirred. "Katherine?" I moved my hand slightly, smoothing her forehead with my thumb, and she stirred some more. "Oh please, God! Let her be all right." Almost as in answer to my plea she raised her head slightly and tried to move. "Careful, Katherine, careful. Please, go slowly."

She finally turned herself over onto her back, and I manoeuvred myself so her head was resting on my thigh. She looked up at me. I stroked her hair back from her face and smiled down at her with relief. "Talk to me please, Katherine. Please talk to me. Let me know you're all right."

"Give me a minute, Connell. Give me a minute," and she closed her eyes.

"No, Katherine. You mustn't close your eyes. Keep talking to me, please."

It was another few minutes before she sat up and looked at me properly, without her eyes seeming to go out of focus. I talked to her constantly, making her look at me and answer question after question, as I was afraid that if she did stop talking she would lapse into unconsciousness again.

By now the sun was beginning to sink low in the sky, and once it was dark we would have great difficulty in finding our way home, especially if there were no moon tonight.

"Bounder? Where's Bounder?"

"I haven't been able to get to him yet. I was afraid to leave you. Do you think you'll be all right for a few minutes if I go to see if can find him? He's quite close by I think."

She started to get up.

"No. Stay right where you are. I don't want you falling again. You may be dizzy still, so wait right here and don't move. Promise me?"

She nodded, and I stood up and set off after Bounder. I found him caught in a gin trap set for rabbits, his front paw covered with blood, caused both by the trap's sharp teeth and his efforts to try to free himself. He had been in it so long, his paw was swollen and obviously had broken bones too. It looked very badly injured.

I took off my jacket and threw it over his head to prevent him from biting me when I removed the trap. I then stamped hard down on the iron bar holding the two vicious jaws around his paw, and still holding my foot down on the bar to prevent it springing back, I bent down and gently extracted his foot, almost losing my balance as I did so. My foot slipped just after I had freed him, and the trap leaped up, snapping its jaws together again, almost as though it were determined to entrap either Bounder once more, or my hand. It missed both of us though, and when I removed my coat from him, he licked my hand, then followed me back to where Katherine was still sitting.

"You're getting some colour back into your face now, although you have quite a lump up there on your forehead. How do you feel? Dizzy? Headache? Any other damage?"

She shook her head slowly. "Well, my forehead certainly hurts. I took some of the water you brought though, and have been wiping it on. It helps."

"I tried to do that, but could find no way of getting it from the bottle onto your forehead without tipping the whole lot all over you."

"Poor Connell. You're a kind man, you know."

I offered her a wry smile. "Useless though, it seems."

"Not at all. You do very well. You're a strong character, and I like that."

I smiled to myself; at least there was something about me that she approved of.

"Well, I think we should try to get ourselves home," I suggested after we had sat there for a few minutes longer, allowing her to recover herself a bit more. "Let's hope the sky stays clear, and maybe we'll even have a moon if we're lucky. I've forgotten what phase it's in. I don't see it anywhere, so with luck it'll rise just after dark, in which case it'll be full. Let's hope that's the case... Can you get up all right. You can pull on me if you like." And I held out my hand.

She got to her feet, and for the moment I thought she was going to faint again. I put my arm round her waist. "Hold onto me. Are you all right?"

"Yes, I think so. As you say, let's get going. Come on Bounder. We're going home."

The horse was still where I had left it, and snickered when it saw us. Poor old Bounder could not get into the gig on his own, though, so between us we managed to lift him in, after which we set off.

Darkness came, but we were fortunate. As I had hoped, before long a huge full, orange moon rose above the horizon and provided us with sufficient light for us to find our way. By the time we reached the place where the path led back to the mansion it had shrunk to a brilliant, lemon white, and David was out looking for us. After first enquiring whether all was well he took off, racing on home to let everyone know we were on our way.

Once back at the mansion, everyone rushed out to greet us, staff as well, and we were welcomed home. Not long after, the physician arrived too, sent for by Mr. Saunders after hearing of his daughter's accident. He asked her questions, and checked her eyes and the lump on her forehead, and as a result decided she should spend the next day in bed, but that someone should be assigned to sit in her chamber with her for the night, and to wake her every so often, to make sure she was just sleeping. He then left and went to see to Bounder, whose paw was in a bad way, and would not be doing much hunting in future. At least we had saved him though, and for that Mr. Saunders was most grateful.

That night, as I lay on my back in bed, gazing up at the canopy, and thinking over all that had happened that day, it occurred to me that seeing Katherine lying there on the ground, blood coming from her head, I did have some feelings for her, and that I cared more for her than I would have ever thought possible. I was willing to believe even that those feelings could almost be considered as affection. Maybe it was just the circumstances; I didn't know, and once she was back to her usual domineering self I might feel less well disposed toward her. I should have to wait and see.

CHAPTER 13

It was a week after our traumatic experience out looking for Bounder, and although Katherine had not been well for the first two days, by the end of the week she was back to her usual vigorous self and looking for something to do. As usual now, that something involved me.

"I know, let's go for a picnic," she suggested at breakfast.

"Good idea. Where would you like to go?"

"Well, we don't want to go anywhere near Carreg Wasted again, so let's go in the opposite direction, down near Trevine."

"I agree with you about Carreg Wasted, but I don't know the Trevine area at all, so it's best you decide. Do you want to take the curricle? It might be easier than trying to carry our picnic on horseback, don't you think?"

I was certainly changing. Now I was even suggesting she made the decisions. This was a whole new experience as far as my relationship with women was concerned, and I was not even concerned about abrogating what I had always considered my privilege and responsibility as a man either.

"Yes. Do let's take the curricle; it makes me feel sporty with the two horses."

I went to the sideboard and helped myself to some more of Mr. Saunders's excellent coffee and a small slice of venison pie -- my second. "Your father certainly has an eye for a good horse. Those two matching greys he has for the curricle are superb. I don't think he's recovered from the loss of his Clevelands yet though, do you? He hasn't replaced them or the carriage, I've noticed that he doesn't even talk about them. Even David doesn't mention them anymore, if it comes to that. Your father hasn't said anything about hiring a new coachman yet either. Perhaps it's all a bit too soon... I'm glad he trusts us with the curricle." I turned. "Can I get you anything? Some more coffee?"

Catherine was smiling, and shook her head. "No thank you."

I returned to the table with my replenished plate, then went back for my coffee. She was still smiling.

"What are you smiling at?"

"Oh nothing, really. It's nice to see you relaxed and chatting about everyday things for once, instead of looking so anxious... By the way, you're highly favoured, I should let you know, Connell O'Keeffe. Father doesn't allow just anyone to take out his curricle; he trusts you."

"Indeed? I'm flattered, especially considering a curricle is the most dangerous vehicle on the road."

"True, but Father sees you as a very calm, responsible man, and respects you greatly. Besides, it's usually flashy young beaus trying to show off who get into trouble driving curricles."

It was my turn to smile. "Flattery, flattery." Mr. Saunders saw me as calm! It was good no-one could see what was going on inside my mind, and what would he have thought if he had known that, not so very long ago, I myself could have been considered a flashy young beau? I sighed to myself. I had changed more than I could ever have imagined. In some ways, I suppose, I could be considered an improvement over my former self, in that I was probably more considerate and understanding now, but I had paid a tremendous price for that improvement... I stopped. "No you don't, O'Keeffe," I told myself. "Don't start going over all that and feeling sorry for yourself again. You're becoming a thoroughly boring misery within the privacy of your own mind, and it's got to stop."

"Connell? Are you listening? You always seem to be going off into a trance, and now you have that anxious look again. What are you thinking about? Cook will need to know what we'd like her to pack for lunch?"

"Oh? Oh yes, of course. The picnic she prepared for us last week was delicious. Can she repeat it, do you suppose?" I ignored her question as to what I was thinking about. To bore myself was one thing: to bore everyone else was another.

Within the hour we were aboard the curricle, along with our picnic lunch. Our bodyguard, Davies, was somewhere behind us, trying not to be too intrusive. Poor Davies, he must find it so tedious following us around all over the countryside, and the one day we *had* needed him -- when we were out looking for Bounder -- he had not been with us.

The air was clear and filled with the perfume of the hawthorn flowers now in full bloom, looking almost as though it had snowed, and I was thinking it would be only a couple of weeks more before Mr. Potter would be back in Haverfordwest. There was word, too, that the Cardiganshire Militia would be returning in the near future, and my thoughts were surprisingly mixed on this. Of course the matter had to be settled as soon as possible. After all, this was one of the things that had been hanging over me and wearing me down all this time, but although it was forever on my mind, I dreaded having to face it finally.

Katherine took up the reins.

I held out my hand. "Katherine...Thank you, but I'll do the driving."

"But, you can't... two horses..."

"No Katherine. Please don't fight me on this. It's important to me. Besides, you said your father trusted me."

I hoped she would not argue with me, or my new resolution to try to go along with her ideas could be in ruins, and we would be back to bickering again, although, oddly, I was beginning to get used to it. It was not spiteful bickering, more bantering really, and I was even getting into the spirit of it. Maybe it was what Katherine liked to refer to as 'spats', and if so, she was right, it *was* fun in an odd sort of way, provided it did not get out of hand, and since discovering how I felt about her teasing, she no longer did that, which had to mean she had never intended it to be hurtful at all.

She set the reins in order and handed them to me, saying nothing, which surprised me, and we set off.

I can even remember the exact spot where we were at the time. We were passing beneath a huge oak growing out of the hedge at the roadside when it happened. Not only did I still feel an affection for Katherine, I loved her! How was this possible?

Maybe it was because she was impossible, or was it that I just *thought* she was impossible? I reminded myself of my thoughts about her during that night, and realized much of the fault was my own, although I did allow myself some leeway here. After all, I had only been reacting according to the way in which I and all men were trained from childhood to think about women and the way they should behave, and Katherine just did not conform at all. To live in harmony with such a woman it was necessary to set aside such fixed notions regarding a women's role. When I took the trouble to listen to her, instead of allowing her to rub me the wrong way, we got along perfectly -- well, perhaps not quite. It was I, though, who needed to get over being so prickly about what I considered her attempts to dominate me, especially as, having been together so much lately, I had come to the realization that I liked her company regardless. It was certainly stimulating, albeit not always in ways I wanted. She was interesting too, and genuine. With Katherine, there were no hidden agendas: she was open and honest, although sometimes brutally so. Even so, I no longer wanted to be on my own. I wanted her to be with me. Yes, I loved her.

I found myself looking at her.

"Are you planning on taking the curricle up over the hedge, Connell?"

I grinned. "You know something, Kate? I'm happy."

"You won't be too happy if we end up upside down in the road because you're not looking where you're going... And yes, I'm happy too... I've been thinking, and have decided you're not quite so impossible as I thought you were."

"Well, thank you... I think. Should I consider that as a compliment then?" Interesting that we each considered the other to be impossible.

She thought for a moment. "Yes, I think you can take that as a compliment, Connell O'Keeffe, but only so long as you don't keep taking your eyes off the road, threatening to kill us both."

A compliment. She could not have said anything to make me happier at that moment. My happiness, however, was short-lived.

I had made no attempt to court Katherine. As far as I was concerned, as I said, my courting days were over as I was convinced no woman would want me now. That still had not stopped me from having the natural urges and feelings that had now made me fall in love with her, and it was the sudden realization that she would never return those feelings that had caused my moment of happiness to evaporate.

Never once had she even laid her hand on me, except when I was helping her up after her accident, and that surely had to mean she could not bear the thought of touching me. Her compliment to me too, such as it was, was nothing more than that she found me not so impossible as she had thought -- not exactly words to suggest she was in love with me. I rode along in silence, my spirits once again deflated.

There was a meadow stretching out towards the sea. The long grass had not yet been cut for hay, and its silver tips rippled across its wide, apple-green expanse like chiffon velvet in the light breeze.

Katherine pointed to it. "Let's go in there. I love lying in the long grass and looking up at the sky. It'll be dry today, too."

I turned the curricle onto the verge at the edge of the meadow, and Katherine tied the horses beneath a spreading ash tree, before we made our way through the knee-deep grass, carrying our picnic and a blanket. She looked around and set down the blanket. "Perfect," and she sat herself down, then lay on her back, hands behind her head. "Perfect."

I stood and looked out over the sea. Boats were passing by on their way to and from Fishguard. Just over the horizon lay my home. With luck, at least some things would turn out right for me soon, and I could at last go back to my family, something even more urgent now that I would be suffering from what was sure to be unrequited love.

Our picnic finished, we both lay on our backs looking up at the cornflower-blue sky. Larks were rising in steep swoops, ever higher, their songs getting sweeter as they rose. Swallows were everywhere too, although flying so high we could hardly see them, a sign of more good weather. I was not completely comfortable though. After being surrounded by those stooks of straw that terrible day down on Goodwick sands, the long grass now hemming us in all sides felt almost claustrophobic. At the same time I was agonizing over my new-found love for Katherine, and whether I should tell her, or not. I tried to ignore the imprisoning grass.

"You're very quiet, Connell. Is anything wrong? Or are you off again in one of your trances? I do have to wonder sometimes what is going on in that head of yours, and could wish you didn't look so sad so often... although I do understand that you do, indeed, have much to be sad about: so much has happened to you."

What had I to lose? If I *did* tell her, the only thing that could happen would be that I could embarrass both of us: Katherine, by forcing her to tell me she could never love me, and myself for having even thought that she might.

"I've fallen in love with you, Katherine." There, I had said it, although more with an air of resignation and regret than with passion. I had even been lying on my back, gazing at the sky, aware of the encroaching grass all around me when I said it. A romantic declaration, it had not been.

"I love you too, Connell." She turned over on her side and looked at me.

I sat up abruptly. "What? You *do*?" It was not what might be called a romantic response to her declaration either.

"Yes, strange, isn't it? I never thought I would. I thought you were impossible and that you would drive me mad."

Then I laughed. Was Katherine telling me the *only* reason she thought she would never fall in love with me was because she found me impossible? That the way I looked had nothing to do with it? "That's exactly how I thought about you. I thought you were impossible too." I grinned at her. "Still do."

"Well, at least we both know how we are, don't we?" she laughed. "And I still think you'd drive me mad too."

I was silent, and lay back down on the grass, staring into the sky. It was an excruciating thing for me to have to ask, but I was going to have to ask it anyway. I had to be sure, because now she had said she loved me, it was the most important thing I had to find out. I almost stammered out the words. "I don't repel you physically then? You love me the way I am now? All lopsided? You don't think I'm ugly because I've been crippled? You're not offended by the way I look?"

She looked at me in amazement. "O my dearest Connell! Lopsided, repelled, ugly, offended? How could you *possibly* think that way about yourself, or that anyone else could think that way about you? You're a beautiful man, all over, every bit of you, even the bit that isn't there. I love it."

She sat herself astride my hips and looked around. Davies, wherever he was, could not see us anyway, hidden as we were in the long grass, and she leaned forward and kissed me on the mouth. It was a warm and loving kiss.

"There, Connell O'Keeffe. That's how I feel about you, all of you, and I don't care if you think I'm a hussy either."

In less than a minute I had gone from being nothing to everything, from the belief that neither she, nor any woman, could ever love me again, to being loved, hugged and kissed so very warmly. I was stunned, but not so stunned that I did not return that kiss with a passion such as I had never, ever felt before.

I needed to find my breath, and opened my eyes. Would she even be still there? Or was this a cruel dream, the long grass as merciless as the straw had been that day? But she *was* still there, and she was smiling down at me. It was a warm, gentle smile, and the long grass continued to wave innocently, and a rush of warmth, love and renewed happiness coursed right through me. For the first time since my disaster, I was aroused.

Katherine moved her hand over me, holding me gently, looking into my eyes as she did so. She gave me a coquettish smile. "What is an arm anyway, Connell O'Keeffe, as long as the family jewels are still intact...?"

I laughed out loud, reached up and pulled her towards me.

"Mr. O'Keeffe! Miss Saunders! Where are you? Are you all right? Where are you?"

I swore, and clambered to my feet. Davies was sitting on his horse down at the edge of the meadow, his hand shielding the bright sunlight from his eyes, looking in all directions.

I gave him a resigned wave. "It's all right Davies, we're here."

He came cantering up. "Oh Mr. O'Keeffe, Sir! You had me so worried. I regret I'd not been keeping a strict enough eye on you both. I'd been watching a fox stalking something, and then when I saw the curricle at the edge of the meadow, but no sign of you, I thought you'd both been kidnapped." He pulled out a large, grubby kerchief and wiped his sweating face. "Oh, I'm so glad you're all right! I'm so sorry, Sir, Miss Saunders, to have been so negligent. I really am."

Poor Davies: not there the one time we *did* need his presence: there the one time we did not.

I did let her drive home, but that was only so I could put my arm around her. She loved me despite my imperfection. My being physically damaged meant nothing to her. I was not repulsive after all, and that knowledge removed one of my greatest fears regarding the loss of my arm. I need no longer have a fear of being rejected because I looked different, or feel embarrassed or inferior in front of her or any woman. I could meet people with self-confidence, and if anyone did reject me, it would not matter, because the most important person to me, my Katherine, loved me as I was. I felt a great weight being lifted off me. I was euphoric even. I was almost happier than I had ever been in my life.

"Why did you never touch me at all?" I asked.

"I was afraid to. You always gave the impression you didn't want anyone to touch you. You even seemed to shrink away. I often went to; I'm a very affectionate person and like to touch, but would stop myself. You were always holding back, and I didn't want to be rejected."

I nodded, but did not answer. *She* did not want to be rejected by *me*! Oh how we had both misread each other! And it had all been my own fault for not being open with her.

We rode along with my arm around her, and we did not meet anyone, so there were no tongues to wag. Besides, we had our newly-watchful chaperone close behind us, pistol and musket at the ready.

That night some of my doubts reappeared. Just because Katherine said she loved me, did not necessarily mean she would want to spend the rest of her life with me. Perhaps she was just feeling sorry for me, and the thought of marrying me might be something different altogether. I had become so unsure of myself these last months, I lay awake all night agonizing, going over in my mind all she had said, looking for hidden meanings, reinterpreting everything. I had to know her true feelings for me. I had no doubt now that I wanted to spend the rest of my days with her. I had no doubt either that it would be fiery at times, and there would be explosions along the way, but just as she said she loved me the way I was, so I also loved her too the way she was.

CHAPTER 14

"Will you take me back to the place where you almost killed me with that musket of yours that day? The place we first saw each other?" We had mounted our horses, and it was the day after our memorable picnic.

Katherine had just gathered up her reins, and looked at me as though I had lost my senses. "What an extraordinary thing for you to want to do. You're not a masochist, I hope. Or are you just trying to make me feel terrible for what I did to you? If so, it shows you too can be cruel, Connell O'Keeffe."

"No, neither of those reasons."

"Why then?"

"I'll let you know when we get there."

"Oh, all right. If you must. Is this another of your demons you feel you have to exorcise?"

"Not telling you." I grinned and set off down the path. "Now, which way do we go? Or are you going to stand there all day bickering with me?"

"I'm not bickering."

"Well, questioning me then."

She pointed her crop off to the left. "Down there. Down that path."

"Right. Let's go."

One would have thought I would remember every inch of that forced march in my bare feet, but I didn't. Maybe I had been too weary and in pain at the time to notice my surroundings, but as we wound our way along the path it seemed all new to me.

"I'm sure you're making me return this way just to make me feel the utmost guilt about what I did to you."

I said nothing, but merely followed her. At least this time, she was in front, and I was certainly not aiming a musket at her back. At last she stopped. It had not been that far after all; it had just seemed that way that day.

"You were lying there, in the heather, and I was hiding behind that big rock over there." She pointed her riding crop at it.

"The rock I remember. I remember you appearing from behind it like something out of Macbeth."

"Not one of the witches, I hope." She dismounted, and I did too.

"Oh, I don't know. Now that I look at you, perhaps..." I ducked as she flipped the crop in my direction. "Can you tie the horses to that tree over there for me, please?" I handed her my horse.

"What are you up to, Connell? Are we going to re-enact what happened, but with you in charge this time? Because if that's what you're planning, I can tell you, there is no chance of you persuading me to remove my boots and walk all the way back."

"Well, I hadn't thought of doing that, but now that you mention it, perhaps that might be a good idea after all. Unfortunately though, I don't happen to have a musket with me, so I can't force you. Anyway, you being impossible, you'd probably refuse to obey me even if I did have a loaded musket pointed at you, just as you did when confronted by poor Gwenda's brothers."

She was standing there in exactly the same place as she had been standing when she had ordered me to put my hands up, and I was standing over the spot where I had been lying. I looked at her.

"Well? Have you gone into another of your trances?"

"No, I'm just looking at you and thinking how you were as beautiful then as you are now, but now your expression tells me that you love me, not hate me. At least, that's what I'm hoping."

"Hmm. What makes you think I could possibly still love you, Connell O'Keeffe, after you've brought me all the way out here to this particular spot to punish me?"

"You do still love me, don't you?" I had never felt so nervous.

She came up to me and put her arms around me. "Of course I do. I'll always love you, even though you're as impossible as ever."

"You too, Miss Saunders." I looked down at her. "You want to know why I really brought you out here then?"

"I'm not going to say, 'yes' now, Mr. O'Keeffe, because I know that's what you want me to say." She looked up at me and smiled.

"Impossible as ever then...Will you marry me, Kate? Be my wife?" All along the way my nervousness had been increasing, still worrying about my fears during the night. What if she did not love me enough to want to make love with me and bear our children? What if she refused me? I was not sure how I would react if she did. I did know her refusal would devastate me now. I could feel my heart beating in my throat, and hear it beating in my ears. It seemed as though time had stopped still. "Please, Kate?"

"But of course I will, Connell. Of course I will." She gave me a cheeky look. "I think I knew all the time why we were coming here."

"You guessed? I'm that transparent? Could you see how nervous I was about asking you too then?" I knelt down, and took her hand.

"It doesn't matter what you were, my love, transparent, or nervous; I'll always love you, whatever you are."

"And that's my promise to you too, my dearest Kate."

I got up, and we stood there on the rocky hillside in the early summer sunshine, holding hands. I grinned at her. "And by the way, your apology is accepted."

"What apol ..? Oh! The one you were keeping in abeyance? Took your time accepting it, didn't you?" And we kissed.

She did truly love me after all, and all my agonizing all this time about how I looked now, had been for nothing. It was obvious to me too that my love for Katherine was nothing like the love I had thought I had for Julia Faraday, and it almost frightened me to think I had thought I loved *her* at all. It had not been true love, but just an empty infatuation with a beautiful woman, who was not even beautiful the way Katherine was: Katherine was beautiful all through.

We rode home side by side. "I know you still think I'm impossible," I joked. "So I do hope you won't find me too much of a trial, under your feet, with nothing to occupy me the way my acting did."

"Well, my dear, if the worst comes to the worst, I can always put you to finishing that embroidery of mine -- the girl in the bonnet."

"The result of that endeavour would be most interesting, I'm sure, always assuming there would be anything left of it at all, including my sanity, by the time I'd finished with it."

"Don't worry, my dearest Connell. I'm sure that between the two of us we can find a way for us both to have fulfilling lives."

"Knowing you, I imagine my whole life will be spent trying to keep up with you and your fervour in attacking each new project you come up with, although the last thing you'll find me doing, I assure you, will be your embroidery." I laughed. "Come to think of it, knowing you, I imagine that embroidery will be the last thing you'll be doing either. That poor girl in the bonnet will never, ever get to look down on whatever it is she's supposed to be looking at."

We continued in silence for a while.

"Will you talk to my father tonight, Connell? I'm sure he'll be delighted to see me happy again."

"What I *am* sure of is that he'll be only too delighted to get you off his hands." And I set my horse into a gallop and raced home before her riding crop came in my direction again.

All through dinner that evening Katherine kept giving me glances, then looking at her father. Did she think I might have forgotten what my duty was to be after she and her mother had retired to the drawing room?

The meal over, she looked over her shoulder at me as the footman opened the door for her and her mother to leave. "Enjoy your port, gentlemen."

"And why shouldn't we enjoy our port this evening?" Mr. Saunders asked of no-one in particular.

"Well, Sir, I do indeed hope we do, as I have something I should like to ask you."

"Oh?" Mr. Saunders held his glass up to the light of the candles set in the silver candelabra before him, and swirled the dark red liquid around, watching it slide slowly down the sides. "Ah! That's good port. Too bad that French wines are all but unobtainable now, but I have to say this Portuguese wine is exceptional. I keep only the Reserve Vintage and, for very special occasions, the Vintage port." He looked at me. "That's ten years old, you know."

"Yes, Sir. My father's cellar is similar to yours."

"Is it now? Well then, let's drink to both our cellars, shall we?"

I raised my glass, and smiled.

"Now, what was that question you wanted to ask me?"

I looked at him through my glass. "My question, Sir, is: may I have permission to marry your daughter, Katherine?"

Mr. Saunders set down his glass with such suddenness, I thought to see the precious contents spill all over the table. "My goodness, Connell! I thought the two of you were always at loggerheads. You mean to tell me you actually love each other?"

I grinned at him. "Yes. Hard to believe, Sir, isn't it? But yes, we do. I love her because she is as she is, and I find her everything I could wish for in a wife. She has spirit and she stands up to me, and that's something I've not been used to... She's good for me..." I hesitated. "And I hope I'm good for her too. I'll certainly do my best to be so. I've changed quite a bit since all this happened. I've quietened down and am more reflective, less impulsive. I've slowed down too -- all this by necessity, I suppose. I have to think some good has come out of it. Emotionally, I think I've matured too." I pointed my glass to where my right arm should be. "Besides, but for this, I'd never have met Katherine in the first place, and now I can't imagine my life without her."

"A hefty price to pay for a wife, I must say... Still, the price was paid regardless, so why shouldn't you receive the reward of your choice?"

"Yes indeed, Sir."

"Well, young man. I have no reason to say 'no'. In fact, I have every reason to say 'yes', and to wish you both every happiness, although I hope you'll keep on hand a plentiful supply of cheap china to throw at each other..."

I grinned. "Yes, we do have what Katherine likes to call our 'spats'. At first this bothered me I have to say. Squabbling with anyone, let alone with a woman was not something I made a habit of. Still, I've come to realize that Katherine's spats are, in the long run, quite harmless, and to learn to go along with them, another sign that I've mellowed a great deal in a very short time... No. I love her much too much to ever have a harmful quarrel with her."

"I'm delighted to hear it." Mr. Saunders leaned back in his chair. "Well, as the father of the bride, I suppose I should ask you the customary questions, shouldn't I?"

I nodded. "Yes Sir. And I hope I can answer everything to your satisfaction."

Mr. Saunders smiled at me. "Considering how far our relationship and this conversation have come, I must say, so do I. So, I might as well plunge right in here, and I think the first question prospective fathers-in-law are supposed to ask is: are you able, financially, to support my daughter in the manner to which she has become accustomed?"

My answer was one thing in which I knew I could have full confidence. "I came into a fortune of £75,000 on reaching my maturity, and also receive an annual income of £10,000 a year. On the death of my father, although I hope that won't be for many years yet, I'll inherit the baronetcy and the very extensive estate in Dunleary. I don't know the value of that, or its current income, but..."

Mr. Saunders held up his hand. As I was speaking, I had watched his eyes widen. I'm sure he had no idea how well I would be able to support his daughter, and I was willing to believe I could, perhaps, support her almost better than she was already being supported.

"I don't think we need to delve any further into your family finances. What I've already heard is sufficient to satisfy me."

I nodded. "Incidentally, I've spoken to Katherine about her coming to live in Ireland, and she doesn't object. However, at this point, I myself have no objection to living in Pembrokeshire either, at least until I inherit the estate in Dunleary. Now that my acting career is over, living in Dublin is no longer a necessity for me. Perhaps I could even buy an estate here?"

"Well." Mr. Saunders stood up and shook my hand. "All we need now is to get your problems with the authorities resolved, and receive some sort of communication from your father, and I'll be happy to celebrate my daughter's marriage to a very worthy young man."

"Thank you, Sir. I'll do all in my power to make Katherine happy."

"I'm sure you will, Connell." He signalled the footman to ask Metcalf to bring a bottle of his Vintage port, and by the time we entered the drawing room to join the ladies, we were somewhat more than all smiles.

CHAPTER 15

The following day, we were sitting, eating dinner, when Mr. Saunders stopped, put down his knife and fork, and looked at me. "Connell."

"Yes, Sir?"

"Now that our two families are to be joined, I think we should invite your mother and father to visit us here in the near future. They should be home soon now. What do you think?"

I hesitated.

"What? It's not a good idea?"

"It's not that, Sir. I've not been looking forward to the moment when I have to see my parents, and when they have to see me. It's a moment I've been dreading. My dear mother is...well...I don't know what reaction she will have when she sees me. I'm her only child, and to her was perfect in every way. I was not of course, but that's how she saw me." I gave Katherine a quizzical look. "And what are you smiling at there, Miss Saunders, may I ask? The fact that I even *have* a mother?"

"Oh no, Mr. O'Keeffe. I'm just smiling because I like the way you truly care about your mother and worry about her feelings, and I love you for it."

I reddened, and did not know what to say.

Mrs. Saunders saved me. "I agree with Katherine. It's a loving son who tries to spare his mother worry, but I do think the sooner you get this revelation over, the better. They have to know sooner or later, and they'll most certainly know at your wedding, but that would be the last occasion on which you'd want your mother to find out. Do as Mr. Saunders suggests, and let us invite them over now. It's June 1st today; what do you think, my dear?" She looked at her husband. "Should we invite them to come over two weeks from today? That's of course, if they're back home yet and have no prior commitments -- and if we can get the invitation to them in time, of course."

"Yes indeed, although it doesn't leave much time for our communications to reach one another, as you say, my dear, but I'll write today. And you, young man, I suggest you write to your father now as well, and tell him everything. Your father can then let your mother down gently, so that when we meet them your mother will be prepared, and it won't be such a shock for her to see you. In fact, I don't just suggest it; as your future father-in-law, I demand it. There! How's that?"

I laughed. "I've lately come to the realization, Sir, that sometimes it's good to have someone else make the decisions, and this is one of those occasions. When I retire this evening, I'll write my letter as you demand."

"Excellent. Do you think you can write it yourself, or would you like Katherine to act as your amanuensis?"

"No, I'll have to start writing proper letters to people sometime soon, so this can be my first effort."

"Tell us what your parents are like, Connell. Whom do you look like?" Katherine asked.

"Hmm. Well, they're both quite tall, as perhaps you'd expect, given my height, and I look like my mother, I'm told; at least we both have the same colour hair and eyes. They both enjoy going out in society, but my father's life is horseracing and racehorses. He has a couple of magnificent stallions at stud, from original Arab stock. You'll have to come over to see them, Mr. Saunders; I've noticed you have an excellent eye for a good horse."

Mr. Saunders smiled and leaned back in his chair. "I like to think I do, I must say, and speaking of which, I'll be sending David off this weekend to pick up some replacements for the horses I lost. He'll be taking a couple of stable boys with him, of course, and..." He paused. "And now we shall be having a wedding in the family, I shall today be getting in touch with my carriage maker to build me a carriage in the latest fashion -- very elegant it will be too, I assure you." He looked at his wife. "And you, my dear, with your excellent taste, shall choose all the interior furnishings. Then we'll be able to meet your parents in style, Connell."

"I'm sure they'll be delighted. I can see that you and my father are going to get along famously, and all the after-dinner talk will be of horses... and horses."

"And a very good topic too."

We were still chatting when there was a knock at the door, and a footman entered carrying a silver salver on which was a letter addressed to Mr. Saunders.

"What is it Father? Who is it from?" Katherine asked.

"My dear daughter, how badly I've raised you, that you should presume to ask about a letter that has arrived for me. Still, I think it's something that will be of interest to all nevertheless." He held up the letter to the light of the candles. "It's from Mrs. Kelly, Mr. Potter's housekeeper. She's writing to let me know that Mr. Potter will be returning to Haverfordwest on 4th June. That's in just three days' time." He paused, thinking. "Yes, the messenger is still at the door, so I'll write right now to let her know I'll be paying a visit to Mr. Potter on the afternoon of the 6th... Of course, I'll let her know also that if this time is not convenient for Mr. Potter, he may not wait in for me, but leave me a message to let me know a time that will be convenient to him." He had stood up and was pacing around, thinking out loud.

I was surprised. "You've been in communication with Mrs. Kelly then?"

"Yes indeed. I wrote asking her to let me know when Mr. Potter might be returning to Haverfordwest."

"She knows then about what happened to me after I left her that morning?"

"No. She knows nothing about the reason why I want to meet with Mr. Potter. It was not necessary for her to know."

"No. I suppose not. Too complicated to put into a letter anyway. Do you want me to come as well?" I asked.

"No. I think it's important you don't show your face in public until this matter is settled. Mr. Potter and I can discuss what steps will need to be taken to exonerate you, and we can take it from there." He folded the letter. "There then, Connell, the ball is finally rolling, and the sooner we can get this trial behind you, the better."

I was alarmed. "You think I *will* be tried then?"

Mr. Saunders smiled. "Oh no. I didn't mean trial in that sense. I meant for your tribulations to be over."

I nodded. It was hard to imagine this ever coming to pass.

That night I sat down in my chamber and began the difficult letter to my father. It was not just the subject matter that was hard to express in writing, but the actual writing itself, and the two together combined to keep me until well past the time when I heard the loud bell of the mahogany long-case clock down in the hallway striking three. During that time I wasted several sheets of writing material, along with rendering at least two quills no longer usable, forgetting, and getting Morgan to sharpen them the way I used to do for myself, which did not suit my left hand, leading to large ink blotches, so my efforts looked like those of a five-year-old child. I had almost finished, when a blob plopped down onto the page, ruining several sentences.

My frustration got the better of me then and I lost my temper, walked away from it, and went over and sat at the window for about fifteen minutes, looking out at the stars and the Milky Way.

I sat there, pondering over their infinite mystery, and came to the conclusion that no matter how my letter came out, it would all be the same in a hundred years. The waves of time would have washed away and obliterated my insignificant efforts, like the incoming tide over footsteps in the sand, and they would be forgotten about, regardless of how or what I wrote, or to whom.

The stars put me in my place in the scheme of things, and I went back to my desk. Regardless of how time would see it, I still had to let my father know about what had happened, and began rewriting my letter once again.

At last it was finished. I folded it, set Mr. Saunders's seal on it, and added the directions. It would be ready to be sent off that day. How my parents were going to react when they read it, I could only imagine, but it had to be done. They had to know sometime.

Two days later, Mr. Saunders set out for Haverfordwest, and I spent the day wondering what Mr. Potter's response would be to the long story that Mr. Saunders would have to tell him.

Katherine and I went out for a walk, but I was not much company, my mind on this whole nightmare, which I had managed to keep tucked away in a corner of my brain in recent weeks, but which now was well into the forefront once again, with all its reminders of terrors past and fears as to what might still be to come. I even began having renewed nightmares, seeing the murderer standing over me, my arm falling to the ground, and had been waking up shrieking. Morgan, who slept in the annexe to my chamber in case I ever needed his services during the night, would come in to me on these occasions.

"It's all right, Mr. O'Keeffe, Sir," he would say. I liked Morgan. He was understanding and sympathetic, having, like the rest of the staff, been told everything. He managed to calm me down without making me feel stupid about my having nightmares, and for that I was grateful.

We were walking through a meadow near the house. All the June flowers were already in bloom, and the long, apple-green grass was a wild tapestry of red poppies, blue cornflowers and big, yellow-eyed oxeye daisies. Katherine took my hand.

"I can tell you're off in one of your trances again, but this time I do know what you're thinking about, and I want to say I'm positive it will all work out well for you, Connell."

"My common sense tells me that too, but after everything that's happened, it's hard not to imagine something else arising to set me back down yet again."

"That's only natural, and of course my own part in this is not something I can contemplate without knowing how much I too added to your misfortunes. If I'd not found you, you'd have been back safely with your family long ago."

"Maybe not. The way the fates were working against me, I'm willing to believe something else might have intervened, if you hadn't." I squeezed her hand. "Besides, if you hadn't caught me, we wouldn't be together now, although I must say you chose an extraordinary way of catching yourself a husband."

"But that's why you love me, isn't it? Because I'm unpredictable... At least I add excitement to your life."

"I hope you don't plan on adding too much of that sort of excitement to my life. There's only so much of that a man can endure."

"I promise never to threaten you again with a musket, if that's what you mean... Of course, I may chase you around the dining table wielding a carving knife now and then. Oh, Connell! I'm sorry! There I am, talking before I think, again."

"That's all right. I understand you better now... And yes, on the night I asked for your hand in marriage, your father did suggest that we keep a good supply of cheap china on hand for us to throw at each other."

"Yes, and if you'd allowed me to continue with your therapy, you might even be able to hit me with it."

"I'd like to toss you over my shoulder, and carry you off, just as I did to that other Kate when I played Petruccio in *The Taming of the Shrew* in Cork last summer." The reminder brought me back down. "Yes... Well..." I shrugged.

Kate read my thoughts again. "Yes, I'm afraid there's nothing I can do to alter that, my dear." And we continued our walk in silence.

Night fell, and dinner came and went, and Mr. Saunders was still not home, and even Mrs. Saunders began to worry as the three of us sat in the drawing room on our own. Finally we heard the clattering of hooves on the driveway, and a few minutes later the master of the house appeared, flushed and smiling.

I leaped to my feet, as did Katherine. At least he was smiling.

"Well, Father. What news? Do tell us! We've spent the day in suspense. Did you get to see Mr. Potter? What did he say? He must have been devastated to hear of poor Connell's experience."

Mr. Saunders put up his hand. "Wait. Wait, my dear. Just give me time, and let me remove my coat and have a bite to eat first." He turned to the footman who was still standing at the open door. "Matthews, would you please have cook prepare me some hot soup with some bread, and a flagon of ale, please? Thank you."

Once on our own, Mr. Saunders sat down in front of the empty summer-fireplace and looked at me. "Well, Connell, if ever I had any doubts about you, which since you rescued me I haven't, they were dispelled by Mr. Potter. We sat in his magnificent library. I have to say I've never seen such a splendid collection, and Mrs. Potter joined us, and they listened, appalled, at what I had to tell them. When I told them what the murderer had done to you, Mrs. Potter had to be given her smelling salts, and Mr. Potter slammed his fist so hard down on the mantelshelf, I

215

expected him to break both his fist and the mantel. I've never seen a man so incensed. Mrs. Potter then began to cry, and had to be comforted by her husband.

"'Oh what a terrible thing to happen to such a charming and talented young man,' she cried. And when I went on to tell them the rest, they were incredulous, even more so when Mr. Potter realized that while he himself was standing on the bridge in Goodwick, watching the French prisoners coming down the hill onto the beach, you were amongst them. Even he became emotional when he discovered that, and said that while he had wondered about you, he had assumed you'd have found out about the invasion while still in St. David's, and would have stayed put until the crisis was over."

"If only I had understood Welsh, I'd have known about the invasion. Unfortunately I didn't, and the innkeeper was so busy, I didn't like to interrupt him."

Mr. Saunders shook his head, and continued. "'Why didn't Mrs. Kelly and Mr. Nash tell us all this when we arrived home?' Mrs. Potter had wanted to know. I suggested to them that it would be best for me to be able to tell them the whole story at once, I explained to her, so they could hear the good news as well as the bad, for, as you know Connell, the last they knew was that you had left Tower Hill, and were heading home to Ireland. I had to admit to my own part in this of course, and to explain the first few unfortunate weeks of your stay with us. Naturally it was unpleasant for me having to tell them that, although they did understand I was under the impression you were wanted for treason."

He had been pacing around all the time he was narrating his story, and it was obvious he had found the whole day one full of nervous tension, and his redder-than-usual face indicated he was still highly agitated by the whole experience. He sat back down, and slapped his knees. "Well, the upshot of this is that Mr. Potter, who is a close friend of both Lord Cawdor and the High Sheriff, Lord Milford, is to meet with them at the earliest opportunity to explain the situation, and -- something I think you will be happy to hear, Connell -- he and Mrs. Potter will be coming to visit here during the time that, all being well, your parents will be visiting as well. With luck -- and I don't see any reason why anything should go wrong -- we shall all be able to celebrate your freedom here together. What do you think of that then, eh?"

"Well, first of all, Mr. Saunders, I can't thank you enough for all your endeavours on my behalf, for all of which I'll be forever indebted. As for all the interested parties meeting here, I think that's an excellent idea... I do still have that other hurdle to overcome, however. I may be in the clear as far as being accused of treason is concerned, but will the authorities believe me when I say I didn't murder McCaffrey? After all, I have no solid proof to the contrary, and neither Mr. Potter nor you can testify to my innocence regarding that. The only argument I have is the absurdity of the idea that I should have murdered him at all. I sincerely hope the real killer can be found, and soon, for until he's captured, I'll always be under suspicion, and never truly free."

Mr. Saunders stood up and came over and slapped me on the shoulder. "Look at it this way, Connell. As you say, the idea is absurd to start with, but I see no reason why, when Colonel Stevens returns with the Cardigan Militia, we can't find the real murderer. After all, you say you'll never forget his face, so I'm sure some arrangement can be made where, disguised so he can't recognize you, you can be given the opportunity to visit the camp and pick out the man responsible without him even being aware of it."

"It'll still be his word against mine though."

"True, Connell, but how is he going to explain how you ended up dressed as an invader, when Mr. Potter can swear to it that you couldn't have been one? And we've yet to get the testimony of the landlord of the Cambrian Inn in St. David's. You stayed there two nights before the invasion, and I'm sure he wouldn't have forgotten the presence of such a distinguished-looking, and well-attired young gentleman as yourself. No, son, I don't think you've anything to worry about now, and can rest easy."

"Yes, I suppose you're right, Sir."

"Yes, of course I am."

CHAPTER 16

Despite Mr. Saunders's assurances, I found it hard to relax in the following days.

"Will you understand, Katherine, if I go out on my own today? I need to be able to concentrate on all that's going on. All of a sudden I can't think straight, and am finding it hard not to allow myself to get into an irrational panic over all this."

Katherine reached up and kissed me. "Of course I understand, although I hate to see you wandering off by yourself. It's so lonely for you to feel you have to face your problems on your own. I know though that, being the way I am, if I were to come with you, I'd probably chatter away, not giving you a chance to sort out your thoughts for yourself." She kissed me again. "There! You see, I'm not bickering with you. I'm getting to understand you well at last, aren't I? And I shall be the perfect and understanding wife, who knows when to keep quiet and let you do what you know is best for yourself... At least, I think that's how I'll be. I'll try anyway." She laughed.

She walked down to the stable with me, and waved goodbye. I felt guilty for not wanting her to be with me, but I did need to get away for a few hours. Everyone was being so supportive and considerate, almost too much so; I felt I was wrapped in a stifling cocoon that prevented me from mentally standing back and taking stock of my situation. My fate was now in the hands of others, although I suppose it had been thus ever since I had witnessed the murder.

I wandered over the moors, climbing towards an area called Garn Fawr. Here I dismounted and dropped the reins over a post someone had put in the ground at some time. It was not clear enough for me to see Ireland today; it rarely was, but I could see across the countryside for miles, with Preseli Mountain in the distance. Now that it was June, all Nature seemed at her most vibrant, with so many shades of green, they were impossible to count, and poking their magnificent rosy spires up through where the heather had burned at some time were thousands of willow-herbs, glowing in the sunshine. In the other direction Pembrokeshire's sheer cliffs dropped into the sea, looking from a distance like richly-embroidered curtains hanging from the moors above, down to the sea below.

Despite being alone, I still failed to achieve any clearer vision of my situation, except inasmuch as it appeared I had no option but to let things take their course. There was nothing I could do to help myself, so my future did depend on others, and my fretting about it would serve me no useful purpose. Mr. Saunders was probably right. I should not worry, but allow myself to rest easy, and with that resolve I returned home just as a fiery sun was disappearing behind a pewter bank of cloud resting on the Atlantic Ocean.

"Guess what, Connell!" Katherine rushed out to greet me. "We've had news that the Cardigan Militia is to be returning on the same day your parents are due to arrive, and Father has sent word to Colonel Stevens, inviting him to visit on June 18th. Isn't it marvellous? So convenient! Now all interested parties will be gathered here together, and we can finally get to work capturing the murderer." She grabbed my hand, dragging me into the house. "Everything will be sorted out at once. I can't wait to see Colonel Stevens's face when he learns that Richard's murderer was not an invader after all, but a member of his own militia. He was so terribly upset about Richard being killed. He'll be appalled when he finds out. I can see him wanting to storm off there and then, and rush back to camp to find the man responsible. As Father said, he'll probably be ready to kill him himself, when he does catch him."

I handed my coat to the footman, and followed Katherine into the drawing room.

"Katherine has told you our news then, Connell? This is a tremendous stroke of luck. I was afraid we were going to have to wait quite some time for us to be able to get Colonel Stevens on the case." He clapped his hands. "But now this whole matter will soon be resolved. At one time, of course, we'd thought it would need Colonel Stevens himself to do some investigating, but that won't be necessary now. All it will take, as we said before, will be for you to go to the camp, disguised so the murderer won't recognize you, and pick him out. There's no way the man can explain how you came to be dressed in an invader's uniform, unless he dressed you in it himself." He slapped me on the back. "Not long now, my boy. Not long now."

I smiled. "All I ask is that you don't disguise me the same way you did last time. I don't fancy traipsing around an army camp dressed as a Welsh woman in a bonnet and petticoats, or anywhere else for that matter."

Mr. Saunders shook his head. "A bad day that. A very bad day. I have my own nightmares about that day."

"Yes Sir. And perhaps I shouldn't have been flippant about reminding you of it. I apologise."

"No, no. Not at all, son. I know you didn't mean it that way. Besides, seeing you trip over your skirts on leaving *The Harp* did add a tone of levity for a few moments, and we both needed that at the time."

"I do wish I'd seen you, Connell. Six-foot-three inches of Welsh woman. You must have looked impressive. From what I heard, you frightened poor old Metcalf almost to death. We must dress you up again one day, just for fun. Next time though, we'll add stays as well. See how you like that."

"Oh no you won't! Anyway, you had your chance at the time, but were so incensed with me, you didn't deign to come near me... I should have you know," I teased her. "I haven't forgotten all those terrible comments you made to me too."

"Oh please, Connell! Don't remind me. You have no idea how ashamed I am now about my behaviour towards you."

"I'm glad to hear it, and shall hold those comments over you so that, whenever we have a spat in future, I can use the opportunity to repeat them to you."

"You wouldn't be so mean, would you? No. Not my Connell. He's not that sort of man."

I put my arm around her. "You're right. I wouldn't. I'll just insist that you make an embroidered sampler with all those comments on it. I'll then have it framed and hung over our bed." I ducked, and put my hand up to fend off her slap, and everyone laughed. I was beginning to relax after all.

"As you well know, Connell O'Keeffe, it takes me so long to finish an embroidery that by the time I've completed it you'll be so old that first of all your eyes will be such that you won't be able to even read the comments when the sampler hangs over our bed, and secondly, you won't remember who made the comments in the first place."

"Too bad we haven't purchased that cheap china yet."

"Too bad for you, you still haven't learnt how to throw it straight."

A few days later -- and time seemed to be moving so very slowly now -- Mr. Saunders received a letter from Mr. Potter. We were all eating breakfast together at the time.

"Ah! From Mr. Potter." Mr. Saunders set down his knife and fork, took the tortoiseshell letter opener from the proffered silver salver, and used it to slit open the letter. I was eating a good breakfast, as usual. There was nothing wrong with my appetite, but when I heard the letter was from Mr. Potter my mouth went dry and my appetite vanished. I put down my fork, pushing my plate away.

Mr. Saunders was scanning the letter, muttering some of the words as he went along. "Ah" he said at last. "Here we are. Potter says, '*I thought you, and in particular our friend O'Keeffe, would like to hear the results of my enquiries now, rather than wait in suspense until our visit, to which Mrs. Potter and I are looking forward with eagerness. I was fortunate enough to meet up with both Lord Cawdor and the High Sheriff, Lord Milford, at a gathering at my reading room this last Wednesday, and am delighted to forward the news to you that, after hearing of the sad events overtaking our friend, a decision was made on the spot to remove his name from the list of wanted traitors forthwith. They agreed as well with the improbability of his being the murderer, given the circumstances, and that he was later found dressed in a French invaders' uniform. What was most helpful was that both gentlemen had already met our friend at the various gatherings held at my own and others' homes, and remembered him well as being not only a talented actor and singer, but as a thoroughly delightful young man as well. To them, the idea that O'Keeffe would have murdered anyone, was preposterous, something with which all the other gentlemen present agreed. They were, moreover, outraged that he could even be considered as being a traitor and murderer!*

'The gathering not being a formal meeting, of course, the official notification of O'Keeffe's exoneration can't be drawn up until the next meeting of the Common Council, at which time such a notification will be prepared, signed, and sent to him. This should be around the 18th of this month' etc., etc...."

Mr. Saunders folded the letter and set it down on the table. "There. That's it then."

"Do please excuse me." I had heard Katherine start to exclaim with excitement, but my relief at receiving this news at long last was such that I stood up and rushed from the room. I pulled open the front door and raced across the lawn, making for the small copse at the end. When I reached the trees, I threw back my head and shouted to the world, "YES!" I felt Katherine's arms around me, and we stood there, hugging each other in silence.

CHAPTER 17

Word had come that my parents would be delighted to accept my hosts' invitation, and had booked a passage to Haverfordwest. All being well, they should be coming in at around noon on June 14th.

"That's the day after tomorrow!" Katherine exclaimed.

"Well I'm glad the new carriage has been here about a week now, and that David has been able to get the new horses teamed up properly and accustomed to working together. I wasn't able to find a coachman I liked, so after some consideration, decided David deserved to be promoted to that position, and I have every confidence that he'll perform his new duties with his usual diligence and expertise. He's a fine figure of a man too, so his livery will suit him well." Mr. Saunders paused a minute. "Now, I know the carriage will take six people, but given that Sir Connell and Lady Frances will have had a tiring trip, and when they get here, will have the business of coming to terms with their son's calamity, I suggest that only Connell and I go to meet them. That way, the trip back here will give them time to compose themselves before meeting you, my dear, and our Katherine."

"An excellent thought." Mrs. Saunders laid her crochet-work in her lap, and looked at her husband. "Most considerate and thoughtful of you as always, my dear."

I too was grateful Mrs. Saunders and Katherine would be spared this particular reunion. As Mr. Saunders had suggested, the fifteen-mile drive from Haverfordwest would give them time to come to terms with their son's 'new look', as I now chose to call it.

On the morning of their arrival, when Morgan came in, he laid out on my bed a whole new suit of clothes. They were identical to those Mr. Nash had had tailored for me during my stay with Mrs. Kelly after my escape from Barnlake, and most of which the highwaymen had stolen from me.

"Mr. Saunders has been saving them for you for today, Sir. He thought you'd want to look your best."

I shook my head. "Mrs. Saunders said he was a thoughtful man. He is indeed." And when I appeared at the breakfast table, everyone applauded.

Katherine rose from the table and ran towards me. "Oh Connell! You look magnificent, doesn't he Mother?" She took my hand and led me to the table. "The blue of the coat matches your eyes, and I love the fashionable silk scarf. Oh, I'm falling in love with you all over again."

"I hadn't realized you'd fallen *out* of love with me."

"Oh, you know what I mean." She clapped her hands. "Oh this is all so exciting. I can't wait to meet your parents."

"Neither can I, now. I'd not been looking forward to it, but now I'm ready at last to face them."

"After your father read that letter of yours, I think they must be only too happy that you're still alive." Mr. Saunders commented.

"True." I smiled. I *was* looking forward to seeing them again now, especially as not only did I no longer have that indictment looming over me, but also no longer agonized over the way I looked. Thanks to my Katherine, I could stand up and be proud of myself once more.

It was our first ride in a coach to Haverfordwest since that tragic day, and when we forded the now peaceful and shallow river, we looked at each other, but said nothing, and the rest of the trip was uneventful, with David making an excellent coachman, and much more to my liking than the poor man who lost his life that day. The new carriage was resplendent in its new paint, and Mrs. Saunders had excelled herself with the supervision of the interior design and upholstering. Mr. Saunders had not replaced his Cleveland Bays, but this time had selected four magnificent black Friesians with which to show off his elegant new carriage. The whole equipage looked most impressive, and he was rightly proud as we drew up at the quay.

The ship was not yet in sight, so while we waited, Mr. Saunders and I spent the time in the Castle Inn. Just knowing I did not need to be looking over my shoulder in fear lest someone would recognize and arrest me, was a relief, and we sat there and chatted over a mug of ale, until one of the footmen came to notify us of the ship's arrival, and that passengers would soon be disembarking.

Despite my newfound pleasure at the prospect of seeing my parents again, by the time we were standing at the bottom of the gangplank, I was still more than anxious to get this meeting over with. No doubt my parents were feeling the same.

"Here they are." I pointed them out to Mr. Saunders, and waved, and then we were all together, me making introductions, and my mother, as expected, weeping.

Not thinking about it, my father shook my hand with his right instead of his left, getting us off to an awkward start.

"Hello son." I could see he was uncomfortable too, so I did my best to deflect attention away from myself, although every time my mother looked at me, she would dab her handkerchief to her nose and turn away. Knowing my mother, though, it was what I had expected.

"Father. What do you think then of Mr. Saunders's taste in horseflesh, eh? An excellent eye, wouldn't you say? Have you ever seen finer Friesians? Come. Look. Mr. Saunders, do tell my father all about them," and I ushered the two of them off to look at the horses while I dealt with my mother. I put my arm around her, which had the unfortunate effect of making things worse.

To my acute embarrassment, she buried her face in my chest, raising her hands and clasping my cheeks, although everyone around was so busy with their own greetings, it was most unlikely anyone even noticed. "Oh Connell!" She was at a loss for words, which was perhaps just as well.

I gave a polite cough. "You're getting me all wet, Mother," I laughed. "Come now. You must at least be happy I'm still alive."

"Yes, but..."

"But nothing, Mother. Enough now. What will Katherine think, seeing my mother weeping all over me?"

"She will understand I'm sure. Any woman would. Your father too. He took it very badly. Besides, you *are* our only child, you know, so you must make allowances."

"Yes, well... At least we're all together now, and I can tell you the indictment has been lifted; I'm no longer a wanted criminal... Oh Mother! Not again! I thought at least *that* news would bring a smile." I took her hand and kissed it. "Come. I can see Father and Mr. Saunders are getting along well. I knew they would, because Mr. Saunders does have some very fine horses. There's a whole stable of them for them to inspect together."

I walked her over to the carriage, and took her hand to help her in, then followed her. It was another fifteen minutes before the other two men climbed in, during which time my mother gradually composed herself, and even began to admire the furnishings within the carriage.

"They were all selected by Mrs. Saunders herself," I told her.

"Excellent taste," she remarked, then out came the handkerchief once more.

"You and Mrs. Saunders will get on very well, I'm sure. She's a sweet, gentle lady. And Katherine..." I hesitated, not knowing quite how to describe my wife-to-be. "And Katherine, you'll find, is very special."

By the time we arrived back at the mansion, everyone was chatting amicably. Mr. Saunders's suggestion that just he and I should meet my parents had been a wise one. Every now and then I could see my mother cast a sideways glance at me, and turn away, her now sodden handkerchief more than doing its duty, but, all in all, things were proceeding very well, and for me, that first, trying hurdle was over.

"Would you do me the honour of introducing my parents please, Sir?" I asked Mr. Saunders as we descended from the coach.

"I'd be delighted to, young man."

I was the last to get out, and poor old Bounder had limped up to greet me as fast as he could on his three remaining paws. Ever since I had released him from that gin-trap, he had seen me as his saviour and hero, and always made the effort to come to meet me. I bent down and patted him. "Hello old boy. You and I, we both know what it's like, don't we?" Bounder wagged his tail, and together we brought up the rear, although no-one but me, I'm sure -- everyone else being involved in meeting one another -- would have noticed the irony of our partnership.

Introductions over, and Mrs. Saunders and my mother already chatting as though they had known each other all their lives, Katherine ran up and clasped me in her arms. "It's all coming together, Connell. I'm so happy. Who would ever have thought it would turn out this way? I now know why you're such a handsome man. Your parents are so elegant and aristocratic looking, and your mother is a beautiful woman."

"Yes, she is, isn't she? But then, your mother is beautiful too, so we're both blessed that way, although I hope mine will soon cease her weeping, and accept things as they are."

"Of course she will. Look. She's already admiring the flower border, and smiling. After all, what are you, a mere son, compared with the delights of my mother's flower border?" She squeezed my hand, and reached up and kissed me, laughing.

"Ah, 'tis a cruel woman that you are, Miss Saunders, but I suppose I'm bound to have you as my wife now. There'll be no getting out of it, alas."

"No. Never, ever."

I grabbed her hand, and pulled her towards me. "Right then, kiss me, Kate..."

My parents were shown to their chambers, where they would rest after their journey, then prepare themselves for dinner, and Katherine and I went for a stroll around the grounds immediately surrounding the house.

"Phew! I'm so glad that's over, and I'm proud of my mother too. I had no idea how she was going to react, but at least she didn't have an attack of the vapours or hysterics on the quayside."

"And your father? How was he?"

"Well, I have a feeling that sometime he and I are going to have to get together on our own, so we can discuss everything man to man, if you see what I mean. I think he'll need to do that. Knowing my father, he'll want to know, and see, every detail, before he's satisfied. I can tell he's holding in a great deal of anger about what happened, and how he would react if ever he came face to face with the man, I dare not think."

Katherine nodded. "It's a bit like the calm *after* the storm right now, isn't it? Everyone assessing the damage, and coping with it in their own way. Soon all will settle down again though, and life will go on."

"And the sooner that happens, the better. And in that spirit, let me ask you: what did you do today while I was gone? Finished off your embroidery perhaps?" I grinned at her, and she laughed.

"As I said before, I'm slow to complete embroidery of any sort, and shall no doubt be confined to my rocking chair before that one's ever completed. Maybe even, my daughter, assuming we have one, will inherit a half-completed picture, leaving everyone in permanent suspense as to what the little girl in her bonnet is looking at."

"And just what *is* she hoping to look at anyway? Just so that I can tell our grandchildren when they ask me about the framed, half-finished embroidery adorning pride of place above the fireplace in our grand drawing room."

"It's a kitten. Anyway, what makes you think they'd ask you, their doddery old grandfather, rather than their spry old grandmother?"

"I think I've had enough of this conversation."

"You started it."

"True, so I have the privilege of ending it. It must be almost time for dinner anyway, and I'm hungry."

To allow my parents sufficient time in which to recover somewhat from their journey, dinner was held later than usual, but when we were all finally seated, it was a magnificent affair. Cook had excelled herself, and all the finest of silver, chinaware and crystal made its appearance on the glowing mahogany dining table. It being mid June, and almost the longest day, it was still not dark. Even so, all the candles were lit, enhancing the sparkle and glow of everything around us. All were dressed in their most elegant and colourful best, and it was a gala occasion, but as depicted by Mr. William Hogarth some years earlier, it was not: behaviour and decorum were of the highest order.

After dinner we three men remained behind at the table while the three ladies retired to the drawing room. What their conversation might have been I have no idea, but ours, as I had already predicted, was about horses. For the most part I was left out of the conversation, not being up to date on the latest racing and breeding news, although Mr.

Saunders found time to praise me for my horsemanship both as a rider and driver.

"There aren't many I'd allow to drive my curricle, Sir Connell," he told my father, "but whoever taught him how to drive, did an excellent job. He and my daughter have taken in several outings, and I'd trust him everywhere."

My father looked at me. "So you can still handle two horses at once then, son? I'm delighted to hear it."

"Ah, Father. You'd be surprised how much I can still do, if not perhaps write a perfect letter yet..." I smiled, thinking about the blotched communication he had received from me.

"Yes indeed," Mr. Saunders added. "We're all very proud of him. You have indeed raised a son to be proud of, Sir Connell."

My father smiled at me. "My wife and I have always thought so."

"Can you go back to horses now? After all your hard work raising a son to be proud of, you don't want to ruin him by making him big-headed, do you?"

They both laughed, and Mr. Saunders looked at the French clock on the mantel. "I think it's time we joined the ladies, don't you? They'll be wondering where we are."

Once in the drawing room, our host suggested some entertainment.

"Oh please have Connell sing for us," Katherine insisted.

"Do you play the pianoforte, Lady Frances?" Mrs. Saunders asked.

"Yes she does," I answered for my mother, "and beautifully too."

"Then why don't we have mother and son play and sing for us?" she suggested.

"Oh yes!" said Katherine.

"What about it then, Mother? Would you like to play for me, or are you feeling too exhausted tonight after your long journey?" I gave her an excuse, as I was not sure how well she would be able to perform in her present state of mind.

"No, Connell. I think I should like to do that. What would you like to sing?"

This required some thought. "I think we should start with something for old-times' sake," I answered after a minute. I needed more than anything, to get over as many hurdles as soon as possible, and what I suggested was one of them. It was risky though, as I did not know if either of us would be able to get through it safely. I was determined to try, however.

My mother had seated herself ready to play, and looked up at me standing beside her. That we should even be together again like this was something I had sometimes thought would never happen, and that in itself was almost too much for both of us at this moment. However, I gave her a look that told her, "This is it, Mother, don't let us let each other down."

"Preab san ol," I announced boldly, and heard my father give a nervous cough, but I was still holding my mother's attention, and although she coloured, she nodded.

Mr. Saunders held up his hand. "I think there are others who would enjoy listening again to Connell sing." While talking he had risen and walked to the door. On opening it, he smiled as several guilty-looking members of staff were seen standing there, all ready to listen.

"Ah! I see the household grapevine is flourishing then," he told them. "All right, if everyone has finished their dinner, tell them they may come into the hall, and we shall leave the doors open. I see no reason why we should not all enjoy Mr. O'Keeffe's fine voice."

I stood looking at my mother, and shrugged my shoulders slightly, smiling. She smiled back. We were going to survive this, although she was not aware, of course, of the last occasion on which some of the staff had heard me sing this song. Mr. Saunders returned to his seat, and nodded. There was silence.

I hesitated. "Mr. Saunders. This is a drinking song which I think the staff will enjoy as well. Last time I sang it, I did so in Gaelic. Tonight though, I'll sing it in English, so everyone can understand the words. May I suggest, Sir, that, since we are all, in a way, celebrating this evening, they each be given a glass of wine with which to toast everyone's good health?"

Mr. Saunders leaped to his feet. "Why yes, of course. This is your special evening, Connell, and you may command whatever you wish." He turned to the servants crowding the large entrance hall. "Did you hear that? We shall wait a few minutes more then, until Metcalf has had a glass each delivered to you all."

In five minutes all was ready, and Mr. Saunders took his seat once again.

"Right mother. Are you ready?"

She nodded, and I sang. Our duet was greeted with a loud 'hurrah' and clapping, and demands were made for an encore. My mother and I, both having leapt the hurdle, were now at ease, and the second time around was even better, both being more relaxed. The tune, being a catchy one, this time others joined in too, giving everyone that much more pleasure.

And so the evening progressed. My mother and I performed two more songs, then Mrs. Saunders entertained us with a couple of lively pieces, followed by a gentle song, at the end of which she stood up and closed the pianoforte.

"And now, ladies and gentlemen, it has been a long day, especially for our honoured guests, and I think it's time for us all to retire."

It was not a suggestion I myself could have made, but had noticed my parents wilting, so was grateful for our hostess's consideration.

CHAPTER 18

The following two days passed quickly. During this time we enjoyed an outdoor picnic, and with the carriage opened up to the fine weather, went on a drive around the area to show my parents the beauties of north Pembrokeshire. My father and I did have our private conversation in which every detail was dragged out of me, and an inspection made of the resulting damage.

"What about your acting career? Is there any chance you'll be able to continue with that, son? I know it means a great deal to you, and you're a highly accomplished actor as everyone knows."

I shook my head.

"Well, as a gentleman, at least you don't have to work for a living."

"That's not the point, Father."

"No, I suppose not. I'm sorry, son. That was thoughtless of me. This whole business has me stunned, I'm afraid." He put his hand on my shoulder, and I raised my own hand and patted his. I did understand.

He insisted too on being taken to the spot where it happened, which was harrowing for both of us. To my mind it all seemed to achieve nothing more than to increase my father's rage at the perpetrator, but presumably he had his own reasons for putting himself though this, and me too, if it came to that. Maybe he thought that by having me share it with him, he could thereby relieve me of some of the hurt. Maybe too, he thought that once fully informed, he too could finally lay it to rest. Only he could know that though.

Saturday arrived, and everyone waited with excitement for the arrival of Mr. and Mrs. Potter. Living in the town of Haverfordwest, the Potters, like many others, did not own a carriage, and used sedan chairs instead to carry them around, Haverfordwest's steep hills and cobbles being particularly hazardous for horses. Sedans, of course, would not do to get them to the Saunders's mansion fifteen miles away, so Mr. Saunders had insisted on sending his own carriage to pick them up.

Just before four o'clock, the sound of the coach was heard, and we all went out to greet them, and once again, I asked Mr. Saunders to do the honour of carrying out the introductions.

The ladies having been introduced, the Potters came up to me. I smiled and bowed to Mrs. Potter, and raised her hand to my lips. However, a loving and generous lady with numerous children of her own, she was so overcome with emotion, she took me in her ample arms and pulled me towards her.

"Come here, my dear. Oh dear! And I told myself I wouldn't cry, but I can't help it. Oh dear, I promised myself I wouldn't..."

I put my arm around her. "Oh, not you as well, Mrs. Potter! Oh well, as my mother will tell you, she too required the services of her handkerchief. I don't know; I think I'm beginning to quite enjoy all this attention," I laughed, and she stood back and smiled through her tears.

"Oh you, Connell!" She wagged her finger at me. "Oh you! Now I'm at a loss for words."

"Perhaps that's just as well, my dear," Mr. Potter broke in, and took my hand. "Connell. Perhaps my wife is right after all though. I too am at a loss for words, for anything I say can't possibly express our horror of what happened."

I bowed. "I appreciate your concern, Sir."

He leaned over and whispered to me. "You and I must get together alone sometime. I think I can safely say I, of all people, as an actor, know what this will have done to you. We need to talk, and discuss it."

"Thank you Sir. Yes. I'd find that most helpful. Acting was not just something I did to keep me occupied."

"Yes, son. I know." He bowed, and moved on to talk to his hostess.

Again that evening a sumptuous dinner was held, and afterwards Mr. Potter asked my permission to use our time together, out of the hearing of the ladies who had retired to the drawing room, to question me more closely regarding the actual murder and its immediate aftermath.

"It's just that I need to get my facts straight. if and when it becomes necessary for me to argue your case regarding the murder itself. Not that I'm a lawyer, of course, but more as a personal friend, a witness."

"Yes, of course Sir. What can I tell you? I'm not sure what you already know, although if Mr. Saunders here explained to you all that I related to him, I don't think

239

there's that much more to say. But please, do go ahead and ask any questions about anything that is unclear to you."

"Well, as you know, that you found yourself dressed in the French invaders' uniform is most important. After all, you left St. David's dressed as a gentleman. Do you remember exactly when the change took place?"

I breathed in deeply. I had already been through this with my father, and the idea of repeating it yet again left me fearing for the fate of the delicious dinner I had just eaten, as the mere contemplation of what he wanted me to describe brought all digestion to a stomach-churning halt. Still, it had to be done; Mr. Potter was my friend, and wanted only to help me.

"At the time the murderer and his accomplice, or friend, or whoever he was, held me up in the road, I was wearing my breeches and boots of course, but because it was a warm day, I'd taken off my coat and waistcoat, so was wearing only my shirt. They tore that off me before... before..." I stopped, and wondered if they could possibly understand how much willpower I needed to get through this.

Mr. Potter nodded. "Yes, I understand. Go on."

"The next thing I remember was waking up being carried over the murderer's shoulder. At that time, I was still naked from the waist up. I don't know what else I was wearing, because I would not have been able to see over his shoulder, but presumably I still had on my own breeches and boots, because they would not have had a French uniform available at that time -- right there in the field -- in which to dress me."

I took a drink of Mr. Saunders's vintage, celebratory port, its special qualities crossing my palate unnoticed, my panic rising, having to relive my terror yet again. I forced myself to sound businesslike. "I lost consciousness again then, and when I next woke up... I'm trying to think... I was lying on the ground in the army camp, and another officer came up and said something about dealing with me. I couldn't think of much else at the time, as I was afraid of what he wanted done with me, but now I remember. I couldn't keep still, and my feet were digging into the ground..."

I stood up abruptly, and walked over to the window, my back to them, staring at my reflection, and took out my kerchief to wipe the sweat from my face, the image in my mind so vivid, I wanted more than anything to run away from it, out into the night. I turned round again, and faced the three anxious faces.

"Yes. I remember. My feet were bare. My boots were gone, so they must have already replaced my breeches too, before taking me to where all the other soldiers could see me and assume I was one of the invaders. Then someone knocked me out by hitting me on the side of the head, which is when they cauterized my arm. I do know that when I woke up in the middle of the night, some sort of coat had been put on me, and the next morning, when I was put in the wagon, I was definitely wearing a French uniform coat and breeches."

I would not be able to continue with this much longer. If Mr. Potter's questioning did not stop very soon, I would be forced to leave the room, and not return.

"From the way you describe it then," I heard him saying, "it would seem as though your clothes were changed after they returned to camp, but before setting you down in the midst of the rest of the soldiers, as you say. I'm using the fact that you had bare feet by the time that officer ordered them to deal with you."

Out of the corner of my eye I could see my father fidgeting. "Father. There really is no need for you to have to stay and listen to this again, nor you Mr. Saunders. Why don't you leave, and go to join the ladies. Mr. Potter and I won't be long, I'm sure." They might be showing the strain of this interview, but how could they possibly understand what it was doing to me, the self control I myself was exercising in all this? I already knew that any time I was forced to relive that day, my night would be followed by nightmares. Tonight would be no different.

"No indeed. I just have a couple more questions of Connell," Mr. Potter assured them, and then we were alone.

"It was the question of the change into the French uniform that I felt was important. There isn't anything else I can think of at the moment, unless you can remember something I should know."

I shook my head, and tried to think of something, anything, with which to take my mind off what we had just been forced to discuss. I felt sorry for Mr. Potter too. To be of help to me, he needed to know the facts, of course; it was unavoidable, but knowing what he was putting me through must have put tremendous pressure on him as well. My voice sounded almost eager. "I have to tell you; I'm glad we had those regular fencing matches, the two of us. If I'd not been practising all those months..." I stopped, and Mr. Potter slapped me on the knee.

"I wasn't as good as you. You were superb." He hesitated. "I'm sorry to have to say 'were', which brings us to your acting career. I felt frustrated when I could no longer act, but at least that was my own doing. I found myself in a place that had no theatre, and stayed there. While you were staying with us, you and I talked so much about your career, and it was obvious you were totally dedicated to it. I want you to know how sorry I am, Connell. More sorry than I have words with which to express myself... and," he smiled, "I'm usually known for never being at a loss for words, typical Dublin actor that I am. I want you to know though, that if there is anything, ever, I can do to help you in any way, you will let me know...To have such a promising career snatched away from you like this is so very tragic, especially for someone so dedicated and talented as you were."

"Thank you Sir." I know he meant well, but he had my mind revolving like a windmill, now reminding me of what I had lost in all this, and I needed to put a stop to it. I changed the subject from the past to the future. "By the way, I don't think anyone has got around to mentioning to you that Colonel Stevens will be arriving here tomorrow."

"That soon, eh? Excellent! Then we can all get together and discuss how to catch this evil man. What does this Colonel Stevens know at this stage?"

"We've not told him anything at all, so, as far as he still knows, Miss Katherine's betrothed, McCaffrey, was one of the very few to be killed by the invaders. He's going to be incensed when he learns his friend was actually murdered by a fellow officer in his own militia."

"Has anyone made any suggestions as to how Colonel Stevens will go about apprehending this man?"

"I'm the only one who can identify him, so it's been suggested that Colonel Stevens take me back to camp on some pretext, but that I should be disguised in some way so the murderer doesn't recognize me, and abscond."

Mr. Potter nodded, and smiled. "Well, with you being as good an actor as any, I'm sure you'll find a way of disguising yourself."

I started laughing. "Did Mr. Saunders tell you how I left *The Harp* in Letterston the day of that terrible accident in the river?"

"No."

I told him, and we laughed at the image of me tripping over my petticoats, then shocking poor Metcalf when I arrived at the door.

"Don't even think it!" I warned Mr. Potter, who had a sly grin on his face. "No-one is going to dress me up in that garb again, especially to have me walk into a camp full of soldiers!"

"Oh I don't know, O'Keeffe. I'm sure you'd charm them all... By the way, going back to our fencing bouts when you were staying with us. I enjoyed that so much that while I was away I decided to see if I could find someone who could take up where you left off."

"And did you?"

"Yes, I even found another young man about your age, who was also an excellent swordsman, and he agreed to take me on. I'm now proud to say that, even though I'm now in my forty-eighth year, and obviously not as good as I was in my twenties, I'm once again a swordsman to be taken seriously. I'm so glad you were around to get me started again. I hadn't realized how much I missed the sport."

"Well, after some of the hair-raising adventures you've experienced in your life, and told me about, I sincerely hope you're not planning on any more similar exploits." I smiled.

" I'm not planning on having any at the moment."

"I'm sure that's a relief to all concerned, especially your dear wife."

He stood up. "On that note, I think perhaps we'd better join everyone, don't you."

I nodded, and we made our way into the drawing room, where they were all playing backgammon. Katherine looked up.

"Tomorrow, my dear Connell, will see the beginning of the end of all of your problems... Well, except the one of course." She got up and came over to me. "And if I could do something about that for you, I would."

I put my arm round her. "See, everyone. See how lucky I am to have such a woman by my side. No man could be happier... Right. Do we have an extra backgammon board, so Mr. Potter and I can join in? Something to take our minds off tomorrow would be good, I think."

CHAPTER 19

The weather being sunny and warm, everyone was outside on the front lawn, enjoying the summer sunshine and strawberries, freshly picked from the walled garden.

Colonel Stevens was not expected to arrive until about mid afternoon, which would give him plenty of time to recuperate after his long ride, and to prepare himself for dinner. Now, at last, his arrival meant the opportunity was almost here for Katherine and me to find and prosecute the man who had wreaked such disaster on our lives, but while I was managing to conceal the turmoil in my mind at the prospect of this long-awaited event and all it was going to entail, Katherine, being Katherine, could not contain herself.

"Oh where is he? Surely he should be here by now! I can't wait to tell him. You wait till you meet him, Connell. He's such a charming man. I've known him since I was a child, and he's always been so very kind to me. He's quite a bit older than I am, of course. He was quite a bit older than Richard too, he being the colonel of the regiment, and Richard just a young captain. It was through him I met Richard too -- at a ball being held at the new assembly rooms in Haverfordwest two years ago. Oh where is he? I do hope he hasn't met with some misfortune along the way. Do you think we should start down the drive to meet him, Connell? I can't wait for you to meet him! You'll really like each other."

"I think it would be better for us to wait here, don't you, Kate? We don't even know for sure when he'll get here. Besides, these strawberries are much too delicious to walk away from." I smiled up at her, standing there on her tiptoes, her hand shielding her eyes from the sun, and peering down the tree-lined driveway.

"Here he comes! I see him! He's here!" Katherine dumped her bowl of strawberries down beside me, and immediately started running to greet him, calling out to him, while the rest of us stood up and began arranging ourselves, ready for introductions. In front stood our hosts, Mr. and Mrs. Saunders, and at a discreet distance behind, Mr. and Mrs. Potter and I stood side by side waiting, Mr. Potter to my right, then Mrs. Potter, and my parents off to one side.

A stable boy was right there to lead his horse away, and we all watched as Colonel Stevens, a man of fine stature, and resplendent in full military uniform, sword at his side, leaped from his horse and gave Katherine an elegant bow, lifting her hand to his lips. Together they made their way towards us, Katherine with her arm resting on his, both chatting like the old friends that they were.

I watched them approach, then, wanting to attract Mr. Potter's attention, I leaned over towards him, putting out my right hand to touch his shoulder. My hand was not there, of course, and as I was a couple of feet away from him, I lost my balance, and ended up crashing into the gravel driveway, landing with my full weight on the side of my head and my still sensitive stump, which I had tried instinctively to put out yet again, this time to break my fall.

My dramatic impact with the ground was sufficiently forceful to cause me to let out a yell, and everyone turned round to see what had happened. Because I was on the ground, however, and Mr. and Mrs. Saunders were in their line of sight, neither Katherine nor the colonel could see me. Katherine, of course, knew where I had been standing, though, and hearing me, left the colonel's side, and rushed up to find me scrambling hurriedly to my feet and brushing myself down, cursing at having embarrassed myself by falling over so dramatically.

By this time, introductions forgotten, Mr. and Mrs. Saunders and my parents, as well as Katherine and Mrs. Potter were all crowding around me, while the colonel stood back where Katherine had abandoned him, not knowing what to do, his grand arrival brought to an embarrassing standstill.

Katherine put her arms out and took hold of me, trying to get me to sit down on the nearest chair.

I shook my head, resisting her efforts. "No, no! I'm fine. You don't understand. It's..."

"It's not all right, Connell," Kate fussed. "It's not all right. Do sit down, my dear. You're not fine at all. You've got blood dripping all down your face. You must have fainted from the heat." She turned to Morgan, who had also come rushing up.

"No! No! I..." I insisted, but no-one was listening.

"Take Mr. O'Keeffe to his chamber, Morgan, will you please? And see to those cuts." She stood on her toes and inspected my face. "There's a lot of gravel in them too."

"Yes Ma'am." And Morgan took hold of me, trying to get me into the house, but I shook him off. "No! No! You don't understand. Will you listen. It's him!"

"Maybe the fall has stunned him," suggested Mrs. Potter who, in her usual, motherly fashion, was also fussing over me, wanting to help, just as though I were her own son. "He's obviously hurt himself, poor dear... All that blood... The sooner we get the physician to see to him the better, don't you think, my dear Lady Frances?"

There was no reply from my mother who, I learned afterwards, was finally having her attack of the vapours.

I stood my ground, and held up my hand. "No! I'm not going anywhere. And will you all stop fussing, and listen to me. I'm trying to tell you... Stevens... He's the murderer! I recognize him. He's the one who did this to me. He's the one who killed McCaffrey."

The silence following my words was sudden and dramatic. All those clustered around me stood as though in suspended animation, then, almost in unison, all heads turned towards Colonel Stevens, who was still standing back, not yet having had a glimpse of me. He appeared not to have heard what I had said either, because he continued to stand there, waiting politely while everyone attended to me. No doubt he assumed people were looking at him now because, having been abandoned in the midst of his welcome, everyone had suddenly remembered he was still there.

Mr. Saunders, as host of this gathering, did not know which way to turn. His new guest was standing there, still waiting to be introduced to the rest of us; my mother had fainted, and I was being fussed over by his servant, blood running down my face. Being a gentleman, he decided to see to my mother first, and rushed over to her.

The first to regain his composure was Mr. Potter, who left my side, and went up to the colonel. "Colonel, Sir," he announced, bowing. "May I introduce myself. I'm Mr. Potter of Haverfordwest. It seems we have a situation that has arisen. A young gentleman staying here fainted in the heat, and has fallen and injured himself." He held out his hand, indicating that the colonel should follow him. "Do come this way, Sir. I fear we have been inattentive."

"Not at all, Mr. Potter." The Colonel strode after him. "We often have situations like this in the militia, when men are standing to attention on parade, and faint as a result of the heat. Think nothing of..."

They had arrived in front of me, and I stood there, looking straight at Stevens.

He started, took a step back, and looked around. "*What!*" he exclaimed, pointing his gloved finger at me. "What's this? How did this man get here? You!" He glared into my face, and poked me in the chest. "You! Fainted from the heat, did we? I think not. You Irish bastard rogue!"

His finger still pressed into my chest, he looked over towards Mr. Saunders, who was still attending to my mother. Where my father was, I could not see. "This wastral, my dear Sir, if indeed he fainted at all, which I doubt, did so out of fear because he recognized me. And why did he recognize me, you might ask? Because *I* was the officer who took him prisoner after he killed my dear friend, Captain McCaffrey, God rest his soul... How did this scoundrel *ever* manage to wheedle his way into your graces, Sir?" he demanded.

But Mr. Saunders, still attending to my mother, had nothing to say, and Stevens then turned his attention to

Katherine. "My dearest Miss Saunders." He poked me in the chest again. "*This* man here is none other than the one who murdered your beloved fiancé! To save you from further heartache, I never revealed to you that I myself saw your dear Richard being killed -- by this man, no less! This Irish traitor to our King!" He emphasised his words by continuing to poke me in the chest, and I was tempted to retaliate, but knowing he was quite capable of finding any excuse to kill me, even though I was not armed, I restrained myself, although my anger was close to exploding.

"To save you from further heartache as well, Miss Saunders," he continued, "I never told you how I myself captured this invader and took him prisoner, sorely tempted though I was at the time to kill him on the spot, but I did the honourable thing: I took him prisoner, only to have others let him escape. I have had those in authority looking for him ever since."

He stepped back, and drew his sword. "Well, at least now we can re-capture him at last." He looked around. "Have someone send for the sheriff's deputy at once, and in the meantime..." He looked again at a speechless Mr. Saunders, still poised over my mother, not knowing which way to turn. "Maybe you have a spare stable, Sir, in which we can lock him until the law arrives. This man is dangerous."

He looked back at me, and waved his sword in my face, something that could not stop the blood draining from my head, remembering the injury he had inflicted on me the last time he had stood before me, brandishing a sword.

Then I saw my father starting to approach the killer, a look on his face such as I had never seen before, and moving much like a cat stalking a prey, ready to pounce.

"No!" I shouted at him. "No! Stand back. This man has murdered once, and will kill you too, as well as me, if given the opportunity."

My father continued to approach, unheeding.

"No!" I yelled at him again. "Listen to me. Please, I beg of you! Stand back. Let others take care of this. Please... for all our sakes. Stand back," I repeated.

My father halted, and looked at me, saying nothing.

The colonel raised his sword, and I heard Katherine scream.

"You! You Irish scum!" he roared at me. "How dare you impugn my reputation, my honour! How dare you accuse me of murder in front of all these good people here, my best friends! I demand satisfaction. Now! Right here!" He poked me in the chest yet again. "Stand on your own two feet, you coward." He moved to push away Morgan, who was still making an attempt to hold onto me. "Stand, I said. Stand like a man, you miserable coward."

I turned to Morgan. "It's all right, Morgan, I'm fine."

Morgan moved away from me, and I stood there in front of Stevens. It was difficult for me to look into that face again. "Not only are you a murderer, Sir," I said, "but it's you who are the coward. You demand satisfaction, knowing very well I can't fight a duel with you, because it was you yourself who stood there, knowing I was unarmed, as I am now, and in cold blood had another man hold me down while you crippled me for life."

Stevens poked his face within inches of mine. "Such insolent lies! In cold blood indeed! We both know I crossed swords with you after you killed McCaffrey. Yes, you lost your arm in that fight, but we were at war. You were one of the invaders, the enemy, a traitor to His Majesty, no less, and I had every right to attack you. I'm a soldier -- and you deserved what happened to you in that fight. In fact, you deserved more; you deserved to be killed."

His face was so close to me I could feel his breath, but I continued to look him in the eye.

"How dare you accuse me of mutilating an unarmed man in cold blood! How dare you!" he ranted. "Me, an officer of His Majesty! I should have killed you when I had the chance! And, by God, I wish I had! I can see you now, standing there, having just killed my friend, his blood still on your sword, standing there over his body in your despicable Frenchie uniform. How I regret it now that I did the honourable thing, and gave you your worthless life. Yes, I should have killed you right there and then, you useless Paddy."

He paused, and looked around. "Right then. If you feel a duel between us would be unequal, and you were no swordsman to start with, let me have my right arm tied behind my back, and we'll fight left-handed. That, you'll have to agree is fair. I refuse to remain unsatisfied after this."

The blood dripping down into my eyes was obscuring my vision, and I wiped it away with the back of my hand. "I have to give you credit, Sir. You're a far better actor than you ever were a swordsman. Yes, I have to give you that... Although given the level of your swordsmanship, I can't say that's much of a compliment... And I shall be only too delighted to..."

Mr. Potter, who had remained silent all this time, stepped forward and raised his hand, interrupting me, and it dawned on me now that he had deliberately led Stevens towards me so as to see his reaction.

"Before we go any further, Sir, may I know what proof you have that this man was the killer of Miss Saunders's betrothed?"

Stevens stood back from me and raised himself to attention. "Indeed, Sir. I'll be happy to tell you. As you just heard me say, I witnessed the killing. I saw this man here, in his filthy Frenchie uniform, kill my friend, whereupon I attacked him. We fought a vicious duel in which he suffered his injury. Then I took him prisoner. It's as simple as that." He looked at me, the corner of his lip curled upward in disdain. "You deserved to be killed outright. No-one would have questioned my actions, you being an invader of our country, but I took you prisoner instead. If I'd known you were going to escape, I *would* have killed you, and as I've said, I wish to God I had."

"I'm sure you do," I said, "because, if you had, you would have got away with two murders, but your fellow officer stopped you, and insisted I be taken prisoner instead. What you did to me then, you did purely out of revenge, because *I* was the one who beat *you* in that duel as you know all too well. I challenge you to tell everyone here what really happened, Stevens -- the truth -- but we both know you're too much of a coward to do that, because, if you did, you would have to admit that it was you who killed McCaffrey, and that I saw you do it. That's why you want me dead. I'm your only witness. No, Sir, I repeat it: you're a coward of the very worst kind. There can't exist a more despicable character."

"You bastard!" Stevens shouted, and raised his sword. "I'll see you in..." but before he could do anything further, Mr. Potter stepped smartly in front of me, putting up his hand.

"So...," he said quietly, then paused. "So, Colonel, you can identify this man as one of the invaders, then, I gather, Sir," he continued in a calm, but authoritative tone. "And specifically as the invader who slew Miss Saunders's betrothed. May I ask you to repeat to us how you could tell he was one of the invaders?"

"As I said, Sir, it was because of the French uniform in which he was dressed. And yes, he was the man I saw kill McCaffrey. His lies about me are outrageous, and the sooner the world is rid of him, the better, and now he's chosen to insult me in every possible way, I shall take the greatest pleasure in dispatching him right here, and now."

No-one had said anything, realizing now that Mr. Potter had set his own trap for the colonel by getting him to repeat in front of everyone his lie about what I was wearing, knowing that for me to be wearing a French uniform at that time was impossible. Out of the corner of my eye I could see my mother still suffering from her vapours, her head bent backwards over the back of the chair where she had been placed, and my poor father, standing as though frozen, his face devoid of all colour, and my hatred of this man boiled over.

I lunged forward, pushing Mr. Potter aside. "Let me..." I roared, but Mr. Potter, grabbed hold of my shoulder, and with surprising strength swung me round to face him -- and winked.

"You," he ordered me. "You stay right where you are, young man, and stop your ranting, while I speak to the good colonel here a minute."

"Sir," he said calmly to Stevens. "Sir, I have a better solution. As a gentleman and an officer, I'm sure you would not want to see yourself win what would have to be a most unequal fight. This man here may be the enemy and, from what you have told us, well deserve his fate, but he'd certainly be no match for someone such as yourself, Colonel -- you, I'm sure, being an excellent swordsman." He waved his hand in my direction as though in dismissal. "He being such a poor swordsman to begin with, I can't possibly imagine him putting up any sort of fight in his present state that would in any way be worthy of your considerable abilities, and your certain victory over him would surely provide you with no satisfaction at all."

"You said you have a better solution, Sir. May I ask what you have in mind?"

"Well, we're all -- except this Paddy ruffian here, of course -- civilized people, are we not? May I suggest to you that I stand in for him, and we have a duel to first blood only, right here, right now? And as we have swords, but no duelling pistols to hand, I suggest we use swords. I pride myself on being a pretty good swordsman myself, and would certainly be able to give you more satisfaction than this sorry excuse for a man." He pointed his finger at me. "That, I hope, should provide you with your satisfaction regarding his insults, after which you may then have the sheriff's deputy carry him off to be hanged as a traitor -- a much more satisfactory solution, don't you agree, Sir?"

The colonel was caught. He could not afford to argue the legitimacy of such a solution before his friends, Mr. Potter's offer appearing to be such a reasonable one under the circumstances. He nodded.

"Right," said Mr. Potter, attempting at the same time to silence his wife's protestations. "Right. Then, as I said, there's no time like the present. The sheriff's deputy has already been sent for, so should be here in a few hours. In the meantime, let us have our duel, my good Colonel." He looked around, and met the still stunned Mr. Saunders's eye. "May I suggest that you, Mr. Saunders, stand as the colonel's second?" He looked at my father, still a stranger to the colonel. "And you, Sir, may I request your services as mine?"

My poor father, in almost as bad a state as my mother, nodded, too bemused to have taken in all Mr. Potter's machinations.

"In the meantime," Mr. Potter said, "may I suggest the ladies retire, along with *you*?" He now felt free to poke me in the chest as well. "Off with you! The servants can see to you, you worthless Paddy," he continued, "while we gentlemen attend to our other business on your behalf, although I'm not sure how much you deserve such consideration on our part," he added, glaring into my face.

The aftermath of my fall was taking over, and every part of me that had slammed itself so unceremoniously into the gravel driveway, was beginning to make itself felt. I stood there staring at him, looking suitably cowed, without even needing to act my part, and it was not until later that I was able to acknowledge what a great actor this man is, and how perfect he was for his current role.

Morgan and another servant, taken in by everything that had been said about me, as well as by Mr. Potter's treatment of me, grabbed hold of me, hustling me roughly into the house, followed by Katherine, who, in the spirit of the moment, was hurling her own insults at me.

The front door shut, Kate turned to Morgan. "Morgan, that was all an act. Please release your grip on Mr. O'Keeffe. He's innocent, I assure you. We can explain later, but for now, please escort him to his chamber... And gently this time."

The other servant, who had been deliberately gripping me as hard as he could, released me immediately. "I'm so sorry, Sir. I thought you were a traitor to our King. I'm so sorry..."

I nodded, and within minutes found myself sitting on the edge of my bed, wondering how Mr. Potter was going to fare, then see to it that the colonel was brought to justice. Meanwhile Morgan and Katherine started their fussing again, but they'd no sooner started cleaning me up than a servant arrived with a letter for me. I held out my hand and took it, then handed it to Katherine. "Would you open it please, Kate, and read it, whatever it is."

Katherine sliced open the letter. "It's an official document," she announced. "And, guess what, my love. It's your official exoneration." She kissed me, and took hold of my hand.

Whether it was because the dreadful threat of being hanged for treason had finally been officially lifted from me I don't know, but I suddenly realized I could not allow Mr. Potter to go ahead and fight Stevens for me. This was my battle, and I was the one who needed to fight it, regardless of my ability or the outcome. I may have won Katherine's love, but I needed to prove to myself that I was still a man who could stand up for myself, and allowing someone else to fight for me would remove any remnants of self-respect that I might have left. I climbed out of bed.

"Connell! What are you doing? Where are you going?"

"To take Stevens up on his challenge. He was no good with his right hand, and I can't be any worse with my left than he is."

"Please Connell. No! Forget first blood: he'll kill you if he possibly can. He... he'll have to; it's the only way he can save himself."

I opened the door. "Then it's up to me to see he doesn't. I'm sorry, my dear Kate, but surely you must understand; I have to do this. I won't be able to live with myself if I don't." I turned to Morgan. "Ask Mr. Saunders if I can use his sword, please, Morgan, then go and tell Mr. Potter to hold up the proceedings for a few minutes."

Five minutes later I was striding out of the front door still wearing my bloodied clothes, my once-white shirt open to the waist to show I was wearing no protective clothing, and carrying Mr. Saunders's sword.

Everyone stared at me as I went up to Mr. Potter.

"I wondered how long it would be before you showed up," he whispered in my ear. "Not that I didn't think I could beat the scoundrel, but I'm glad to see you've lived up to my expectations." He turned to the astonished crowd, which now included all the servants as well.

"Well," he announced. "It seems our worthless Paddy has insisted on entertaining us with another show of his poor swordsmanship after all." He looked at Stevens. "Your challenge, it would appear, Sir, has been accepted by this... this..." He flipped a disdainful hand in my direction. "The rules will be the same, of course -- to first blood -- and I shall stand as his second. Mr. Saunders, I suggest you still be the good Colonel's second."

It was decided to hold the duel right then and there on the lawn in front of the house, but Mr. Potter insisted that all distractions in the form of an audience should be removed, leaving only the two seconds in attendance. This was something for which I was most grateful. The last thing I wanted was for any of the ladies, in particular, to witness the fight because Katherine was right; this man had no choice but to kill me, and he could still claim it legally as long as the first blood he drew from me was from my heart.

I watched the colonel remove his jacket and open his shirt, then tie a handkerchief around his left hand before putting his right hand behind his back. Even in this he still showed himself to be dishonourable, because he deliberately left a corner of the handkerchief hanging loose, knowing that my sword could easily become entangled in it during our fight. Mr. Potter, though, an expert swordsman

259

himself, as I already knew, was quick to notice the attempt to cheat, and asked Mr. Saunders to make sure the end of the kerchief was tucked in before securing Stevens's right arm behind his back.

Mr. Potter tied my handkerchief around my hand for me. He then ordered us to take our stance and to hold out our swords to make sure there was the regulation two-foot space between the points. As Stevens held out his sword, I recognized it. It was mine. I knew I could prove right then and there that it was mine because it was the sword my father had given me when I reached my majority, and had my name engraved under the hilt. Now, though, I could not wait to fight him, not only to satisfy my desire to gain some sort of revenge, but also to satisfy the need to regain my own dignity and self worth as a man. I should have liked nothing better than to kill him in the doing, but the fight was to first blood only, so in the spirit of that, I, at least, as a gentleman of honour, would abide by that rule.

We stood there, waiting for the signal. "Be prepared," Stevens sneered at me quietly, out of hearing of our seconds. "The first blood will be from your heart, O'Keeffe, I'll guarantee that."

"We'll see about that."

"Allez!" Mr. Potter barked the order to begin.

I knew that although I was in good shape physically, I was out of practice as I had not wielded a sword for many months now. I also found that, without my other arm, my balance was off. I considered the field level, however, in that I doubted Stevens had fought with his left hand for some time either, if indeed he ever had, so his balance would be off too, probably more than my own, I myself having had to live this way for a considerable time already.

He was the first to lunge. It was a crude and hasty move, and I avoided it easily, and it very quickly became obvious that whatever he did as colonel, it was not particularly strenuous. Agile he was not, and I soon had him red in the face, and puffing. I was several years his junior too, and it was also clear that my years of regularly performing realistic duels onstage -- frequently using two swords -- was paying off, for after a hesitant start it soon all came back to me, and I settled down to a performance I knew would rival any I had ever exhibited, determination adding to my skill. I was sufficiently confident, moreover, to toy with him, thus frustrating and infuriating him, making him careless.

Even so, it would be foolish for me to push my good fortune too far, so leaving myself open perhaps to a lucky strike on his part, so when I had satisfied my honour and my need to teach him a lesson, and proved to myself that I was still capable of making an adequate defence of myself, I simply nicked him on the arm, drawing enough blood for Mr. Saunders to call a halt to the fight.

I put my sword up immediately, but then Stevens, enraged, and ignoring the command to cease, lunged at me, aiming in desperation straight at my heart. I saw it coming, but did not have enough time to avoid the thrust completely, and catching me off balance, his sword pierced my left shoulder, knocking me over backwards. He raised his sword again, ready to kill me, but this time I was ready, and rolled over, dropping my sword as I did so, and grabbed him by the ankle, causing him to tumble. By this time both Mr. Saunders and Mr. Potter had joined in, the latter wresting Stevens's sword from his hand.

I clambered to my feet, and within minutes, servants were taking charge of Stevens, and Morgan was seeing to me, blood seeping out through my shirt and spreading across my chest and down my arm. "Oh Sir!" he was exclaiming. "Oh Sir!"

"It's all right, Morgan. I'm all right."

"But Sir!"

Having made sure Stevens was no longer a threat, Mr. Potter and Mr. Saunders came up to me. Mr. Saunders was aghast at the colonel's behaviour, and shaking his head, at a loss for words.

"Let me see the damage." Mr. Potter pulled back my shirt. The point of the sword had pierced my shoulder, but apart from bleeding rather profusely, did not feel as though it had done anything too serious.

I looked at them. "Pierced by my own sword even!" I commented.

"What do you mean?" Mr. Potter asked.

"As soon as I saw the sword he was pointing at me, even before we began, I knew it was mine, the one he stole off me that day."

"Why in Heaven's name didn't you say so at once? You could have stopped the fight right then and there, Connell!"

I grinned. "I was ready to fight that murderer, and nothing would have stopped me at that point. I was determined to beat him too, and was not going to let him get off without being taught a lesson in swordsmanship. He showed his true colours too, didn't he? You didn't hear what he said to me right before you shouted 'allez' either. He threatened me, saying that the first blood was going to come from my heart. After that pronouncement, there would certainly have been no stopping me, I can assure you."

Mr. Potter clapped me on the back. "Well, son, you certainly proved you're still a swordsman to be taken seriously. Congratulations. I..."

"Connell! Oh Connell!" Katherine was running towards me. "You're bleeding! You've been hurt! What did he do to you? I knew you shouldn't have tried fighting him. I knew it! He..."

"I won."

" How? I thought it was to first blood only."

"It was supposed to be, Miss Saunders," Mr. Potter told her, "but the dear colonel proved himself to be no honourable gentleman. Your betrothed here nicked him first, and drew blood, and when Mr. Saunders called a halt to the fight, Connell, a true gentleman, put up his sword at once. The colonel didn't, and lunged at him. If Connell hadn't been quick on his feet, the colonel would definitely have killed him, because he was aiming for his heart. Even then he tried to kill him before he could regain his feet, but your young man here was too quick for him, and brought him down."

Katherine put her arms around me, her head on my chest, and started crying.

"Come Kate, you're   beautiful dress is being ruined."

"I don't care. I don't care. That dreadful, dreadful man! How could I ever have thought him to be an honourable gentleman? A friend?"

Her father patted her on the shoulder. "I think it's time we let cook take care of that wound of his, my dear. You don't want him to end up bleeding to death after all this, do you? The physician should be here any minute."

Some time later we were all sitting in the drawing room, wine being served all round. Even the servants were being offered something to calm their nerves, most having apparently witnessed the whole fight from a room in the attic. My mother was still weeping, and Mrs. Saunders was comforting her, my father having come to me and quietly congratulated me while cook was busy seeing to me in the kitchen.

Mr. Saunders raised his glass. "To our dear, courageous Connell." He looked at me. "Well you most certainly showed us what you're capable of today, young man. You were magnificent. It all seemed to come so naturally to you too. It was so obvious you were even toying with him, making a complete fool of the man, and could have finished the fight in the first minute, had you chosen to... No wonder he became so incensed that he lost all reason and assaulted you as he did!"

I grinned. "Yes, in a way I suppose I was asking for that. After all, I, more than anyone, knew that he's no gentleman, and should have been prepared for him to behave true to form, the coward."

Mr. Saunders then raised his glass to Mr. Potter. "And to Mr. Potter here. What can I say? What a great actor you are, Sir! You almost had *me* fooled too."

"So it was back to the stable with me, was it then?" I laughed.

He shook his head, serious. "No, Connell. Let's not even joke about that."

"By the way," I asked, "tell me what happened after the sheriff's deputy came. What about the invader's uniform? Did anyone prod Stevens more about that before he arrived?"

"No." Mr. Potter was pacing up and down the salon, obviously still in the grip of excitement. "We didn't want to alert him to the fact that we knew he was lying. As far as he was concerned, we were waiting for the sheriff to come to take *you* into custody, he still under the impression that he'd convinced us that you were the one to have murdered McCaffrey... The man had obviously lost all reason, still claiming that he had every right to kill you by whatever method, regardless of the rules...!"

"O dear," Mr. Saunders sighed. "So much to take in. Too much. Too much. To think that Stevens should have killed poor Richard. Such a shock. Such a dreadful shock."

"Believe me, it was a shock for me too to discover it was your good friend who was the villain in all this!"

"Going back to the fact that he was using your sword, I'm not sure now that that would have proved anything one way or another. He could have argued that when he took you prisoner after fighting you in battle, as he calls it, he had a right to take it as a trophy," Mr. Saunders suggested.

"Yes, that's true, but if that other officer, who saw what he did to me, is honest, he'll refute Stevens's claim that he injured me in battle. After all, he saw Stevens take my sword right after the two of them pulled me off my horse."

Mr. Saunders came over and patted my knee. "Well, we have enough evidence now against Stevens without that other man's testimony, so let's not worry about him... By the way, I haven't thought to ask you before, but why did you come to fall so heavily like that right after the colonel arrived? Did you have a giddy spell, or something?"

"No. I recognized the visitor as the man we were looking for. In my surprise I forgot, and went to grab hold of Mr. Potter's arm with my right hand, then lost my balance when it did not support me as I was expecting it to." I gave him a wry smile.

"I've heard of that happening," Mr. Saunders mused. "I remember hearing of a man who'd had his leg amputated, then went to stand up on it, with similar results, of course. But eventually, I understand, you get used to it, and remember not to try to rely on what's no longer there."

Small consolation, so I changed the subject. "That was a very brave thing you did to be prepared to stand in for me in that duel, Mr. Potter, Sir. There aren't many who would have done that, and I'm indebted to you. I don't even know how to thank you..." I grinned at him. "Although word has it you were quite disappointed to have your fight denied after all."

"Ah! News travels fast, doesn't it?" He stopped his pacing, and laughed. It was obvious he was enjoying every minute of this. "No need to thank me, Connell. No need. It's true, though; I was itching to give that man his comeuppance, and yes, I might have been taking a risk in offering to take him on, but I'd pretty much regained all my old expertise, and I was a damned fine swordsman, you know. You ask any of the old theatre people in Dublin. I just knew I could beat him, and he could not refuse the first blood suggestion. After all, no true gentleman fights a duel nowadays with the intention of actually killing his opponent, as he was all set to do to you. It's just a case of settling issues of honour." He picked up a sword from off a nearby table and handed it to me. "By the way, here's your sword, the one he tried to kill you with."

"Thank you... So where is Stevens now?"

"He's on his way back to Haverfordwest, manacled and in the care of the sheriff's deputy, as I'm sure you'll be delighted to hear."

"He is? Tell me what happened then. I was busy being fussed over by cook while you were all involved with the sheriff." I pushed back my shirt, and peered at her handiwork. "She's done a good job... No more bleeding, and plenty of her marigold salve, I see."

"Well, the arrival of your official exoneration helped, as it proved, along with my sworn statement -- and that of the St. David's innkeeper, which they had also obtained -- that you could not possibly have been one of the invaders. Even so, we let Stevens repeat to the sheriff's deputy his version of events, before producing that proof. Then, of course, when he was asked to explain how you ended up in an invader's uniform, he couldn't, and had dug himself in so deeply with his lies that, faced with the evidence, he couldn't refute it, and ended up confessing. When asked then *why* he had murdered Captain McCaffrey, Miss Saunders, he admitted he was jealous, and had always wanted you for himself. They had got into an argument over you, and in a rage, he had killed McCaffrey, all which of course you witnessed, Connell."

Katherine leaped up. "What! Richard was murdered on account of *me*?"

"Apparently so. He had wanted to kill you too, of course, Connell, but, as you said, was prevented by his fellow officer. Asked if his fellow officer had been an accomplice, he at least had the decency to admit he wasn't, but that the man had naturally believed Stevens's version of the slaying. We have the officer's name, so he'll no doubt corroborate all that, although, as your father has already said, we don't need his testimony anymore."

"So now I really *am* free. I can hardly believe it. All over. Just like that. So suddenly. In the end it has seemed to have come to an all-too-easy conclusion...Well, not all too easy, of course. None of this has been easy at all, and all because I happened to be in the wrong place at the wrong time! I wish at least I could have seen Stevens being carted away. Were you there, father, there to witness it?"

"Oh yes indeed, I was. I think that given the chance I'd have murdered the man myself. Indeed, if my invective could have killed, Stevens would have dropped dead on the spot."

I looked over to where my mother was seated, silent. "How are you now, Mother? Are you recovered from the ordeal? I'm so very sorry to have put you through all this. I could tell you were in trouble, but there wasn't much I could do about it, I'm afraid."

I stood up and went over to her, holding out my hand. She took it, then reached up, pulled me towards her, and kissed me. "I'm still so worried about you, Connell. You look so pale. I'm sure you lost much too much blood at that man's hands."

"I'm fine, Mother. It's all over now... There's nothing more to worry about, nothing at all," I added, when she began to cry. "It's truly all over."

"It's been a most harrowing time for us all, the last few hours beyond description even," my father said. "Come, my dear." He took her hand. "Let's leave Connell and everyone now. I'm sure that he, like us, needs to call an end to this extraordinary day."

My mother rose and kissed me again. "Good night, my dear. We'll see you in the morning. A new beginning," she smiled, and allowed herself to be led away through the door.

I raised my hand in acknowledgement, and they were gone.

Mr. Potter then came up and took my hand. "Your parents are right, Connell, so Mrs. Potter and I shall take our leave now too, and see you in the morning. In the meantime, get a good night's rest if you can, and you, Miss Saunders, look after him. You have a very special man there, you know."

Katherine, who had been reduced to a most uncustomary silence ever since the drama unfolded on the arrival of Colonel Stevens, nodded. "Yes, I know."

CHAPTER 20

The next day was spent by everyone, including the staff, recovering from the drama of the preceding day. I came down to breakfast, and on the way was greeted by smiling servants, all congratulating me, but not before poor Morgan, who, almost in tears the preceding night for having treated me so roughly, begged forgiveness yet again.

"I'm so very sorry, Sir. I thought Mr. Potter meant what he was saying, and if true, then I felt..."

"That's all right, Morgan," I continued to reassure him. "It just proves what an excellent actor Mr. Potter is. Did you know he was one of the best-known actors in Dublin before he came here to Pembrokeshire?"

"No, Sir. I didn't."

"Then you didn't know he was also one of their finest swordsmen too?"

"No."

"Ah well then. It never does to take people at face value, does it? Not everyone displays their talents every day to show the world how clever they are."

"No, Sir. You're right."

"Well, let's consider the matter closed then, shall we? And help me get dressed. I admit to being still very sore, and have a stiff neck to boot, so go gently will you, please?"

"Of course, Sir."

Unusually, everyone was already gathered at the breakfast table, and I was given a hero's welcome.

Katherine, usually a late riser, came rushing up to me, and flung her arms around me. "Oh Connell! What a great day this is! To think it's all over. We must celebrate. How shall we celebrate? It must be a grand celebration!"

Her head was buried in my chest, and I looked over her shoulder at everyone. " *I* have a suggestion for a grand celebration."

Katherine stood back and looked up at me. "You do?"

I grinned. "Yes, I do. How about we celebrate by getting married as soon as possible, right here, before everyone leaves?"

The approval for such a plan was unanimous, and when the chatter subsided, Mrs. Saunders said, "We can't wait for the banns to be announced then, so we must apply right away for you to be married by special licence. A special license is much more discreet anyway."

"That's how Mr. Potter and I were married," said Mrs. Potter. "We were married in St. Martin's Church in Haverfordwest by special licence." And from then on all talk, at least on the part of the women, was about the upcoming wedding, about which they all had something to say.

"You and I, Katherine will talk to the vicar, Mr. Jeffries, as soon as possible," Mrs. Saunders announced. "And you, Connell, should come with us too to declare there's no impediment to your being married." She laughed. "We take it you're not already married?"

I smiled, and bowed. "No Ma'am."

"There we are then. Are you well enough to make it to the vicarage this morning?"

"Yes, of course, Ma'am."

"Well, then. As soon as we're ready, let's go."

So while I was hurried off to the vicarage, the rest of the men went back to discussing their favourite topic, horses, and as I was being ushered out of the door, could hear Mr. Potter recounting the story of his magnificent Irish horse, Hercules, which he had owned for many years.

The wedding arranged, my father took me aside to ask me if I had decided yet what to do to occupy myself in the future. "I know it's still early days, not yet five months since your whole life was turned upside down, son, but now you're to be married, it's time to rethink what you intend to do, and where you intend to do it... Given your character, I know the idle life of a gentleman will not be for you."

We were walking through a glade in the woods near the mansion at the time. Summer was here, and everything was still fresh and green, untinged as yet by August's mellowing effects on the countryside.

"I've discussed it with Katherine, and she has said she doesn't mind whether we live here or in Ireland. For myself, living back in Ireland will be emotionally harder for me, as I'll be forever thinking about my lost career. I think it would be easier for me to make a fresh start right here in Pembrokeshire. I know some terrible things happened to me here, but I've already managed to return to some of the

271

places where I suffered the most, and having done that, have been able, to some extent, to rid myself of the demons associated with those places. I still have a couple more I need to deal with though, and intend to do that as soon as possible."

"And where in Pembrokeshire do you intend to live then?"

"I haven't said anything to Katherine yet, but there's an estate on the market not so far from here. I thought we could take a look at it, to see if she'd like the house, and whether the land is to my liking."

"Is there anything special you want to do with the land?"

I stopped walking, and turned to look at him. "Well, I thought I might like to follow in my esteemed father's footsteps, and breed some fine horses. I think Pembrokeshire is ready. What do you think?"

My father slapped me on the back. "Why yes indeed! An excellent idea, son. You know a good horse as well as I do, and you're still an expert horseman. Then there's your future father-in-law too; I'm sure he'd be delighted at the idea, seeing that he, too, is a connoisseur of horseflesh. An excellent idea!" he repeated. "Well done! Well done! I could not have thought of a better plan myself... I knew you'd pull through all this in fine style, son. I expected nothing less of you... I... I'm proud of you." He turned, and started walking ahead of me, emotion taking over.

My parents, of course, extended their stay so as to attend the wedding, although the Potters returned home to Haverfordwest in the meantime, Mr. Potter having some business that needed to be attended to. Two weeks later, and two days before the event, I went to pick them up again in the carriage. I had insisted that Mrs. Kelly, the Potters' housekeeper, come as well, and at a discreet moment, repaid her all the money I owed her, with interest.

The little church was crowded for the ceremony, which was followed by a grand wedding celebration, held at the Saunders's mansion, and eventually my beautiful bride and I were able to escape to our own, newly-decorated chamber together, although I think I could be forgiven for not noticing the decor at the time.

That night, we lay in bed together, our arms locked around each other, having come together so perfectly in every way, and spending the night, our bodies and our spirits united in complete harmony. To me it was all doubly special and filled with a whole range of emotions, and the next morning, while we were out walking together under the light, dappled-green shade of the tall beech trees down in the folly not far from the house, I had to tell my Katherine the reason for this special feeling. I stopped and pulled her towards me.

"I've thought about this a great deal, and it takes some explaining, but I need to tell you this, my dearest Kate. I feel so very emotional, and not just because I love you more than anything in the world, and couldn't imagine my life without you, but because I'm blessed with an extra joy as well." I paused. Not being used to opening up my thoughts like this, it was difficult for me, and I still hesitated, but I had changed, and it no longer seemed unmanly to lay bare my soul, at least to Katherine. I knew she would understand, and this gave me courage, so I continued.

"That extra joy is being able to experience something I had led myself to believe would never, ever be possible again. My dearest Kate, if only I'd been able to express to you the anguish of believing I'd never again feel the warmth of a woman's body next to mine, feel her sweet breath on my face, have her respond to my advances. Kate, I never in my life felt so lonely, so isolated and so desperate. Not being able to share my fears with anyone, only added to my despair. That, coupled with the need to give everyone the appearance of coping, almost drove me out of my mind. Then, when I found myself in love with you, that anguish became almost unbearable, sure as I was in my own mind that you would never want me. Now, to have you next to me like this, the only woman I would ever want this way, it's overwhelming. It is indeed a double blessing, so very precious, and I just want you to know that."

She reached up and kissed me. "My dearest, sweet, gentle Connell, if only I'd known the true extent of your pain, my love! I know I chastised you for not being open with me, but that particular pain, I know now, of course, was something you couldn't possibly share with me at the time. You must have thought me so very callous and cruel, not understanding. I wonder even that you ever fell in love with me." She put her hand up and smoothed my cheek. "You must understand too though, my dear, that as I myself never, ever considered you in any way unattractive, there was no reason for me to think you might consider yourself to be so. You should know that, regardless of how I felt about you otherwise, even when I was on my worst behaviour with you, I always considered you to be a highly attractive man." She kissed me again. "Oh my dearest Connell. I do indeed love you so very much, and you must realize now that all those fears and anxieties are truly gone forever. You are at last free in every way, your self-esteem and your confidence, restored, and I see it in your eyes, in your smile and in your carriage. You are so very beautiful, my love."

I pulled her close to me, her hair light and fragrant against my face. "It's taken me a long time to learn this, but knowing I can always share my feelings with you and be open with you, is a wonderful freedom of itself. Not to have to try to pretend to you to be what I'm not, gives me a sense of comfort and wellbeing I never knew could exist, and if we were ever to be separated again, I should feel as though a huge part of me had been ripped away, so much so, I don't think I could even survive."

She stood back, and held me at arms' length, smiling up at me. "It's not going to happen, my love. You'll not get rid of me now, ever."

I laughed and pulled her back to me again, holding her tight against my chest. "I'm delighted to hear it my dear Kate. Now I can truly lay it all to rest." And we walked arm in arm, in silence, beneath the tall beeches.

The wedding now over, the Potters and Mrs. Kelly returned home again, and my parents stayed on for a few extra days, during which we all took off in Mr. Saunders's fine new carriage, and went to inspect the estate, which was still on the market, and situated about five miles away.

Once there, the ladies went to look over the mansion, while my father, Mr. Saunders and I went to see the stables, the home farm and the land around it. Several hours later we all met up on the front lawn.

"Well," I asked my wife. "How is it? Is it liveable?"

She grasped my hand. "Oh yes indeed, my love! It needs completely redecorating, but that will be such fun. Oh please, Connell, can we have it? Please?"

"Of course you can. You may have anything you want, my dearest Kate."

I bought the property, and after my parents had returned home to Ireland, we stayed on at Carregowen, making the trip almost daily to our new home to supervise renovations to the house and stables, and for me to get to know the tenants still in residence, including the farmer running the home farm.

A few weeks after my parents' departure, we were sitting at breakfast, Katherine, as ever, full of excitement about furnishing her new home, her mother equally enthusiastic about, and involved in, the project.

Mr. Saunders stood up. "Well, I think I'll leave you two ladies to your fabrics and designs, and take myself off down to the stables to take a look at a new arrival." He looked at me. "How about you, Connell? Would you care to accompany me?"

I stood up at once. "Of course. A new arrival, eh? You've bought yourself another horse then, Sir? Right away then, let's go. When you buy a new horse, I know I'm going to see something special." Morgan brought me my coat, and the two of us made our way to the stables, where David greeted us.

He gave Mr. Saunders a proud smile. "He's all ready, Sir. Would you like me to bring him out now?"

"By all means, David. Let's see him."

I was surprised. "You mean you've purchased a new horse, sight unseen. That's very brave of you."

"Ah well, Connell. I have the greatest faith in the source."

I gaped. David had brought out the finest-looking Arabian stallion I had ever seen. I was speechless.

"Trot him up and down a bit, David. Let's see him move."

I finally found my voice. "Sir, you have outdone yourself. I've never seen such a fine animal."

A wide grin spread across his face. "Neither have I, son, so I hope you'll follow your father's wishes, and put him to good use."

"He's for us? From my father?"

"Yes indeed, son. He's your parents' wedding present to the happy couple, and his name is Darius."

CHAPTER 21

About a month after the estate was finally mine, and renovations were all in hand, I decided the time had come to set about laying my other demons to rest. There were two in particular, and I told Katherine about them as we lay in bed, our arms around each other.

"I need to go back to St. Mary's Church in Haverfordwest," I announced. "And I have to find Mrs. Beynon, the old woman who saved my life, and helped me to escape from Barnlake. Will you come with me, Kate? Do you feel you could do that for me, please?"

"Of course, my love. You know I'll do anything for you. Maybe we could ask Mr. and Mrs. Potter if we might visit them, and go to Sunday-morning service with them. That would be a good reintroduction to St. Mary's, don't you think? Then, while we're there, perhaps we could go to Burton and find this Mrs. Beynon of yours."

So that's what we did. It was, of course, difficult for me to re-enter the church where I had ended up that midnight, scarcely aware of what was happening, but on this warm August Sunday morning, with the sun shining through the high windows, it was all made easier, escorted as we were by Mr. and Mrs. Potter and their children.

I looked around. The church had been fully restored, so nothing remained of the devastation that had been wrought during my stay there, nor of the stench that had filled the air. I pointed out to Mr. Potter the pew where I had lain for so many days.

"You were privileged, if being here then can be in any way be called a privilege," he whispered. "That's the sheriff's pew."

"I have to say I didn't feel very privileged," I whispered back.

"No, I imagine not."

During our brief stay at the Potters' house on Tower Hill they held a dinner for us, which many members of the local gentry attended, along with Stephen George, the landlord of the Blue Boar Inn, where I had acted the part of Romeo almost a year ago now.

Unusually, Mr. Potter insisted that all should have arrived and be seated in their drawing room, before Katherine and I were allowed to enter. The moment came, and the doors were opened.

Mr. Potter himself announced us, then said: "Ladies and gentlemen, you're all aware of the dreadful tragedy that befell this young gentleman after he left the safety of our home last February." There were nods and murmurs. "Well, so that our dear Mr. O'Keeffe does not have to spend his whole evening accepting one by one all your condolences for his misfortune, which I know you all wish to offer him,

I've decided that we should, here and now, express our thoughts all together, and wish him and his beautiful wife every happiness by giving them a loud round of applause, something, actor in his heart that he still is, I know he will appreciate."

To my astonishment, everyone rose and gave me a standing ovation, and even Katherine stood out in front of me, turned, and joined in the applause. I had never felt so proud, now so fully exonerated, and gave my audience a deep bow of appreciation. Only Mr. Potter himself could have thought up such a magnificent and, of course, dramatic, welcome.

As planned, while there we rented a single-horse gig from the livery stables, where Mr. Potter had stabled Hercules for so many years. It was another warm August day, and we set out for Barnlake. In a way, it was like driving over new territory, as when I had travelled the road the first time, I had been in no state to take note of my surroundings. Besides, it had been foggy and pouring with rain. The second occasion had been by night, so I did not recognise anything along the way, which was a relief.

Finally arriving at Burton, we found a narrow lane leading to the old farmhouse, where I had ended up so ill that awful day, and had been put into that tiny stable on my own.

The summer having been quite dry, the ground was no longer six-inches deep in mud, and as we approached the farmhouse, a woman came to the door, wiping her hands in her apron. I came to a stop, and she walked towards us.

I raised my hat. "Good afternoon. I was wondering if you could tell me where I could find someone by the name of Mrs. Beynon. She was here in March of this year, helping to tend to the wounded and sick prisoners."

She looked surprised at my request, and hesitated before answering. "Well, once they were all shipped off to the prison hulks, those that were still alive, that is, and there weren't many of them by that time, his lordship took the farm back, and made us tenants. A right mess it was too. No wonder so many died... Now, Mrs. Beynon, you say? Yes, I knew her. Local she was, but soon after we moved in, she lost her home for some reason, and she's now in the workhouse in Haverfordwest. That's where you'll find her."

I raised my hat again. "Thank you for your help." She started to return to the house, and I turned the gig around, ready to leave, but then stopped, reining in the horse. I looked at Katherine. "I'm sorry, Kate, but I have to do this," I said, and called out to the woman just as she was about to disappear. "Excuse me, but would you mind very much showing me something while we're here?"

She came back. "What is it you'd like to see, Sir? We don't have much worth looking at, I'm afraid. It's taking time to get the place back in order and, as you can see, we're not wealthy farmers here."

I shook my head. "That doesn't matter. I know it's an odd request, but could you show me the stables, please?"

"A very odd request indeed, if you don't mind my saying so, Sir. But yes, by all means, although we don't have any stock in them, and they're in pretty poor condition."

I helped Katherine down from the gig, and we followed the woman, who explained that the stables were used for storage. "We keep our turnips and potatoes in them."

I stopped. "It's this one I need to see, please."

"What! This little one? That's hardly even a stable. May I ask, Sir, why on earth you would come all this way to look at this ramshackle place?" She turned to look at me, smiling. "You've not got hidden treasure in here, have you?"

I shook my head, not able to return her smile. I opened the door, and led Katherine inside. She did not have to ask me anything about this place, and just stood there, squeezing my hand, and looking round at the still moss-covered walls and rotting thatch above, where some bats were sleeping, hanging upside down from the rafters. She turned to the woman, who was waiting outside with a bemused look on her face.

"My husband was wrongly accused of being one of the French invaders," she explained to her. "He nearly died in this stable."

I noticed Kate's eyes welling up with tears, and kissed her. "It's all right, my love. I'm sorry to have done this to you, but thank you."

The woman shook her head in sympathy. "Every time I come past here now, I shall think of you," she said as we made our way back to the gig. "I'm so glad, Sir, that you survived your ordeal."

This time I smiled at her. "I too."

We returned to Haverfordwest, me worrying lest Mrs. Beynon's kindness to me had been discovered after all, and she had lost her home on my account, which would have been a terrible tragedy.

The following day we were to return home to Carregowen, so having said our goodbyes to the Potters in the morning, we took sedan chairs, and stopped off at the workhouse on our way to Castle Square, where we were due to pick up the stage coach.

"Jemima Beynon!" The caretaker shouted across the big communal room. It was a sad place, where women were separated from their husbands, and forced to live with other women, and to work until they almost dropped with fatigue, a way of earning their keep. "Company here to see you." We waited in the doorway, while Mrs. Beynon made her way towards us. She had lost weight, and appeared exhausted. I stepped forward, and she looked up at me. Her eyes opened wide with pleasure, and she gave me one of her toothless smiles. "Mr. O'Keeffe, 'un'! You escaped! I knewed as 'ow you would. An' are you all free an' clear now, 'un'? By the look of you in your fine clothes, I'd say as 'ow you mus' be. An' you've come back to see ol' Mrs. Beynon." She took my hand, and squeezed it. "An' your arm now? All healed is it?" Still grasping my hand, she turned to look at Katherine. "An' who's this beautiful young lady with you, 'un'?"

"Katherine, I should like you to meet Mrs. Beynon. It's Mrs. Beynon to whom I owe my life and my freedom. Mrs. Beynon, please meet my wife, Mrs. Katherine O'Keeffe."

Contrary to what a gentlewoman would normally do in the presence of a woman of Mrs. Beynon's status, Katherine curtsied, and held out her hand. "Mrs. Beynon, my husband has spoken so much about you, and I'm delighted to meet you at last."

"My dear. You be a lucky young woman. You couldna 'ave found yourself a more thoughtful, brave an' carin' 'usband, an' meetin' you now, I can see as 'ow 'e too 'as found 'isself the perfect wife." She looked at me. "A proper end for all you've went through, 'un'." She looked puzzled. "But you didna get 'ome to Ireland after all then, 'un'? What 'appened?"

It's a very long story, Mrs. Beynon."

"Wot! Even longer than the one wot you told me to start with?"

I laughed. "Well yes, almost, in fact, come to think of it, I think it's probably longer."

We chatted for a few minutes, then I called the caretaker, and asked her to bring three chairs. Once seated, I looked at Mrs. Beynon. "Mrs. Beynon, first of all, I need to ask you something. Did you lose your home on my account? Did they discover that you helped me escape?"

She took my hand again. "No, 'un'. I told you. Jemima Beynon be too wily for that. No. Ol' Mr. Beynon died, an' they needed the cottage so someone wot could work the land could move in."

"So they turned you out?"

"Ah, 'un'. That's the way it be, ain't it? 'Is lordship 'as to 'ave somewhere for 'is workers to live, an' if 'e clung onto all us ol' 'uns, well..." She spread her fingers out on her lap.

I was disgusted at the landowner, whoever he was. My father never turned out those who had worked faithfully for him for many years. "I don't like to see you in this position, Mrs. Beynon. It's not right."

She held up her hand. "Now, young man, not you worry yourself about ol' Mrs. Beynon now. As I told you afore, she be well able to take care of 'erself, 'un'."

I shook my head. "I don't consider this taking care of yourself, Mrs. Beynon, and I have a suggestion to which I know my dear wife will agree... In a couple of weeks, we'll be moving into our new home in the north of the county, and we insist that you come to live with us."

"Oh Mr. O'Keeffe, 'un'! I be gettin' way too ol' now to earn my keep. Wot would I do? Your other servants wouldna like an ol' woman in their midst, doin' nothin' to 'elp make 'er way. No, I couldna impose like that, 'un'." She shook her head. "No I couldna do that."

"Nonsense," Katherine spoke up. "Nonsense, Mrs. Beynon. When you saved my dear husband's life and set him free, you made all the contribution you'd ever need to make for the rest of your life. I assure you, you've paid your dues. You owe nothing, nor ever will."

I took Katherine's hand. I was so proud of her, and before Mrs. Beynon could come up with anything further, I stood up. "Right then, it's settled. If you can just wait it out here another couple of weeks, I myself shall come to fetch you, and you'll come to live with us."

Mrs. Beynon was speechless, but her face told us all we needed to know. I took her hand and kissed it. "We'll see you soon then."

She nodded, and we left.

"Katherine, my beautiful wife, I've always known it -- well perhaps not always." I grinned at her. "You're beautiful right through."

Our mansion was ready, as were our stables, and come September, we all, Katherine and I and our stallion, Darius, and Bounder too, moved into our respective lodgings. In the meantime Mr. Saunders and I had amused ourselves, as only two horse-loving men could possibly amuse themselves, by travelling around the country, securing three of the best mares to complement our stallion, and to publicize his availability at stud.

Morgan had come with us too to our new home. Mr. Saunders, knowing how much I relied on him, had willingly let him go, and one day, Katherine came to tell me something about him.

"Morgan, unlike another pupil of mine, is proving to be such an excellent and rewarding student, and I'm enjoying teaching him so much." She paused and gave me a quizzical look.

"And now I'm to guess who that other pupil was, I suppose?"

She smiled and held my hand. "No need to. We both know already, don't we? Anyway, I have an idea."

"Nothing that involves me having to obey orders, undergo therapy and get browbeaten into the bargain, I hope."

"No, not this time. I'll think up something along those lines later."

"No hurry."

"No, my love. I've been thinking. There are quite a few children on the estate here, and we are so far from anywhere where they could go to school, I'm thinking that perhaps I could teach them. You know that old barn, the one you said you won't be using? Well, I thought we could do it up and I could use it as a schoolroom. What do you think?" She looked up at me, that look of enthusiasm in her eyes that I knew so well, and that had hitherto filled me with such trepidation as to what might be coming.

"I think that's an excellent idea. As soon as we've got the horses settled, I'll transfer the workmen to converting the barn for you."

"Oh thank you, my love! I knew you'd agree with me."

"Don't I always?"

"Well, not as often as my father, but then, he does spoil me."

"And I don't?"

"Not so much, yet, but you will."

"We'll see about that." And I kissed her.

Our new staff were learning to work as a team. We now had a new coach of our own too, nothing as grand as Mr. Saunders's, but plenty to satisfy our own needs. It required only two horses, so most of the time, I drove it myself, although I would get the head groom to stand in for me on more formal occasions, as well as on the occasion when I set out to collect Mrs. Beynon.

Forewarned that I should be coming to collect her that day, she was ready and waiting, although she had nothing in the way of baggage, having been obliged to part with all her belongings on entering the workhouse. Katherine must see to it, I thought -- as I was sure she would do anyway -- that Mrs. Beynon would be outfitted with sufficient new clothes to keep her comfortable, as all she had was her workhouse uniform.

I helped her into the coach, and it was obvious she was most pleased with her turn in fortunes. As I said, I had got my head groom, Robert, also taken from Mr. Saunders -- with his permission, of course -- to drive us so I could keep Mrs. Beynon company on the drive back, and tell her the various things I thought it necessary for her to know.

"'un'?"

"Yes, Mrs. Beynon?"

"You said as 'ow what 'appened to you after you left Barnlake was an even longer story than wot you 'ad to tell when you arrived there." She shook her head. "Oh dear, I were so afraid I were gonna lose you that day, 'un'. You was in such a bad state." She took hold of my hand, and I held hers. She was silent for a minute, then: "Would you like to tell me the rest of the story then, 'un'?"

So I did, and towards the end of the trip, when I had finished my tale, I said, "Now. Let's not talk any more about the past; let's talk about the future. I want you to know that the staff are all aware you're coming to join us, Mrs. Beynon, and you do have a role to play after all, so you won't feel as though you're not contributing. They have been told, all of them, butler and housekeeper included, that you're very special to me, and that should they have any problems, cuts, bruises, or any other problems at all, they are to come to you, and that if you're unable to deal with them, then you will go to Mrs. O'Keeffe to seek her help. And, of course, if you yourself ever, and I mean *ever*, have any problems of your own, then you come to either Mrs. O'Keeffe, or to me. My door is open for you any time... Oh! And by the way, I'll always be 'un' to you, Mrs. Beynon."

She smiled, and patted my hand, and turned away. I think there were a few tears, but I pretended not to notice.

Then, in mid-October, I was looking out of our chamber window at the golden autumn leaves gathering on the green grass of the lawn, and realizing that I had finally come to terms with all that had happened to me, when Katherine came up behind me and put her arms around my waist. "You said yesterday that one of the mares is pregnant."

"Yes, and she..."

"She's not the only one."

I swung round. "We're going to have a child?"

Katherine nodded, and I pulled her towards me, and kissed her. "Wonderful, my dear Kate!..." I lifted her chin, and looked into her beautiful eyes, smiling. "Does that mean too," I teased her, "that one day I am indeed going to have the chance to explain to our son or daughter what it is the girl in the bonnet in that unfinished embroidery of yours should be looking at?"

She backed up, and wagged her finger at me. "I should have you know, my dear husband... that cheap china I ordered will be arriving shortly..."

THE END